To. Dick a
w/ love
Peggy T. Winstead

The Picture

A Teenage Girl in the Shadow of War

Peggy Aileen Taylor Winstead

ISBN 1-4196-6188-4

Cover and Layout Design:
Pamela Meyer
Granite Publishing
P.O. Box 1429
Columbus, NC 28722

Printed in the United States of America.

The
Picture

THE SEARCH

Toys
To
Boys

Sixteen and now the seeking,
Who, when, where, and why?
Is what's she's thinking.

Boys
Are
Dogs
They're all out there,
Out there searching,
She feels it so - but where?

Dogs
Or
Frogs
They came — they went.
The search goes on.
That's how, her youth was spent.

Frogs
To
Prince
She kissed them all,
She didn't wince,
And so it was — she found her Prince.

By Katie Winters

Introduction

January 16, 2004, was Maggie McGee Winters' eightieth birthday, and her whole family would arrive shortly to celebrate this special day. She felt very nostalgic and decided to go to her bedroom for a little quiet time before everyone arrived. She pulled up a chair beside her cedar chest, opened it, and began looking at the keepsakes and letters she had kept there for more than 50 years. She was deep in her thoughts while reading an old letter, when her 20-year-old granddaughter Katie came and stood beside her.

"Grandma, what are you doing?"

"I'm just reminiscing a little about my younger days."

Katie knelt down beside her grandmother and picked up a red-quilted satin box, which had once held stationery, but now held an assortment of old keepsakes from her dating years. "May I open this?"

"Certainly, it's filled with old memories that I've kept all these years. I really don't know why, but they still seem very important to me." Katie picked up a ring box, and looked at her Grandmother questioningly. "That was the box my engagement ring was in," said Maggie.

"You saved a lot, Grandma. Why didn't you ever show me these things before?" Katie said, as she handed her the box.

"You weren't interested before."

"Well, I am now. Tell me about all these things?" she said excitedly.

Maggie took the satin box and lovingly took each piece out of the box. "These are ribbons from a wrist corsage my boyfriend gave me on my sixteenth birthday. Oh, and this is from the first orchid corsage your grandfather gave me."

"Grandpa?" exclaimed Katie. "And you still have it?"

"Yes, and much more." Then Maggie pulled out a small compact that was blue and had a raised Citadel insignia on the top and chuckled, "This was given to each girl who attended the dance at the Citadel in Charleston. What an exciting weekend that was for a young girl!" Maggie sighed. "Oh, Katie, here's an invitation to the Engineers' Brawl at NC State, where I fell in love with your grandfather." Her hands passed over several letters from a Cpl. Ken Winters. Maggie smiled wistfully as she said, "These were some very special letters from your Grandfather." She showed Katie pictures of old boyfriends, Paul, John, James, Tim, Jake and the special ones - Ken and her brother Bill dressed in soldier's uniforms. As she shuffled to the last picture, she smiled and gave out a big sigh. Katie thought she saw her grandmother become younger and younger as she reminisced over old times.

"I just love hearing about your life, Grandma. There's so many stories here."

Maggie began placing each picture back in the box, but Katie stopped her.

"Grandma, is that your picture?"

"Yes, dear, that's me, when I was oh, so very young."

"How old were you?"

"I was 17 and my parents let me have a studio picture made. I thought I was a big deal. I had six prints made, one for them and five for my boyfriends."

"You had five boyfriends at one time?"

"Kinda." Maggie said sheepishly.

"Oh, wow, Grandma! How did your parents let you do that?"

"Well, things were different then, Katie. Boys and girls dated more casually."

Katie reached down and picked up a bundle of letters, tied with a blue ribbon. "Who were all these letters from?"

"Those boyfriends I was telling you about. You see after Pearl Harbor, our lives were disrupted in so many ways. All the boys either enlisted or were drafted. We kept in touch by writing letters, and each one of them wanted a picture to take with them when they went into the service. That's why I had so many pictures taken."

"What are all those loose letters?"

"They are three years of daily letters from your grandfather to me, and three years of my daily letters to him."

"Wow! That's a lot of letter writing. This is all really amazing." Katie straightened herself on her knees and said, "Grandma, what's in this chest would make a great story! You really should write a book about these letters and that picture."

Maggie patted her granddaughter on the head, stroking her auburn hair and said, "Honey, I'm too old to start a project like that. You're studying journalism, and want to be a writer, so maybe you should write a book about these letters."

Katie jumped up and said, "I'd love to, if you'll be my collaborator."

"That I will surely look forward to. We'll start as soon as you can, if you like."

"I like," said Katie, hugging her grandmother. "This is going to be fun."

Ken came into the room and asked, "What are you girls up to?

"Oh, Grandpa, we're collaborating, me and Grandma."

"Well, it's time to stop collaborating with her and get ready to go to her birthday party! Everyone is here."

Maggie closed the chest, locked it, and gave Katie the key. "You can come anytime you want, Katie. I'll help you all I can."

As Katie left the room, she looked back at the Hope Chest and felt a tingle go through her body. She was so excited to begin this project, and really get to know her grandparents as young people. The brief glimpse she just had on their past gave her a whole new perspective of grandparents whom she previously always thought of as "old." All of a sudden she could resonate with their lives.

Thus started months of Katie and Maggie pouring over the letters and mementos. Maggie never tired of telling Katie stories of each young fellow and how she finally met Ken Winters, the love of her life.

Chapter 1

January 16, 1924, was cold, with snow falling silently on the house at 300 Cascade Avenue. For weeks the household had been awaiting the arrival of a new member. It was before dawn, and the snow had turned the world into a white wonderland, when Dr. Michaels finally arrived. He had made it to the McGee house just in time. A scrawny little girl with a head full of dark hair finally came into this world. This was just what Ruben McGee wanted, as he had been saying for six months: "I want a dark-haired, dark-eyed, little Irish girl."

After the doctor finished delivering the baby and making the new mother comfortable, Annie had drifted off to sleep. He turned to Ruben and said, "Let's get out of the room and let Annie and the baby sleep."

Ruben directed the doctor to the kitchen and reached into the cabinet where his wife kept the good crystal. He took out two of her cut-glass high ball glasses, poured two shots of brandy, handed the doctor one, raised his glass, and said, "Here's to the answer to my prayers — a dark-haired, brown-eyed baby girl."

"She's beautiful and she's healthy," the doctor added.

After he made one last check on the mother and baby, Ruben showed him to the door.

After several weeks of trying to come up with the right name, Annie and Ruben named her Maggie Eileen McGee. They were not sure they could handle a new baby, because times were pretty bleak. Jobs that could support a family of four were hard to find. Ruben was working two jobs, so they were making ends meet and saving a little. Nevertheless, they were very happy to have a girl to add to their two-year old, tow- headed, little boy, William Edwin. Annie's mom called him Will, but everyone else called him Bill.

As Maggie grew up, life was very simple, but good. The family increased by two more - a sister Elisa Marie, (Lisa) five years later, and Jean Kathleen, (Jeanie) 14 years later. Annie always called Jeanie, "the surprise of my life."

Maggie grew up in a neighborhood full of children of all ages. She was called the tom boy of the crowd. She would climb the highest trees and dare the boys to climb up after her. She loved to help her mother in the garden, and her favorite job was to watch the smaller children. Maggie was always in the middle of whatever was being planned, which got her into trouble sometimes, but she took her family chores very seriously.

Her parents moved the family to a new home in Maggie's early teen years, to make room for the expanding family. Maggie still had to share a room with her 12-year-old sister, Lisa, but she didn't mind most of the time.

On January 16, 1940, Maggie's mother and father gave her a fancy party for her sixteenth birthday. That morning dawned overcast with a hint of snow in the air. Maggie jumped up, ran downstairs, and exclaimed excitedly, "Momma, if it snows, we can't have my party. It won't snow, will it?"

"No, dear, this is your day, and it will be perfect."

Maggie went back up to her room, confident it would not snow. After all, her mother had assured her, it was to be perfect, and her mother was always right. She jumped on her sister Lisa's bed and began tickling her. "Wake up! Do you know what day this is?"

Lisa rolled over and answered, "NO!"

"Well, it's my sixteenth birthday, and I don't want you to sleep it away."

"Please Maggie! Let me sleep a little longer. It's not my birthday."

"OK, but just a little longer, because Momma needs us to help her."

Chapter 1

Maggie ran back downstairs and found caterers taking over the kitchen and the house crawling with people bringing in tables and chairs. Excitement filled the air every where she went. Momma and her friends had turned the recreation room into a fanciful garden. The corners of the room were banked with large potted plants...and colorful lanterns of pink, green and lavender were strung around the room.

The three-car garage had been scoured clean, and tables and chairs were set for 100 guests. She knew that by evening it would be a wonderland. She swirled around and around, she was so happy. Dinner was to begin at six, followed by a dance.

Maggie came down from her room about 5:30, dressed in a white circular skirt, with a pink appliqué on it. She wore an Angora sweater that matched the appliqué perfectly. The pink sweater set off her long auburn hair in all of its glory. She wore white Angora socks with brand new saddle oxfords. She felt like a princess as she descended the curved staircase to the front hall.

She went straight to her parents' room to show her mother how she looked and, Annie said, "Maggie, I do believe you are growing up to be a beautiful young lady."

Maggie looked at her mother, and thought, "How lucky could a young girl be to have such a wonderful mother?" She crossed the room, hugged her mother and whispered, "I love you and Daddy. Thank you for my party!"

Right then the front door bell rang. Maggie thought as she ran to the door, "Now my party can begin!" As she opened the door, there stood her date, James, a tall, handsome young man with dark wavy hair and a ruddy complexion. His smile was infectious. It made you feel like something good was about to happen. He was smiling that wide smile of his and holding out a wrist corsage of white roses for her to wear. "Hi, Maggie! Happy birthday! You sure do look gorgeous tonight! Are you the same Maggie I saw this morning?"

Maggie stood on her tip toes and gave him a quick kiss, "Yes, silly boy! Come on in, James. I want you to see how pretty my party is going to be."

She reached out her arm to him and asked, "Can you tie on my corsage? It is so beautiful. Thank you so much! I love it!" She looked at James and gave him that smile that sends a sparkle into the air.

James fumbled with tying the bow, but after starting over a few times, he finally finished. "How does that do for the birthday girl?"

"Fine." She hugged him, grabbed his hand, and said, "Come on! Let's go downstairs."

As they descended to the rec room, a steady stream of school friends began to arrive. She ran right back upstairs to greet her guests, among whom were Nancy and Doug, her brother Bill, and his date Anne Delaney, Jake, her brother's best friend, and his date Bonnie, a friend of Anne's.

The party was quite a success. After a delicious dinner was served, they went to the rec room and danced to the music of Harry James, Artie Shaw, Kay Kyser, and Glenn Miller. The party did not end until after 11:00, because every one was having a marvelous time. As Maggie said good-bye at the door to her last guests, her world began to be covered with a soft, white blanket of snow. For a few moments, she gazed out the door at the beautiful snow falling and thought, "What a fabulous evening this was."

Before going to bed, Maggie went to her parents' room, jumped on their bed, and kissed them for giving her a wonderful party. She danced out the door, all the way up the stairs into her room, and kissed a sleepy Lisa.

She flung herself onto her bed and said, "Lisa, this being 16 is going to be great."

"Do you know how late it is?" Lisa said half asleep. "Your birthday is over now. Get undressed and go to sleep, please!"

"Oh, ok." Maggie said grudgingly, as she began to undress and accepted the fact that her birthday was really over. "But," she thought, "my dating years have just begun."

Chapter 1

Up until her 16th birthday, Maggie had not attracted too many boyfriends, probably because she was scrawny and looked more like a boy than a girl. Her redeeming features were her long, dark, auburn hair, her ready smile, her eagerness to learn new things and to meet new people, especially boys. Her mother often consoled her when she complained of not having a boyfriend. As her mother brushed Maggie's lovely hair, she would tell her, "My sweet little Maggie, don't be in too much of a hurry. The boys will find you soon enough."

Soon enough came several months later when Annie's sister Estelle called and said, "Annie, I have a problem, and I need some help."

"Of course, Estelle. I'll help you any way that I can. What can I do?"

"Well, you see Gary's nephew, Paul Stark, has come to visit us for a month from Spartanburg, South Carolina. What am I going to do with a 16-year-old boy for a month, when I am so busy working and looking after twins? I'm too busy to entertain Paul." She sounded desperate.

"Estelle, don't worry. I think Maggie can help you with your problem. She is bored to death since school has been out. So, how can we get them together?"

Estelle had it all figured out. She worked at Sunset Pharmacy right across the street from a big city park, which boasted tall oak trees, a meandering stream running through it that passed eight tennis courts, an oval track, and a ball diamond used for baseball and football practices for the nearby high school. There was a playground for children, and the best feature was the park stretched between Annie's and Estelle's homes.

"Send Maggie over to the pharmacy this afternoon, and I'll have Paul there. We'll see how it goes. Annie, cross your fingers - I need all the help I can get."

Maggie was just coming in the door from a trip to town, where she had been buying supplies for a new dress. She had taken the city bus to town, went to the fabric store and shopped. She was so proud because this was the first time her mother had let her go to town all by herself to buy a pattern and fabric to make a dress. She burst in saying, "Momma, look at my pattern and fabric! Do you think I can make it without any help?"

"Calm down, little lady, and let me have a look." Annie took all the purchases, looked them over, and said, "You've made a real good choice, and yes, I do think you can handle this project, with very little help." Momma went on, "Someone else needs your help."

"Who, Momma, who?" asked Maggie. Somehow, she felt it might be fun; by the way her mother was smiling.

"Aunt Estelle called this morning."

Maggie interrupted, "Not baby-sitting again, Momma?"

"No, and if you will be quiet, I'll tell you what she wanted."

Maggie hugged her purchases to her chest as if they were long-lost treasures, went over by her mother, sat down, and said, "OK, I'll be quiet. What does Aunt Estelle want?"

"Uncle Gary's nephew, Paul Stark, has come to visit them for a month, and she wondered if you could help entertain him?"

"Momma, he's not some little kid, is he?"

"No, honey. He's 16 going on 17, and he loves to play tennis. I'm sure you will like him. Aunt Estelle wants you to come over to the pharmacy this afternoon around 3:00, and she will introduce you to Paul."

As she flew up the stairs, two steps at a time, Maggie shouted back, "That sounds great! Now, just what should I wear to make a good impression?"

Momma called after her, "I'm sure you'll figure that one out by yourself."

Maggie dashed into the room and excitedly announced, "I'm going to meet Aunt Estelle's nephew down at the Sunset Pharmacy, Lisa. What should I wear?" Maggie pulled out one outfit after the other. She tried each one on, deciding why she didn't think each one would do. One was too old, one was too little. She had grown since last summer, and she didn't like the blue one. As she pulled out one after another, she flung them on the bed, with some landing on the floor.

Lisa, being the neatnik sister, said, "You better pick those clothes up and hang them back in the closet, or Momma will be mad."

"Yeah, and I'll bet you'll tell her," Maggie said, as she pulled out a little white tennis dress, with a flouncy little pleated skirt. She decided this was the very outfit for a warm afternoon in June. Lisa stormed out of the room and went straight to report to their mother what a mess Maggie was making in their room. She was a little ticked off that it was Maggie getting to go out, and she was not included.

Before Lisa could finish her tattling, Maggie came downstairs in that little white tennis dress with an apple green tie under the collar, and with it she wore brand new white socks and sneakers. She looked so fresh and excited. Out the front door she hurried, saying, "Momma, I'll see you about five!"

Annie said to Lisa, "Honey, don't spoil her fun. She can hang them up when she gets home."

Lisa stomped her way back upstairs to their room and began hanging up Maggie's discarded dresses. Not because she wanted to help Maggie, but because she couldn't stand a messy room.

Chapter 2

Maggie raced by the tennis courts, over the foot bridge, and by the track, where young boys were sprinting, and on through the park, afraid she would be too late to meet this new boy. When she arrived at the door of the pharmacy, she had to stop and catch her breath so she wouldn't appear too anxious to meet Paul. As she opened the door, she flipped her dark auburn hair so it fell loosely around her shoulders.

As Maggie entered the Sunset Pharmacy, she saw her friend Ray behind the walnut-carved soda fountain. He was standing there in his starched white jacket and his cap sitting saucily on his red hair.

"Hi, Ray," Maggie said in her friendliest manner.

"Hi, Maggie, Looks like you've been playing tennis. Come on over here, grab a stool and I'll fix you a cool drink, on me," Ray called to her.

"Sorry, Ray. Today I've come to see my Aunt Estelle. How about giving me a rain check."

"You've got it, anytime."

Maggie headed to the prescription counter in the back of the pharmacy, where her Aunt Estelle was helping a customer. As she waited she looked around. The pharmacy was a large building with walnut paneling and high ceilings. The ceilings were covered with patterned squares of metal. On these hot days it was cooled with large ceiling fans that went swoosh, swoosh in a constant rhythm. As she looked about her eyes caught sight of a young boy sitting over by the front window away from all the other customers. She was wondering to herself if this might be Paul Stark.

Aunt Estelle finished with her customer and turned to Maggie, and said, "Hello Maggie." She took Maggie by the hand and led her over to the table where this young man was seated. As they neared the table the young man rose and came around the table to meet Maggie. She thought, "He's mighty good looking, blond-curly hair and blue eyes that twinkle when he smiles, but he's a little short."

"Maggie, this is my nephew, Paul Stark. Paul, this is my niece, Maggie McGee."

Maggie quickly asked her aunt, "Does that mean we're related?"

"Only by marriage, and that doesn't count," her aunt answered and quickly excused herself to go wait on another customer, leaving Paul and Maggie to get acquainted.

As Paul turned to go to the fountain to get them a cherry coke, Maggie quietly smiled to herself, "Gee, this is going to be great!"

Paul returned and set the cherry coke in front of Maggie, and as he sat down, Maggie asked, "Paul, how long will you be visiting Uncle Gary?"

"I'll be here a month, and I hope I can see you often," Paul replied.

As always happens, when two teenagers meet they begin to ask questions. "What year are you in school?" Paul asked.

"I'll be a senior in the fall," Maggie said proudly.

"Me, too," Paul said. "What's your favorite subject?"

"Math. I just love playing with numbers. This fall I'll be taking Geometry II; it's just like working a puzzle. What's yours?"

"I can't believe it, but Math is my favorite subject, too. Now don't tell me Latin is on the bottom of your list, like it is for me."

"Oh, of course it's Latin," Maggie agreed, and then she went on, "Latin is a language, dead as it can be. It helped to kill the Romans, and now it's killing me."

They both cracked up in laughter.

With academics out of the way, they quickly found themselves on the subject of sports. Paul asked, “Which sport do you like to watch best?”

Maggie quickly answered, “Oh, I like them all, if the players are boys.”

Paul found that amusing, and as he laughed, he asked, “Do you like tennis?”

Maggie came right back, “To play or to watch?”

“To play of course,” Paul answered and eagerly awaited her reply.

“That’s great, because if you haven’t noticed, I’m dressed in the proper attire.”

Paul smiled and retorted, “The outfit hasn’t gone unnoticed, I assure you.”

Maggie smiled and felt her cheeks begin to flush. Before she could think of something to say, Paul seized the moment and asked, “How about us playing some tennis tomorrow morning?”

Hoping she would not sound too anxious, she answered, “OK, I’ll meet you at the first court right across the street in the park at 10:00 in the morning.”

Paul was more than delighted, and as he answered, he reached over and touched her hand, “Alright then, Maggie, it’s a date.”

The afternoon had passed by so quickly and before she knew it, it was time to go home. Maggie went over to the counter to say good-bye to Aunt Estelle, and to thank her for introducing her to Paul. “I had a wonderful afternoon; I’ll see you again real soon.”

Estelle looked up from what she was doing and said, “It was nice having you here to meet Paul.” Maggie looked over at Paul with a beautiful smile on her face, which you could never forget once you’ve seen it. “Paul, why don’t you walk Maggie home? It’s just on the other side of the park, and I’m sure you can find your way back.”

Paul jumped up and took Maggie by the hand, “Come on, Maggie! Let me see you home.”

Chapter 2

Out the door they went talking and giggling. Estelle smiled and thought, "I believe my problem is solved."

They crossed the street and descended the steps to the path that led across the park.

Maggie skipped ahead and turned around walking backwards. "Paul, what do you want to be when you finish college?"

"A fireman."

"Silly, you don't need to go to college to be a fireman."

"Well, I'll be an educated fireman."

"Can't you be serious, for a change?"

Paul smiled, "Would you like me better if I told you, I really don't know? Maybe an engineer or an architect?"

Maggie turned around and joined Paul on the path. "I think you would do well at whatever you decide to do."

"Now it's your turn to tell me what you intend to be."

"Well, I plan to go to college to study voice," Maggie replied gleefully.

"Oh, you sing, do you? What will you do then?"

"Get married, have a family, and sing wherever I can."

Maggie looked up, as they neared the side gate to the backyard. She saw her mother and Jeanie pulling weeds in her mother's flower garden.

As they entered the yard, her mother said hello.

Jeanie ran to Maggie and asked, "Who's that?"

"He's Aunt Estelle's nephew, Jeanie. She turned to her mother, "Momma, this is Paul Stark. Paul, this is my mother, and my little sister Jeanie."

Paul extended his hand and said, "I am so glad to meet you."

"Please excuse me for not taking your hand, but my hands are too dirty from pulling these weeds. If you will give me time to wash up a bit, I'll fix us some lemonade. I was just about ready to quit. Jeanie has been begging for lemonade and cookies, and we would love for you to join us."

"Thank you very much," Paul answered, "but I think I had better get back to the pharmacy and walk Aunt Estelle home. I'll take a rain check on that. Lemonade and cookies sound good to me."

"Please do come again, and we will have some," Annie said.

"Yes, and we can play." Jeanie called after them.

Maggie walked to the side gate and told Paul good-bye.

As Paul started walking away, he waved and said, "I'll see you at the first tennis court."

"I'll be there right at ten." She turned and went into the house.

For the next several weeks, they spent every morning playing tennis. Anyway, Maggie came dressed in her cute little tennis dresses and hit enough balls back over the net to keep Paul interested. He found it hard to let her win a few games each day, as any young gentleman knows he should, but he did not tire of watching Maggie run after the stray tennis balls. When she stopped and spun around, those little pleated skirts flipped out to reveal her skinny legs. Paul didn't notice they were skinny; instead, he found them very exciting.

Their days together were filled with tennis in the morning, swimming at the club in the afternoons, perhaps walking downtown to see a movie, and several nights a week, baby-sitting for Aunt Estelle's and Uncle Gary's twin boys, or baby-sitting for Maggie's little sister, Jeanie. They took the children to the park to play on the swings and slides. They didn't look forward to their baby-sitting jobs, but it gave them a little extra change to spend when they went out. Uncle Gary let Paul use his car sometimes, and when he did, they always went to the drive-in movies. On their first trip to the drive-in, Paul kissed her, which caught Maggie by surprise. She didn't mind his presumption at all, but it was a little unsettling.

Before they knew it, it was the 1st of July, and Maggie made plans with Paul to join her family and friends at the country club's July 4th celebration.

On the 4th, Paul picked Maggie up and they arrived at the country club around 1:00 and met all their friends for a swimming party. After several hours of playing in the pool, they changed clothes and joined the picnic for barbecue and corn on the cob. After it got dark, the glimmering fireworks lit up the sky, giving an exciting end to a perfect day.

On th e ride home, it struck them that there wasn't much time left before Paul had to go h ome. They obsessively began making plans for Paul to visit again the next summer. Each promised to write regularly.

The next morning, Paul and Maggie met in the park as usual for their tennis game. Neither had their heart in the game, so they walked over and sat in the shade of a giant oak tree. They talked about what it was going to be like to be seniors, and especially graduating and then going off to college. Paul suddenly became serious.

"I can't believe I'm a senior and have only one year left before college. I know I can always be a fireman, but I think I would like to be an architect."

Maggie giggled and punched him on the shoulder, "You can be whatever you want to be."

"It's a pretty hard course of study, and it is hard to get into architectural school."

"Come on, Paul, you're pretty smart. Don't sell yourself short. Go for it."

"Thanks, Maggie. Sometimes I don't believe in myself enough."

Maggie's stomach started growling,, so they headed to the pharmacy to have a light lunch. When they finished, Paul walked Maggie home. As they neared the door, he said, "Uncle Gary is letting me use the car tonight, so I want to take you somewhere special."

Maggie spun around, giving her little skirt a whirl and chattered excitedly, "Oh, let's do go somewhere special, so I can wear the new dress I just made."

"Gee whiz, she's pretty and talented too," Paul said. As he turned to go he called back and shouted, "I'll pick you up promptly at seven!"

"I'll be ready and waiting," Maggie said, as she closed the front door behind her.

Several hours later, Paul drove up in his Uncle's car. Maggie peered through the slit in her bedroom curtains, and her heart turned a flip. There was Paul getting out of the car dressed in a coat and tie, with his sandy curls combed to perfection. Maggie hardly recognized him as the same boy with whom she had spent the better part of a month. Gone were the tousled curls and the sloppy summer attire. Now he looked like a grown-up young man.

Maggie turned to take one last look at herself in the full-length mirror on the back of the bedroom door. To her surprise she also looked like a grown-up young lady, in the new dress she had made in her spare time these past four weeks. It was an aqua polka- dotted, chintz sun dress, with an elongated waist and a full-flared skirt that rippled as she walked. As she descended the stairs to the front door, she felt very pretty. Opening the door, she saw Paul looking so handsome, but still just a little too short!

"Hi handsome! Where are you going so dressed up?"

"I'm taking my best girl out tonight for dinner and dancing to the Hotel Robert E. Lee Roof Garden Restaurant," he said, smiling at Maggie. "Could that be you?"

"It better be," she said as she winked.

Paul grabbed her hand. "Then let's go."

Maggie called back to her mother as she closed the door, "Momma, we're going! I'll be home by 11:00."

Paul and Maggie virtually ran, talking and giggling, all the way to the car. Paul opened the door and made sure she was settled in her seat before he closed the door. He ran around and jumped behind the steering wheel. Both were smiling to themselves and not believing the adventure on which they were setting out.

Maggie squealed with delight and said, "Paul, do you know how grown-up I feel?"

He reached over and touched her hand and answered, "Yes I do, and did I tell you how pretty you look? Is that the dress you made?"

"Yes it is. Do you like it?"

"You bet I do, and I like the girl in it, too."

Maggie sat silent for a short while thinking, "He sure is a nice guy, if only he was taller...." She smiled at Paul as he drove up to the hotel's front door. The Robert E. Lee was the biggest hotel in town built in the 1920s. It was a nine-story hotel, with a restaurant and roof garden on the top floor. He gave his keys to the valet parking attendant. Paul came around and helped Maggie out of the car. When they entered the lobby, they were both taken by the beauty of the dark-stained walnut paneling. All around were leather chairs and sofas. In the center was a large marble table with a huge urn of mixed summer flowers. Waiting for the elevator, hand in hand, Maggie thought, "What a way to spend our last night together this summer!"

The doors opened, and they entered the elevator to be carried to the roof garden. As the doors opened again, she saw the most elegant restaurant she had ever seen, except in the movies. They were met by a white-gloved waiter, who took them straight to their table near the dance floor. The orchestra was playing Little Brown Jug. The other couples were on the dance floor doing the "jitter bug." Maggie's feet were itching to get out there and dance. They sat down as sedately as they knew how and looked over the menu. Maggie remembered her father telling her, "When you go out with a young man, always read the menu from right to left, not left to right." So, she ordered the baked chicken. This would have pleased her father since it was the least expensive item on the menu.

After they finished their dinner and were waiting for their dessert to be served, Paul stood up and took Maggie onto the dance floor. As Paul put his arms around her, the orchestra began to play "Polka-dots and Moonbeams," and outside a full moon was shining. Maggie thought, "How could the orchestra know she was wearing a polka-dotted dress for this special night, and the moon was shining?"

Paul glided her around the dance floor until they were by two large French doors leading to a balcony. Out on the balcony, Maggie found herself in Paul's arms being kissed as she had never been kissed before. Chills went up and down her spine and down into her finger tips. Maggie thought, "Could I be falling in love? Oh, but he's still too short."

They danced their way back to their table, and by then the waiter was serving their dessert. As they were finishing their baked Alaska, Maggie broke the silence by saying, “I’ve had the most wonderful evening of my life, but I think it is time that we should go.”

Paul rose and took Maggie by the hand. They held hands all the way out of the restaurant and until the parking attendant brought the car. The ride home was pretty quiet, each one thinking, “This was a great way to spend their last night together this summer!”

Paul broke the silence saying, “Uncle Gary says I may come back next summer as soon as I graduate from high school. I’d like to know that you’ll be available.”

“That sounds great! Now be sure to write to me this winter.”

Paul pulled up into Maggie’s drive, and for a while they both sat there without speaking, holding hands. Paul got out, came around the car, and opened Maggie’s door. As she rose to get out, Paul kissed her. Hand in hand, they strolled to the front door. They stood there a few more moments, not wanting to say good-bye, but suddenly Paul took Maggie in his arms and kissed her one last time. As he turned to go, he called out, “Be sure to write me often!”

“I promise!”

As Maggie went through the door and closed it behind her, she was smiling and remembering what a wonderful evening this had been. “Gosh, I wish he was a little taller,” she thought. Up the stairs she went two steps at a time and right to the window so she could watch Paul drive out the driveway.

Maggie thought, “Now what will I do the rest of the summer?”

Chapter 3

Maggie had been Jeanie's nursemaid ever since she was born, because their mother's health had been declining, and it was feared that Annie would have to have an operation if her health did not improve. Maggie was glad to take over the care of little Jeanie; it was something she loved to do. Her little sister was two and a half now and she was changing so quickly — going anywhere she pleased and getting into whatever she could find — mostly Maggie's stuff.

Since meeting Paul, Maggie had been so preoccupied with her summer romance and the new dress she made all by herself that she wasn't even aware of what was going on around her. One day it began to dawn on her that she was missing something — Jeanie. Even though Maggie and Paul were around the house quite often, Jeanie would drag him off to play with her. This sometimes aggravated Maggie, but she also admired Paul because he gave Jeanie this attention. It also began to dawn on her that her mother was lying down on her bed more often, and she decided she better start paying attention to what was going on around her house.

She had been wondering why Jake Holden was always around, and lately, he was at their dinner table every night, but she never bothered to ask until she saw him moving in more of his clothes and personal effects. Then she decided that she had better find out what was going on. She had dated Jake off and on, but he was several years older, and he seemed more like a big brother than a boyfriend.

"Momma, I need to know what's going on. Jake is moving in here, bag and baggage."

"I'm so sorry, Maggie. I meant to tell you, but you were so busy, and gone so much, and I have been feeling so rotten that I just didn't find the time. Obviously, you know Jake has been in and out of here for the past six months. He and Bill have become such good friends, and Jake seems to like staying here with Bill. Then last week Jake came to your father and me and asked if he could move in and live here for a while. It seems his mother has a new husband, and he and Jake don't get along. Your father and I thought it over for a little while, then I called Mrs. Holden. I explained Jake's request and after a long silence, she thanked me for calling and agreed it would be best for everyone."

"Whew, and all that has been going on right under my nose, and I didn't even suspect."

"Well, Maggie, you've had your head in the clouds lately, haven't you?"

"I guess I have, but, now I have to get used to another brother and another person to share the bathroom with," Maggie mumbled as she started for the door.

Her mother chastised her, "Maggie, we have so much to be thankful for, and I don't want you to forget that. There is always room for one more."

As Maggie left the room, Annie shook her head and wondered, "When is that girl going to become more serious about the world around her. It's just boys, boys, boys."

Maggie marched upstairs with her mother's words in her head. She went to Bill's door and tapped. The door opened and there was Jake, sandy haired, blue-eyed, and smiling. Maggie stuck out her hand, "Welcome to the McGee family!" Jake grabbed her and placed a great big kiss on her. It wasn't like Paul's, but it was good enough. It said it all. Jake was glad to be there.

For the next several weeks Maggie settled into days of sewing and tending to Jeanie. Occasionally Jake and Maggie went to a movie, double dating with her brother Bill and his girlfriend, Anne Delaney. She always had fun with Jake, but it was no longer like a real date since he moved in to live with them.

Chapter 3

After her whirlwind adventures with Paul, Maggie just wasn't interested in the mundane world that circled around her anymore. Unless she was busy with dates, she seemed glum. Annie noticed how unhappy her daughter seemed to be and wondered how she could help her become the happy-go-lucky young girl she always was. It seemed the more Maggie dated, the more miserable she became when she wasn't dating, and this greatly concerned Annie.

Chapter 4

The perfect solution to Maggie's doldrums came when Annie's brother, Walter called to say he and his family would be in Winston-Salem for a couple of days. He went on to ask if Maggie could go home with them to Charlotte and spend a couple of weeks with Emily, his oldest daughter.

Annie said, "I think Maggie would love to go for a visit, but how will she get home?"

Walter had the solution, "I'll put Maggie on the bus, and you can meet her at the bus station. It's only a three to four hour trip."

"Walter, let me talk to Maggie, and I'll be back to you today. I'm sure she'll be excited to visit Emily," Annie replied.

When Annie hung up the phone, Maggie was right there waiting to see what her mother was talking about. "Momma, what did Uncle Walter say?"

"He and his family are coming tomorrow to stay a few days, and Emily wants you to go home with them and spend a couple of weeks."

Before her mother finished, Maggie headed upstairs to pack her suitcase. Emily was Maggie's favorite cousin. She was only six months older than Maggie, blonde, blue-eyed, beautiful, and well developed. She was quite a contrast to Maggie's dark eyes, auburn hair, and undeveloped frame. They did not seem to notice the difference as they grew up. They had always loved spending time together.

Emily came, and they spent the next two days in the park, dressed in their tennis dresses and carrying their tennis rackets, which was a good way to meet cute boys.

Chapter 4

Sunday arrived, and it was time to load up and drive to Charlotte with Uncle Walter and Aunt Betty. They had never spent two weeks together, but they loved each other, and the thought of spending that much time together excited them both. They had visited each other every summer since they had gotten big enough, but this would be the longest time they had ever spent together, and Maggie had so much to tell Emily.

As Maggie crawled into the car, she shouted good-bye to everyone. Then she noticed little Jeanie hiding behind her mother and looking mighty sad. Maggie got out of the car, went to Jeanie, picked her up, and with a great big hug and kiss, said, "Jeanie, I won't be gone too long. You be a good girl and help Momma. You know Maggie loves you oodles, and I'll bring you a surprise."

"I will, I promise," said little Jeanie.

Maggie wiped a tear from her eye, and got back in the car, and off they drove. After asking several times how long the trip would take, and numerous other questions, the girls began to sing.

"She'll be coming around the mountain when she comes, when she comes."

Uncle Walter chimed in with, "She'll be driving six white horses, when she comes."

The girls sang, "When she comes, when she comes."

"She'll be driving six white horses," Uncle Walker sang.

The girls sleepily sang, "When she comes, when...she... comes

Uncle Walter finished singing, "She'll be driving six white horses."

(Silence)

Aunt Betty touched Uncle Walter's arm saying, "I think you sang them to sleep. Now you can stop singing and pay attention to your driving."

"Why Betty, I'm a good driver. By the way, don't you like my singing?"

"Of course I do, but it's best in the shower."

Three hours later, Uncle Walter pulled into their driveway and announced, "Girls, wake up! We're home!"

The girls sat up, rubbed their eyes, and groaned a little. Lily, Emily's little sister, jumped out and ran to the house screaming, "Daddy, open the door! I need to go see about Stanley."

Maggie looked at Emily and asked, "Who is Stanley?"

"That's Lily's pet duck. You see, Lily has asthma real bad, and she can't be around furry animals, but she can be around fowl, so Mother and Daddy got her a duck."

"That sounds neat," said Maggie.

"Well, my parents thought it wouldn't live but maybe six months, but Stanley is almost three years old now."

"Where do you keep him?"

By now Maggie could hear the constant quacking of a duck, and out the front door came Lily with Stanley waddling right behind her.

Emily answered, "On our screened-in back porch. You'll get tired of being waked up at dawn by a quacking duck, but at least he goes to sleep at dusk."

"How interesting," said Maggie.

Maggie and Emily were getting their suitcases out of the trunk of the car when Maggie heard a young boy calling from across the street.

"Hey Emily, where have you been? Dave's been calling me for two days to see if I knew where you were, and how long you would be gone."

"We went to see my Daddy's sister, Aunt Annie, in Winston-Salem. Come on over, John! I want you to meet my cousin who came home with us. She'll be here for two weeks."

Maggie couldn't stand it any longer, "Emily, who is Dave?"

"He's my new boyfriend, Dave Willis, but I don't call him that in front of Daddy. You know how strict he is."

Maggie sighed, "I know."

Chapter 4

Maggie looked up, and across the street came the best-looking boy she had ever seen - tall, dark, and handsome, with brown eyes so dark they seemed to be black. She thought, "This is going to be a good two weeks." Her thoughts were interrupted as Emily said, "Maggie, this is my good friend John Ereland. And John, this is my cousin, Maggie McGee."

"It's a pleasure to meet you," they said in unison and laughed at the coincidence.

John picked up their bags and followed them into the house. Maggie said to herself, "and he's a gentleman too!"

That night after dinner, Dave and John came over, and they talked on the front steps until they pretty much knew everything there was to know about each other. They were going to be seniors in high school; John and Dave were on the swim team at their school; Maggie studied voice and sang in the church choir; and Emily played the piano. They all planned to go to college, but none was sure where they were going, except John. He had been accepted in the early admissions program at the University of South Carolina and planned on studying medicine. Dave wanted to be an architect and had applied to Clemson's School of Architecture. Maggie had applied to Florida Southern in Lakeland, Florida, to study music, along with several other schools, but she really hoped to be accepted at Florida Southern. Emily was applying to Queen's College in Charlotte, to study business and minor in music.

It was an exciting time in their lives - filled with hopes and dreams of their future. They talked excitedly until late in the evening when Uncle Walter came out and gave them the ten-minute curfew warning. He was pretty strict about dating at night, but the good thing was that he didn't mind the boys hanging around. Quick plans were made to meet at the municipal swimming pool at 10:00 the next morning, where the boys would be practicing.

The boys rose to leave and as they strolled down the path, John said, "We'll see you at ten."

As Maggie and Emily went inside, Emily asked her mother if they could meet the boys at the swimming pool the next morning. She hesitated for a bit and then gave her permission.

As the girls went upstairs to their bedroom, Maggie thought to herself, "I've been here just one day, and look what has happened. I just met a hunk."

The next morning at dawn, Stanley started calling for Lily, "Quack, quack, and quack."

Maggie sat straight up in the bed and punched Emily, "Emily, what's that?"

Emily rolled over and said sleepily, "That's just Stanley, go back to sleep."

Several hours later, Maggie and Emily rushed down to the kitchen to eat a late breakfast.

"Where are you girls going?" Aunt Betty asked.

Emily replied, "We're planning to meet John and Dave at the pool at 10:00. Remember?"

"Oh yes, I remember, but I'd like for you to take Lily and Stanley to the park this afternoon."

"Alright, we'll take them at 2:00," answered Emily.

Maggie and Emily weren't too happy with that idea, but Aunt Betty was being very nice to let them go meet the boys. Maggie understood about looking after little sisters. She was already missing Jeanie.

The girls raced back upstairs to put on their swimsuits and cover-ups, and out the door they went with Lily begging to go with them. Emily called back, "Lily, we'll be home at lunch, and then Maggie and I will take you and Stanley to the park."

Lily ran back into the house screaming, "Momma, Emily and Maggie are going to take Stanley and me to the park after lunch!"

"That's nice, honey; now why don't you take Stanley out in the back yard and play with him for a while?"

Chapter 4

The girls arrived at the pool and found the boys working hard on their swimming and diving. Maggie and Emily sat there and watched the boy's well-tanned bodies dive into the glistening aqua-colored water. When John surfaced, he waved to his audience. Soon the coach ended the practice. The boys yelled, "Come on in girls, the water is fine."

The girls ran and jumped in the water, making a big splash. For the next two hours, they swam, dunked, splashed water, and did all the crazy things that make going to the pool fun. The whistle blew to clear the pool at 12:00. It was time to dry off, don the cover-ups, and walk home. The boys insisted that they walk the girls to their front door, and of course, Maggie and Emily didn't mind at all.

On the way, John asked, "Would you girls like to skate some this afternoon? We can skate in the street in front of our houses."

Emily answered quickly, "That would have been so nice, but we promised Mother we would take Lily and Stanley to the park after lunch. Maybe you all would like to go with us?"

They both answered, "We'd love to! When are you going?"

"Around 2:00."

As they arrived at Emily's house, and the girls waved good-bye saying, "See you at two."

Lily was ready to go as soon as the girls got home, but they reminded her that they needed to eat lunch. "We are going at two," Emily said. Lily stood on one foot and then another, and never took her eyes off of the clock.

The minute the clock hands moved to 2:00, "It's 2:00, and Stanley and I are ready to go," Lily said.

"OK, we're on our way." Emily and Maggie came downstairs dressed in shorts and halters. Emily called back to her mother, "We're on our way to the park, and we have Lily and Stanley with us!"

Outside, the boys were waiting, dressed in white shorts and collared tee shirts. Maggie thought to herself, "Boy, they sure do look good, and John is tall enough!" Three blocks away, their street ended at Washington

Park. Down the street paraded John and Maggie, Dave and Emily, and Lily, with Stanley waddling behind.

They walked through the park, visited the playground, swinging and seesawing and watching Lily go down the tall slide. Maggie thought how nice it would be if she had Jeanie there. While Lily was playing in the sand, John said, "Maggie would you like to go sit in the pavilion for a while?"

Maggie immediately replied, "I sure would!"

John led her to a secluded corner and took her hand as they sat down.

"I've wanted to talk a little, just you and me," John said. Then he added, "How long will you be visiting Emily?"

"Two weeks," Maggie answered.

"I hope I can see you often; today was fun!"

"As often as Uncle Walter allows." Maggie went on, "John, you said you want to be a doctor. How did you make that decision so soon in your life?"

"Well, I've always liked to look after sick animals. My grandparents live on a farm, and there is always something there to look after."

"Why not a veterinarian?"

"I don't know, I just think I would like healing people."

"That's sweet! You're lucky you already know what you want to be."

"How about you?"

"Oh, I just want to get married and be a mother."

"That sounds like a pretty good life to aspire to."

They sat there quietly a while, and before Maggie knew what was happening, John had kissed her right on her lips. She felt a little dizzy and a little bit surprised.

"Why did you do that?" Maggie asked.

"Because I like you, and I wanted you to know," John told her.

Maggie blushed a little and gave him a great big hug.

Chapter 4

Emily called to them and announced, "It's time to take Stanley to the lake."

"We're coming!" Maggie answered.

They all followed Stanley to the lake side; it was as if he knew exactly where he was going. When he reached the lake, he took off, flew a few feet, and landed on the water with a splash. Lily squealed with delight. His splash alerted the resident ducks that a newcomer had arrived, and they came half swimming and half flying to where Stanley had landed. As they approached him, Stanley scurried to land and back to Lily, as if he wasn't sure he was one of them. After a few minutes he went back into the water and swam around with the other ducks, but when it was time to go, Lily called Stanley, and he came to her as fast as he could swim. Maggie could not believe her eyes.

On the way back through the park, John took Maggie by the hand, and that made the afternoon perfect. They strolled hand in hand until they were in sight of Emily's house, and then he let her hand go. John knew how strict Emily's father was, and he didn't want to do anything to upset the next two weeks.

The rest of that week the girls kept busy with meeting the boys at the pool, skating on the block, taking trips to the park, and talking on Emily's front steps in the warm evenings.

Saturday, they were confined to the house to help Aunt Betty get ready for Lily's tenth birthday. Emily and Maggie were in charge of decorating the back yard for the party. John and Dave came over to help out, but they really were more hindrance than they were help. That afternoon when the children arrived, Emily and Maggie organized the games and played with the guests, which made Maggie miss her little Jeanie more than ever.

Sunday the family went to church and then home for a family dinner. The day was miserable and rainy, but Maggie didn't care anyway because she wasn't going to see John, as he had gone to visit his grandparents. Dave wasn't around either, because he stayed home and looked after his little sister, so the girls had a day to themselves and enjoyed playing different games down in the rec room. However, as it approached supper, they began to fret about what the weather would be tomorrow. If it was still pouring, they wouldn't be able to go to the pool.

There fears were unfounded anyway, because Monday morning dawned bright and beautiful, a perfect day to meet the boys at the pool and start the week's routine again. It seemed the past week went by much too fast for Maggie. She hoped her last week would go a little slower. As one day led into another, John found more occasions to hold Maggie's hand and steal a kiss. They swapped addresses with each other and promised to write often. Maggie thought, "I'm going to have a lot of writing to do, but then I'll get a lot of letters, I hope."

The day to leave came all too soon, and Maggie felt sad about going, but she was also excited inside at the thought of being home again. As they loaded up the car to go to the bus station, John ran across the street to say good-bye one more time and cried, "Remember, you promised to write!"

Maggie assured him, "I won't forget."

Uncle Walter said, "Come on, girls. Climb in. We don't want Maggie to miss her bus."

On the way to the station, Maggie began to feel a little sick. This was her first time riding a big bus on a long trip all alone. As she boarded the bus, Uncle Walter gave her the book, *Little Women*, to read. They all kissed good-bye, and she stepped up into the bus, finding a seat near the door. The engine roared, and the bus jerked, and finally Maggie was on her way home. She settled into her seat and opened up the book, but somehow she couldn't get interested. She closed the book, and her eyes, and savored the memory of the past two weeks. She and Emily had had so much fun and she had added another fellow to her list of beaus. She reached into her pocketbook and took out John's address. On it was scribbled, "Don't forget to write. You promised. Love John." She smiled then closed her eyes and slept as the wheels of the bus rolled on and on.

Maggie was awakened by a jostling bump as the big old bus lumbered into the station and came to a rather sudden stop. She rose up in the seat, rubbing her eyes, and took a look at the people standing on the ramp by the bus. There was her father holding Jeanie, and her mother holding Lisa's hand. Her eyes filled with tears. She didn't know how much she had missed them until she looked into their smiling faces. She wanted to jump right out the window, but she would have to wait her place in line to get through the door. As she emerged, her father put Jeanie down, and she flew into Maggie's arms saying, "Did you bring me a present, Maggie?"

"I surely did, cutie, but you'll have to wait until we get home for me to get it out of my suitcase. Then I'll give it to you," Maggie said as she picked Jeanie up and followed her family to the car.

As they coasted into the drive, Maggie could help it no longer. Tears welled up in her eyes again; she was so happy to be home. Her father brought in her bags, and Maggie opened them in the front hall. She began dispensing the gifts she had so carefully selected for each one of them. Jeanie ran off squealing with delight, hugging a new stuffed puppy in her arms.

Annie said, "Let's get your bags up to your room and put your clothes away. Throw your dirty clothes down the laundry chute so I can start washing them."

"So much for being the center of attention," Maggie thought. "It's back to the old routine, but I like it."

Sunday morning, her father called up the stairs, "All you sleepy heads! It's time to rise and shine! Breakfast will be ready in 15 minutes."

With that the rush began for the 2nd floor bathroom. After breakfast everyone managed to get dressed and piled into the car for Sunday school and church. Maggie had been warming up her voice all morning, for she had a solo part in the offertory at the 11:00 service. Her parents always loved to hear her sing, so this was a special day.

After church everyone gathered around the big table in the dining room. It had always been a full table, but now with Jake included, they were elbow to elbow. They bowed heads, and Ruben said the blessing. He added a special prayer for peace in the world, and Maggie wondered why. She had been so busy having a fun-filled summer that she was unaware of what was happening on the other side of the world.

After lunch, Jake asked Maggie if she would go with him to the movies that night, and Maggie said that she would love to go. On the way, Jake said that he was thinking of joining the Army Air Corps in the fall. Maggie was stunned. Her father was praying for peace and Jake was talking about joining the Air Corps. She spoke up and asked, "Jake, what's going on? Why would you want to go into the service?"

"Maggie, honey, you haven't been paying attention to what's happening around the world. We will probably get in this war before the end of the year. The turmoil in Europe is boiling over."

"Come on Jake, let's not talk about that any more. I want to have a good time with you tonight."

"That's exactly what I had in mind."

When they returned home that evening, it seemed strange to get out of the car, go into the house together, go upstairs together, and say goodnight at the top of the stairs. Once again, Maggie realized that this had not been like a real date, but more like a night out with her big brother. But that was OK, too.

Chapter 5

The end of August was always a time to begin thinking about going back to school. Maggie called her best friend, Nancy Hanes, to catch up on what had gone on for the last few weeks.

"Nancy, this is Maggie. Can we get together today and talk about our summer vacations?"

"Sure, but where have you been? James has been bugging me the last two weeks as to where you were," Nancy said, rather exasperated.

"I'm sorry I didn't let you know, but I went to Charlotte to visit my cousin, Emily. It came up suddenly, and I forgot to call you. I'll tell you all about it when I see you."

"Ok, I'll meet you at the park around two, and we can go to the drug store and catch up. I've got a lot to tell you, too. Be sure to call James. He's real angry with you."

"Pooh on James! I'll worry about him later."

"Maggie, you shouldn't take James for granted, you know what a good friend he is," Nancy admonished her.

"I know, Nancy, I'll call him as soon as we hang up. I really do like James a lot. I better go now, so I can get dressed and meet you in the park at two."

Maggie and Nancy spent the afternoon relating their summer romances, and talking about what they thought it would be like to be a senior in high school. They even planned what they were going to wear the first day of school. Before the afternoon was over, they had laid plans for which boy they were going to set their cap for. It was a very busy afternoon, but very productive for soon-to-be seniors.

The first week of September, Ruben took Bill to Charleston to enter the Citadel. Maggie could hardly believe that it was time for Bill to attend college, but, she thought, it will only be one more year before I'll be going off to college. I really hope I will be accepted at Florida Southern.

School started the day after Labor Day. Maggie took a look at her schedule and was relieved to see that it was a light load, because her mother was having serious health problems, and she had begun to take over more and more of Jeanie's care. She thought that she would be needed to continue helping her mother as much as she could. Maggie got up early everyday, bathed Jeanie, and fed her before leaving for school. Since they lived near the school, Maggie was able to come home at lunch time to feed Jeanie and put her down for a nap. She realized her mother was not well, and soon her mother told her that she would be going to the hospital in a few weeks to have her breasts removed. Maggie began crying and begged, "Why, Momma?"

Her mother hugged her tightly and whispered, as if afraid to say the words, "Because, Maggie, I have cancer."

The words burned a hole in Maggie's heart, and she just began to sob. She could say nothing. No words came.

Her mother held her close and said, "Maggie, you will have to take over as much of little Jeanie's care as you can. I hope it won't interfere with your school work."

Maggie assured her mother that she and Lisa could look after their little sister and go to school too.

"Thank you, honey. That will take a lot of worry off of me."

The day of Annie's operation Maggie went with her father to the hospital and waited with him. The waiting seemed interminable. Maggie sat there beside her father and remembered all the things her mother had said to her. "Maggie, you don't take things seriously enough. Maggie, you need to grow up. Maggie, life isn't just playing." These motherly admonitions spun round and round in her brain.

"Daddy, how serious is this operation?" Maggie asked.

"Very serious, but your mother is a very healthy woman, and, with God looking after her, she will be all right," her father answered, as if he were trying to convince himself.

The doctor entered the waiting room and came right over to Maggie and Ruben.

"Annie came through the operation very well. We had to remove the right breast, but the good news is that we were able to get all the cancer. She's in recovery right now."

"May we see her?"

"She'll be sleeping for a couple more hours. Why don't you go get something to eat, and when you get back, you may see Annie." The doctor went on, "I'll need to talk to you before you leave. Annie will be just fine, but she will require a lengthy recovery."

When they returned from lunch, they were allowed to go in and visit Annie. Maggie thought her mother looked so pale and exhausted, but when she managed a smile and a weak, "Don't look so glum; I'm going to be fine," Maggie began to feel better.

It was reassuring to Maggie to hear her mother's voice. She looked at her father as he wiped tears from his eyes.

The doctor came in and said, "Good, you are all here. I am happy to tell you that Annie will be fine, but she will need to stay in the hospital about a week. Then she will need lots of rest when she goes home."

Maggie spoke right up, "Don't worry! We can look after Momma, and she won't have to lift a finger until you say she can."

"That sounds good. Annie, you have a fine daughter here!" The doctor said as he patted Maggie on the head. He spoke to Ruben, "I think it's time to let Annie get some much-needed rest."

Ruben went to Annie's bedside, stooped, kissed her, and whispered, "I love you. We'll take care of you."

Annie smiled and closed her eyes.

While Annie was in the hospital, Ruben assumed the role of their mother. One day, Maggie asked her father if it was all right to go to the movies with James the following Saturday night. Her father said that would be fine, and promised her that he would be home in time for Maggie to leave on her date. When James came to the door to pick Maggie up, her father was there in the front hall, reminding them to be in by 11:00. Maggie gave her father a big kiss and said, "Don't worry. We'll be home on time."

James and Maggie got out of the movie and went into the nearby soda shop for cherry cokes. They were watching the time, and they left in plenty of time to be home with minutes to spare. Then it happened. James heard the fire-truck sirens, and he turned to follow them. Maggie cried, "James, I've got to be home in ten minutes."

"I know. I just want to see where they are going." He had a devilish grin on his face.

Maggie kept pleading, but James kept following the fire trucks. Maggie said, "I'm going to be in real trouble, and it's your fault." She sank down low in her seat and began crying. James realized she meant business, so he tried to turn around, but by then he was blocked in by the fire-truck chasers. James wheeled into Maggie's driveway 30 minutes late, and her father was standing on the front door steps.

"Where have you two been?" he cried, "I've been worried sick!" He sounded just like her mother. And then he added, "With your mother in the hospital, I'm the one who has to worry about you."

Maggie realized that it had always been her mother who worried, and Daddy had let that be her job, but now it was his job, and he was finding out what it was like to play Momma.

Ruben sent Maggie inside and began to reprimand the "young man," as he called him.

Chapter 5

Maggie ran upstairs crying, and as she burst in the door, Lisa said, "What in the world is the matter with you?"

"Daddy is outside yelling at James, for bringing me home late." She snubbed and ran on, "I know he'll never ask me out again, and we weren't that late!"

Lisa, the quiet and more serious one of the sisters, reminded Maggie, "You know Momma's in the hospital, and Daddy feels all the responsibility for us, and he really doesn't know how to handle it. Don't blame him, Maggie."

Maggie dried her eyes and slowly went downstairs. She hugged her father as he came in the door. She said, "I'm sorry if I worried you, Daddy."

He gave her a great big hug and kiss and said, "James explained it was his fault. Go to bed now. We'll talk about it tomorrow."

Sunday morning as Maggie arrived at church, James was waiting for her on the lawn in front of the church. He came up to her and said, "I hope I didn't get you in too much trouble. I told your father it was my fault, but he was so mad I don't know if he heard me."

Maggie assured him that her father had cooled down by the time he got in the house, and he seemed all right this morning. She told him, "You know my mother is in the hospital, and he is so worried about her, and he feels responsible for all of us."

"Maggie, I want a date this weekend. I want to prove to your father I can take you out and get you home on time," James pleaded.

"OK. Make it Friday night. Mother is coming home Saturday, and I want to go with Daddy to bring her home," Maggie said.

Relieved, James answered back, "It's a date! Thanks!"

Friday night, James arrived right on time. As they turned to leave James said to Mr. McGee, "I promise we will be home on time."

"Thank you, James, go on and have a good time," Mr. McGee said.

Saturday morning, Maggie was up bright and early helping her father fix breakfast. As they all assembled in the kitchen, there was an air of excitement among the family, especially their father and little Jeanie. Today their mother was coming home.

As Ruben finished clearing the table, he said, "OK, all of you get in the car; we're going to bring your momma home."

Jeanie squealed, and Maggie grabbed her hand as they ran to the car. It seemed like a long time since their mother was home.

By November, the leaves were falling, and the lawn in front of the house looked like a carpet of gold. Maggie's mother had been home a couple of weeks and was beginning to feel much better.

Thanksgiving and Christmas were not the same that year because everyone had to chip in to make the dinners, but there was a new appreciation of all the work their mother did for these holidays. No one really minded though as the family was together, and Maggie was grateful that her Mother was doing well.

The New Year of 1941 rang in with our nation at peace, but the world around was in a state of upheaval. Maggie's 17th birthday was January 17th and as it approached, it began to dawn on her that her wonderful, happy life might be threatened.

Even her birthday would be different this year. She couldn't have a birthday party, because her mother was still not able to take on any extra activities, and she wondered what she would do.

But James, as always, came through and asked to take her out. Nancy and Doug went along with them to celebrate her birthday, which ended up being just as much fun as a party. As she mounted the stairs to her bedroom after this night of celebration, she wondered, "What will seventeen be like?"

Chapter 6

It was getting close to Easter, and Annie was busy sewing their Easter outfits — a frilly little dress for Jeanie, a jumper dress for Lisa, and a dress and coat ensemble for Maggie. Maggie helped when she could, cutting them out, basting, pressing and whipping in the hems. She liked sewing with her mother, because it gave them time to talk. One afternoon when the dresses were nearly finished, her Mother announced that after school that day she was taking the girls to town to buy their Easter bonnets and shoes. Maggie was so excited she could hardly get through the school day. She loved to go shopping better than anything else.

That afternoon they all rode the bus to town, and when the bus stopped in the center of town, they headed straight to the shoe department of the Anchor Store. Jeanie couldn't wait, so she was fitted first with little white Mary Jane shoes. She cried when Annie wouldn't let her wear them home. Next Lisa was fitted with a pair of black- and- white low-heeled sandals, which would go very well with her black-and-white checked jumper and white blouse. Now it was Maggie's turn. Before Maggie could tell her mother what kind of shoes she wanted, her mother said, "Maggie, I think you're old enough to have a pair of high-heeled shoes. Would you like that?"

She hugged her mother, ran over, picked up a pair of black patent leather sandals, and said, "Momma, I'd love a pair like these. May I try them on?"

Her mother smiled and replied, "I think those would look stunning with your new pink coat and dress." Soon the salesman came back carrying a shoebox in his hands, and as he opened it, there was a pair of black patent leather sandals in Maggie's size.

Maggie stuck her foot out, feeling like Cinderella waiting for the glass slipper to be put on her foot. She knew it would fit. He placed the other shoe on. Maggie rose up on her high-heeled sandals, and she couldn't believe how grown-up they made her feel. It was like walking with your head in the clouds. She ran over to her mother and said, "Thank you, thank you, thank you!"

The next purchases were their Easter hats, but this was not nearly as exciting as getting a pair of high-heeled sandals. Finished with their shopping, they headed back to the bus stop, and boarded their home-bound bus. Maggie hugged her box of shoes to her chest like a precious treasure. She could hardly wait to get home and call Nancy to tell her about the shoes.

Easter weekend arrived, and plans were made to attend the Moravian sunrise service. Bill was home from the Citadel for the holidays, and he and Jake were taking Maggie and Anne out Saturday night and to the sunrise service, Sunday morning. Anne was home for the Easter holidays from Greensboro College, and since she started dating Bill, she had become a good friend of Maggie's as well. And to Maggie's amazement, Bill wasn't so much the pesky older brother he used to be, but now was more of a friend.

Anne came over Saturday night to spend the night with Maggie. The girls dressed up to go out to dinner with the boys, followed by an Andy Hardy movie. Maggie looked over at her black patent-leather sandals sitting right beside Anne's black patent-leather sandals, and smiled as she left the room.

When they got downstairs, her mother said, "Girls, the radio is predicting a cold front to move in tonight. You two had better take a sweater tonight, and you need to dress warm for the early service. Particularly, put something warm on your feet."

As they raced upstairs to get sweaters, Maggie thought, "I can't leave my sandals behind tomorrow morning." Out the door all four of them went, laughing and giggling. The evening was fun, except that the boys kept talking about the possibility of the country going to war, and what branch of service they wanted to go into.

Maggie said, "Let's not talk about that war stuff anymore. Let's go to the Dairy Bar and see who we can find there."

"OK, Maggie. You never think about anything serious, do you?" Bill chided.

At the Dairy Bar they joined a group of their friends and finished off the evening. They arrived home on time and headed up to bed. Her mother called after them, "Don't forget to dress warm in the morning! They say it's going to snow."

"Snow!" Anne exclaimed.

"Don't worry. My mother has a way of worrying about things that never happen."

They all laughed and headed for their beds. The four of them were up at 3:00 the next morning. With only one bathroom to use, there was a lot of scurrying around in order to get dressed. They needed to be at the Moravian Church before sunrise, which was 5:00 A.M. Anne and Maggie dressed in their Easter outfits- hats, gloves, and straw hats, and, yes, they had to wear those black patent-leather sandals. They all piled into the car laughing at what their mother had said about snow. They parked at the square, and walked up to the church where the crowd was assembling. The Moravian bands were playing the traditional Easter music which was echoing back and forth from the church to the cemetery. It was hauntingly beautiful. The sun began to rise over the cemetery gates as the minister said, "The Lord is risen."

The mass of people responded, "The Lord is risen indeed." The people began to follow the band up the cobblestone street to the crest of the hill in the cemetery. By then the sun had risen and the world was eerily beautiful. The service continued with the bands playing and the people singing. Half way through the service a black cloud rolled over the sun, and it began to snow-yes, snow. When the service was over, the four young people began to follow the procession back to the front of the church. First one inch fell, then two inches, and before they could get back to the car, three inches of snow covered the ground. It was as if the snow flakes were falling down in layers. As they walked back to the car, Maggie and Anne could not see their black patent-leather sandals, and their feet were so-o-o-o cold. Their beautiful straw bonnets were keeping the snow off of their heads, but the hats were beginning to droop. Anne didn't say a word about what Maggie's mother had said about snow, but Maggie spoke up and said, "I guess Mother knows best. Next time, I'll listen to her even if it's in June." They all laughed.

It was a quiet ride home because they dreaded to hear what Annie would say. As they came in the house, Annie surprised them all by only saying, "Go take off those wet clothes and come back downstairs. Daddy has built a fire in the den, and you can warm your toes there. I am warming two pans of water for you girls to soak your feet in. I know they must be frozen."

Maggie was so grateful that her mother had not said, "Girl, I told you not to wear those sandals," and had refrained from an "I told you so" scolding. The girls supposed she knew they had already figured out that Mother knew best. Maggie and Anne warmed themselves by the fire until it was time to dress for church. This time they dressed warmly and left those black patent-leather sandals at home. They arrived at church just in time for Maggie to don her choir robe and join the choir in the singing of the beautiful Easter music that they had been practicing for the past two months. It was a good thing Maggie was not singing a solo, because she was still too cold to take a deep breath.

Chapter 7

Two few weeks after Easter, Maggie came home from school, and her Mother called to her as she came in the door, "Maggie, the mail came and you received four letters. They're on the front hall table."

Maggie excitedly grabbed the letters, ran to her room, and jumped on the bed. Lisa wasn't there to complain that she had messed up her bed, and she thought, "I'll smooth it out before she gets home."

Maggie sat straddle legged on the bed and began to open the first letter. It was a letter from Jake.

Dear Maggie, *April 16, 1941*

I am now in Florida with my mother. We will be at my grandmother's for the next month. Mother wants to visit all of our relatives while we're there. I kinda dread it, but it means so much to her that I consented to go with her. I will be enlisting in the Army Air Corps when I get back to Winston.

Oh well, I'll get to soak up a lot of sun and do a little girl watching, but I'll probably be here for the next month, so please write. I miss the McGee household, tell them all hello and give them a hug for me.

I hope I'll have some time to take you out when I come back. I'll let you know when I find out exactly when we will be coming home. I am missing you and the rest of the McGee family.

Love to all of you, Jake

The second letter was from Paul. She thought to herself, "He has really been regular in his writing, a letter about every three weeks, which is better than I've been." The thought made her feel a little guilty. Paul wrote that he was looking forward to graduation and planned to be in Winston-Salem June 10th. He went on to write that he could only stay three weeks because he was going to be a tennis instructor at a day camp in Spartanburg the rest of the summer, and he hoped he and Maggie could spend a lot of time together during his visit to Winston. Maggie thought, "OK, I'll graduate June 6th, and Paul will be here June 10th for three weeks, so that takes care of what I will do in June." She smiled as she opened the third letter.

The next one was from John, who had not written quite as regularly as Paul, but often enough. He wrote:

Dear Maggie, *April 19, 1941*

Graduation is almost here, and I was hoping to hear from you as to when you will be visiting Emily this summer. I remember how much fun we had last summer, and I hope you won't disappoint me by not coming. Please write soon and let me know of your plans. I talked to Emily yesterday, and she said she hoped you were coming, but that no date had been set. Hurry up and set that date.

Love, John

Maggie lay back and smiled, "Well, it will have to be in July. I'm booked all of June." She let out a squeal of delight.

Annie heard it and called to Maggie, "Is everything all right up there?"

"Everything is wonderful up here! I'll be down in a minute to tell you all my news!" Maggie shouted back.

She sat and held the last letter awhile, wondering what her brother Bill was writing to her about. She ripped open the fourth envelope, and was pleased when she began to read.

Chapter 7

Dear Sis, *April 13, 1941*

Everything here at the Citadel is going well, I'm making good grades and have finally learned how not to get demerits. They're no fun because you have to walk them off on the weekends, and I love my weekends too much.

Here at the Citadel the spring fling will be May 1st, and I thought you might like to come down to Charleston and attend the dance weekend with my new girlfriend, Miriam Gill and me. She's a cute girl, a lot like you, but nicer. I think you will like her, and she says she would like for you to stay with her at her home. Tell Mom I'll take real good care of you. Let me know as soon as you make your plans, that is, if you want to come. Write to me and let me know, and I'll make the arrangements and get you a date.

Love, your "dear" brother, Bill

"Do I want to come?" she said aloud as she bounded off the bed, and down the stairs calling, "Momma, where you are?"

"Maggie, don't be so loud, you'll wake Jeanie. I'm here in the kitchen," her mother answered.

Maggie ran in the kitchen shaking a letter in her mother's face, "Do you know who this letter is from?"

"Paul, John, or which ever boy you are writing now?" Her mother guessed.

"No, it's from Bill. He has asked me to come to Charleston to attend the Spring Fling Weekend at the Citadel." She was breathless when she finished. But went on asking, "Can I go? Please, please, please?"

"Of course you can. He asked me if you might like to go to a dance weekend at the Citadel, and I said, "Do birds like to fly?" Her mother went on, "I checked on the bus schedules, and you can ride a bus straight there and have only one change coming home. Bill will meet you at the station."

Maggie could not believe her ears. Her mother and brother had everything all worked out for her to attend a weekend at The Citadel with all those boys dressed in handsome uniforms. Maggie reached over and hugged her mother so tightly that she said, "Honey, I need to breathe a little."

Maggie turned to go back upstairs, suddenly realizing what a mess she had left in their room. Lisa was due home any minute, and she would hit the ceiling if she found their room untidy.

"Honey, who were the other letters from?" her mother asked.

Maggie called back, "Oh, Paul and John wrote about this summer, and oh, by the way." She turned and went back into the kitchen, "I had a letter from Jake. He was writing to tell the family where he'd be for the next several months. He asked me to write him and to give the family his love." She went on, "I think that was all, but I'll bring Jake's letter down so you can read it. I gotta go now and clean up our room so Lisa won't have to run to you to make me clean up my mess."

As Maggie left the kitchen, Annie smiled and said, "How could I raise daughters that are so different?"

Before her mother got that thought out, Maggie was bounding down the steps, calling, "Mother, do you realize, I'll need a new evening dress, and what else, I don't know?"

"Yes, I have, and I thought tomorrow we could go pick out a pattern and some material, so I can make a new dress for you. I was going to make you a new one for the junior-senior dance later in the month, and this dress can be worn for both."

"Oh Mother, you are so smart. You're always one step ahead of me. You know I love you, don't you?"

"Yes, honey, I know you do, but please keep telling me."

"Well, if I forget, please remind me to tell you."

"You bet I will," her mother said as she pointed the way back up the stairs. "You had better get back to your duties, or Lisa will be hopping mad."

Maggie stomped back up the stairs, but she was smiling all the way.

Chapter 8

Time always seems to creep by slowly when anticipating something exciting, and that's exactly what Maggie experienced the two weeks before her trip to Charleston. She looked after Jeanie so her Mother could finish her lovely ball gown, with its royal blue velvet tight-fitting bodice that extended to the hipline. The skirt was multi-layered with different tones of light blue to darker shades of royal blue. The taffeta petticoat under the net skirt made a swish, swish sound when Maggie walked. It was the most beautiful dress she had ever seen. She went over to her mother, sitting at the sewing machine, and hugged her. "Thanks Momma, you've done it again."

"I've done what?"

"You've proven you're the best mom and the best seamstress in the whole wide world!"

They both smiled. "Maggie, take that dress off so I can sew on the hooks at the neck, press it, and hang it up. It's finished."

Maggie began the next week by making a list of things she needed to pack. In anticipation, Maggie had all her bags packed by Thursday night. She was up and ready early on Friday and caught the bus for Charleston at 9:00 A.M., with her heart pounding with excitement and apprehension over the coming weekend.

After an uneventful trip, the bus rolled into the station, and there was Bill - standing there with the cutest little girl- she wasn't as big as a minute. Bill grabbed Maggie as she descended the steps of the bus, and gave her a brotherly kiss. Maggie thought as he kissed her,

"Hey, Bill's a pretty neat brother. He's pretty nice, blond-haired, blue-eyed, and good looking." Bill grabbed her again and hugged her so tightly, she knew he was glad to see her, too.

"Maggie, this is my girlfriend, Miriam Gill. Miriam, this is my sister, Maggie."

Miriam was petite with a head full of brunette ringlets around her face and her hair tossed on top of her head. When Miriam smiled, Maggie saw she had piercing, unforgettable, green eyes.

Miriam smiled, saying, "It's so nice to meet you, Maggie. I feel as if I know you. Bill talks so much about you."

"Really," said Maggie. "Good or bad?"

"Always good," Miriam answered.

"Are you sure you're talking about my brother?" Maggie leaned over and hugged Bill. They all went off laughing.

Bill hailed a cab and they drove to the old section of Charleston, where Miriam lived. It was so enchanting. One entered her home from the sidewalk through a wrought- iron gate and into a garden area, then down a long path leading into the front hall at the middle of the house. There they entered the parlor, which was furnished with a Victorian sofa and chairs, covered in royal blue velvet. The windows were heavily draped with damask and lace curtains on the windows to give a sense of privacy. Maggie had never seen anything like this before; she felt as if she were going back in time.

Bill returned to the Citadel, leaving Maggie and Miriam to get acquainted. As Maggie followed Miriam up the ornate staircase, Maggie said. "Miriam I love your home. It is so sweet of you to ask me to stay with you and your mother."

"I was so happy to have you come, it's more fun when you have someone to share going to all the activities. Here's our room, come in and make yourself at home."

They dropped the bags and flopped on the bed. They spent the rest of the day telling each other about their lives. Maggie found out Miriam was an only child, and her father had died when she was very young. She and her mother lived there alone, but her grandparents lived close by. She was a senior in high school, as was Maggie, and they both loved music. Maggie was really struck by the differences between her family and Miriam's — she had so many brothers and sisters around her all the time and Miriam's life seemed that it would be lonely. And, yet, it wasn't.

They discussed what they were wearing for all the weekend activities. Miriam told Maggie that there was a dress parade at the Citadel at 2:00 Saturday, and that Bill would meet them after the parade and show them around the school. Maggie shivered as she realized how exciting this weekend was going to be. Miriam also told her that Bill had asked Jim Arnold to be her escort after the parade and at the dance. Maggie thought, "This is sounding better all the time. I hope he's tall enough. Oh well, that doesn't matter. He'll be in uniform and anyone looks good in a uniform."

"Miriam, I'm worried I won't know enough guys to dance with me, and I'll end up being a wall-flower, or Jim will have to dance every dance with me," Maggie confessed.

Miriam laughed. "Don't worry, the boys take care of that. They have a dance card for you which they get their buddies to sign, so that each of your dances are spoken for. You meet a lot of nice guys that way, and no one ends up being a wall-flower. In fact, that's how I met your brother Bill."

"Boy, that's a relief!"

Bill called when they were getting ready for bed, "Hi, Miriam, how are things going?"

"Every thing is going great! Maggie and I haven't stopped talking since she got here, Bill. She's a real fun gal, and she loves her brother!" Miriam answered.

"Let me talk to her a minute, please."

"OK. Maggie, your brother is on the phone and wants to speak to you."

Maggie grabbed the phone and said, "Bill, I am having so much fun, and I love Miriam; she's one cute girl!" She turned and smiled at Miriam.

"Calm down, Maggie, and let me tell you the plans. It's almost lights out, so I can't talk much longer. You and Miriam will come to the Citadel parade grounds at 1:30. Miriam knows where to go because she's been here before. Your date, Jim Arnold, will meet you and Miriam after the parade. Got it?"

"Thanks, Bill. I got it, especially since Miriam already filled me in. Don't worry. We will be there and we will be on time. I love you." Maggie hung up the phone with a little tear of happiness in her eyes. "How could I be so lucky to have such a caring brother? And here all the time I've been thinking he was such a jerk. I guess I was born under the right sign to get a brother like Bill." She closed her eyes and began dreaming of the next day's adventure.

The sun rose warm in the Charleston skies. As it streamed into the bedroom window, the girls began to stir. Each lay there thinking about what they had to do that day, each reluctant to make the first move.

Finally, Miriam sat up in bed, stretched, turned to Maggie, and asked, "Are you awake?"

After a few seconds, Maggie rolled over, and weakly said, "I think so."

They both laughed and Miriam asked, "You ready to put on a robe and go down for breakfast?"

Maggie jumped out of bed, threw on her robe, and answered, "Show me the way; I can always eat, especially in the morning."

Downstairs, Miriam's mother invited the girls out into the garden where they feasted on a wonderful breakfast. Around them were blooming an array of delicious smelling flowers and overhead, bougainvillea hung heavy with blooms. The air was warm, and it seemed like the beginning of a perfect day. Miriam's mother came out and reminded the girls to go upstairs and begin getting ready. "You know your hair has to be washed and rolled up. You know how long that takes."

The girls headed to their bedroom to lay out their clothes for the day's affairs.

Chapter 8

Maggie unzipped the hanging bag that covered her ball gown and Miriam gasped, "Maggie, it's just beautiful, and Bill said your mother made it for you."

Maggie smiled, "Yes, Mother made it; in fact, she makes most of my clothes."

"You're a lucky girl," said Miriam, as she headed into the bathroom to wash her hair. "Maggie, I won't take but a minute, and then you can be next."

Before long both heads were shampooed and rolled up in rollers, making the two of them look like they were wearing large helmets. It would take at least an hour to dry, so they went down to the parlor. The night before, Maggie and Miriam had realized that they had more in common that just being high school seniors on the eve of graduating, and, of course, pursuing young men. They both loved music. Miriam played the piano, and Maggie loved to sing. In the parlor, time rolled on as they played and sang the morning away. Miriam's mother came to the door and called to the girls, "You two sound beautiful, but you had better scoot upstairs to get dressed for the parade. It will be time to leave in 45 minutes. You must get there on time."

When they began to dress they could not believe how similar their outfits were. They each had chosen plaid, pleated skirts, frilly white blouses and cardigan sweaters to match their skirts. They looked a little like twins. Forty-five minutes later the girls were downstairs giggling in anticipation.

As Mrs. Gill drove the girls to the Citadel, Maggie asked Miriam, "Would you like to visit me in Winston-Salem this summer? We could have so much fun! Bill will be home, and we could double date!"

Miriam was delighted with the idea and asked her mother if she might go and visit Maggie. "Girls, let's talk about that in the morning." Her mother said. "After Maggie makes sure it is all right with her mother."

Maggie piped up and said, "I know she'll say it is OK for Miriam to come."

In front of the Citadel, the girls jumped out of the car, thanked Miriam's mother for getting them there on time, and proceeded to the parade grounds.

Maggie looked up at the imposing entrance, and even though she had seen pictures of it, she was still totally impressed with the grandeur of the building. The girls followed the arriving crowd into the inner courtyard, where the band was playing. This raised goose bumps on both of the girls. They clasped hands and squeezed each other's hand until it hurt. They were ushered to their seats by a cadet in parade dress uniform, and Maggie caught a glimpse of Bill, and winked at him.

As the parade began, the cadets looked very handsome in their grey dress uniforms with their chests covered with gold buttons. Their white-gloved hands carried rifles with bayonets that glistened as the sun flashed on their surfaces. The band played marches as the soldiers performed their intricate maneuvers.

When the parade was finished, the commandant yelled, "Dismissed!" There was bedlam on the field as the cadets dispersed to find their dates and families. Through the mass of people, Maggie saw Bill coming toward her. He was grinning, and following right behind him was one of those good-looking cadets. Bill stopped right in front of her and said, "Maggie, this is Jim Arnold." He turned and added, "Jim, this is my kid sister, Maggie."

Bill kissed Miriam and said, "you and Jim know each other, don't you?"

"Oh, yes," they both quickly responded.

Jim was tall, which pleased Maggie. His red hair glowed in the sun, setting off his warm green eyes. He had an easy smile that made Maggie feel as if she had known him forever. He proudly took Maggie by the hand and led her on a tour of the Citadel.

The boys escorted them all over the campus, even showing them their barracks rooms. Maggie could not believe how bare they were, with not a thing strewn around. Maggie said, "Bill, I can't believe this is your room. Do you have a maid?" They all laughed.

Chapter 8

"You keep it this way or you walk off demerits every weekend, and you know I'd rather not miss my weekends."

Jim agreed, "It's not that hard after you get used to doing it their way."

"You girls sit down on the bench here and wait for us to get changed," Bill said. "Then we'll walk down to the Battery before dinner."

The boys disappeared up the iron steps to get out of those "straight jackets," as they called them. They were back almost immediately, and the four of them ran off to catch the streetcar and then take a long walk along the Battery. The Spanish moss-covered trees made a canopy over the street along the Battery, and the sun peeped through the leaves, sending intricate patterns of sunlight dancing all around them. The wind blew a soft breeze off the river, making the afternoon pleasant for a walk. Time sped by so quickly that they could hardly believe when it was time to find a place to eat and get the girls home to dress for the ball. They dined in an old house right on the Battery. They all ordered seafood cooked Cajun style and enjoyed fruit crepes for dessert. Bill went outside to hail a cab, which was ready and waiting when the others came outside.

The cab drove them along the Battery and through old Charleston. Maggie was wide-eyed. Seeing all the old, large, colorful mansions that lined the streets made her feel that she was back in the 1800s. When the cab pulled up in front of Miriam's, the boys took the girls to the door and bade them farewell. They went back to the waiting cab, and returned to the Citadel to dress for the dance. Two hours later Bill and Jim were knocking at the front door, and when Miriam opened the door, she saw two very handsome fellows. Miriam invited them into the parlor, and as they entered, Maggie followed.

Bill began to tell the girls about the etiquette for girls entering the grand hall. "When you enter, you will be on your escort's arm, like this." He took Maggie by the hand and showed her how to place her hand lightly on his arm.

Maggie giggled and said, "Oh, this is going to be fun!"

"This is serious," Bill said, a little irritated. "You don't want to embarrass Jim, do you?" He went on to explain, "You move through the receiving line, and at the end you will meet General Summerville. To each one you meet, you will say, 'I'm so glad to meet you,' and when you get to the General, most times the girls do a little curtsy."

By then, Maggie was practicing a bow, and nearly fell.

Everyone laughed. "No, Maggie," Bill said. "Not a bow, just a curtsy." He went on to show her how, and she thought, "He looks so silly, and where did he learn all this stuff?"

"Miriam, show Maggie how to curtsy, so she won't embarrass Jim," Bill said. Miriam proceeded to demonstrate a curtsy, and in no time Maggie was doing a curtsy like a real lady.

When Miriam came back in the parlor with their wraps, Bill said, "You girls won't need those wraps. It's a very warm evening."

"Oh, Bill, you don't wear these wraps for warmth. See how light they are? They're just made out of velvet."

"Well, why do you need them?"

"Silly, to cover our bare shoulders."

"That sounds silly to me."

"Well, a lady covers her bareness with a shawl or a cape, even if it is warm, or at least that's what Momma says"

"I guess if Momma says so, it's got to be right."

By now the cab had returned, and the boys held the wraps for the girl, with no more questions as they escorted them to the cab.

Miriam's mother called to them, "Have a wonderful evening!"

Once again Maggie looked out of the car as they were arriving and was excited by the vastness of the Citadel. She felt chills run all over her as she climbed out of the cab and saw Jim extend his white-gloved hand to her. Maggie thought, "This can't be me. I feel like a princess, or maybe, Cinderella, going to a ball!"

By now they were inside, and Jim offered his arm. As Bill had shown her, she laid her gloved hand lightly on his arm and proceeded down the receiving line. Her heart was in her throat as she neared the end of the line and her curtsy was coming up. Maggie thought, "Don't let me flub this curtsy. Bill will never let me forget it."

"General Summerville, my date, Miss Maggie McGee," said Jim.

Maggie made a small, perfect curtsy, and then smiled as she said, "I'm so honored to meet you."

Jim squeezed her hand and winked at her as he led her onto the dance floor. The band was playing a waltz, and as Jim took her into his arms and began to sweep her across the floor, Maggie felt like Scarlet O'Hara in Gone with the Wind dancing in Ashley Wilkes's arms.

Bill and Jim had filled her dance card with all of their friends, to make sure she had a good time. It was a beautiful and exciting sight looking across the dance floor at all the cadets in their dress uniforms and the girls in their ball gowns. It was like living in a dream world. The band played waltzes, slow two-step pieces and a few fox trots, but no jitterbug music. Maggie thought to her self, "I sure would like to cut loose with one jitterbug, but tonight I must be a dignified young lady."

The band began to play "Star Dust," and Jim came to dance the last dance with her. She looked up at him and thought, "Boy, he is good looking and he's tall enough!"

"I've had a mighty good time today, Maggie! I hope I can come to see you sometime."

Maggie smiled up at him and said, "I think that would be lovely; maybe you could come home with Bill one weekend."

"Sounds great," Jim said as he led Maggie off the dance floor and over to the side to join Bill and Miriam.

Bill had called a cab, and had rescued the girl's wraps. The boys helped them put on their wraps, and then they strolled outside into the warm moonlit night. Maggie ran over to Bill and gave him a great big sisterly hug and kiss.

Bill was shocked and asked, "What was that for?"

"Just because you are the best big brother a girl could ever have, and I love you." Maggie was shocked too as she heard her own words. This had been one of the best days of her life. They all climbed into the cab, exhausted.

Bill and Jim saw them to Miriam's front door, and after thanking each other for a lovely evening, they received a goodnight kiss and the evening ended.

The girls went in the house and ran up stairs. After they took off those lovely ball gowns and let their hair down, they sat in the middle of their beds until the wee hours of the morning. They were so excited about the whole day that sleep did not come until very late.

Morning came much too soon and they quickly regretted their chatting the night before. The girls had to scramble to get Maggie ready to go to the bus station for her trip back to Winston-Salem. Bill came to pick them up, and on the way to the bus station Maggie told Bill, "Miriam is coming to visit me in Winston the last week of July! Isn't that great?"

Bill was more than delighted because he would be coming home the last of May, and he would miss seeing Miriam. Bill said, "That's a great idea. I'm so glad you girls got along so well."

Maggie's bus was just pulling into the station, as they arrived at the bus station, Bill ran and checked her luggage for her and when he returned, it was time for her to leave. Maggie boarded the bus and waved good-bye to Bill and her new friend, Miriam. She settled into her seat for the long trip home, with many wonderful memories whirling around in her head. Maggie fell asleep so soundly that when the bus arrived at the stop where she was to change buses, she missed getting off to make the change. The bus pulled out and headed on its way, but after about an hour it rumbled into a small station and everyone began to get off. Maggie gathered up her things to change busses, only to find out that this bus was carrying only college students, in fact only female college students. She was in Rock Hill, S.C. All the girls were going back to college after a weekend away. She decided something was wrong; there was no other bus there for her to change to. She asked the bus driver, and he informed her that she had missed getting off the bus back at Beaufort, and that this was as far as this bus was going.

Chapter 8

Now Maggie was scared and at the point of tears. She went inside and blurted out her dilemma to the station master. He assured her that there would be another bus coming in that would take her to Charlotte, where she could change for Winston-Salem.

"But how much will that cost? I don't have much money."

He quickly assured her she had a through ticket and there was no extra charge.

"I'll be happy to call your parents and assure them you're all right, and I'll see that you get on the right bus."

Maggie thanked him profusely, "That will be ever so nice of you." She went over and found a place to wait for the next bus. Two hours later the bus lights woke her up and her heart began to feel a little relieved.

The station master came over and said, "Little lady, this is your bus to Charlotte. Now don't go to sleep and miss your change in Charlotte."

Maggie thanked him, gathered up her belongings, and headed for her bus.

She didn't dare go to sleep, even though she wanted to. She managed to stay awake to Charlotte, and got on the right bus to Winston, and at 2:00 PM Monday afternoon, she called home and was very relieved to hear her father's voice.

"Well, Maggie, you finally decided to come home, did you?" Ruben teased. Maggie began to cry, saying, "Don't tease me now, Daddy. I'm tired, hungry and scared. Please, just come and get me."

"Honey, I'll be right there." That was music to Maggie's ears.

The ride home was quiet, and when her father pulled the car in the garage, Maggie bounded up the stairs, hardly taking time to hug her mother. She was in her bed so quickly that she was nearly asleep when she heard her father come in.

Next morning Maggie's mother decided to let Maggie sleep in, since there was so little time left in the school year, and Maggie didn't have to take the year-end exams.

Maggie woke up around three in the afternoon and raced downstairs to tell her mother all about the weekend. She told her about the good-looking cadets she had danced with, how Jim Arnold, her date to the dance, wanted to come to visit her this summer, and especially how wonderful Bill had been to her. She talked about liking Miriam and how she and Miriam loved music, and about Miriam coming to visit in late July. She went on breathlessly, "Momma, I learned to curtsy, and the ball was wonderful and...."

"Maggie, stop and take a breath. There's plenty of time to tell me all about your weekend. I am so happy you had such a good time, but I am happier that you arrived home safely. Were you frightened when you found out you missed making your change in Beaufort?"

"You bet I was, and home never looked as good as it did this morning," Maggie declared.

"Now that you have had some breakfast, you go on upstairs and unpack your suitcase. Throw down your dirty clothes, and bring down your evening dress so I can have it pressed for your junior and senior prom. Oh, by the way, James called all weekend wanting to know where you were. Maggie you should have let him know you were leaving town. It's too near prom time to chance him getting mad and breaking up."

Maggie answered, "I hadn't thought of that. I'll call him right now and make sure he isn't mad."

"James, this is Maggie. Momma said you have been calling," Maggie said in the sweetest manner she could.

"And where have you been?" James answered curtly.

"Oh, James, I'm sorry I didn't call you and let you know, but I went to Charleston to visit Bill at the Citadel."

"The girls said you went to a dance."

"Yes, Bill asked me to their spring weekend parade and dance. It's not like I went with anyone I knew. Bill asked one of his buddies to escort me to the dance."

"Well, you should have told me before you went. I was left here high and dry. Are we still going to the prom together?"

"I'm counting on going with you, James, and I have a new ball gown to wear."

"OK, Maggie, just don't do that to me again. I'll see you at homeroom in the morning."

"I'll be there, good-bye."

Maggie went into the kitchen and assured her mother that she still had a date for the junior and senior dance. As Maggie went back up to her room, Annie shook her head and said to herself, "Maggie's a sweet one, but I sometimes wonder when will she start taking things seriously."

Chapter 9

The night of the Junior and Senior Prom was warm, and the moon was large enough to illuminate the night and make the world seem magical. Maggie put her hair up, which made her feel like a grown-up young lady, and then she donned that gorgeous blue ball gown her mother had made for her. Annie was there to zip her into the gown, and she realized what a beautiful young lady her daughter was becoming. She noticed Maggie had begun to acquire a more mature figure, and her hair was lovelier than ever. She whispered to her daughter, "Maggie, be careful with your actions, or you might break some young man's heart."

"Oh, Momma, don't worry. I'm just having fun."

"That's what I'm afraid of."

"Maggie," her father called. "There's a fine-looking young man waiting for you in the parlor!"

"Tell James I'm on my way," she replied, turning to her mother she asked, "How do I look?"

"Beautiful."

Maggie picked up her sequined blue purse and royal blue-velvet wrap and headed down the stairs.

James took one look and exclaimed, "Maggie, is that you? You look gorgeous! Come on, let's go have a ball." Out the door they went into the warm May evening.

When they arrived at the gym, they were excited to see how the juniors had decorated it for the prom. To their amazement, as they entered the gym, it had been transformed to look like a garden outside of Tara, Scarlett O'Hara's plantation. Couples entered under the tall columns of Tara and on through the front hall out onto the veranda. Maggie thought, "Oh boy, and I'm dressed like Scarlett." Make-believe trees hung heavy with Spanish moss. Imitation mint juleps were being served, and everyone seemed to be transported back in time. When the evening was over, everyone agreed that the juniors had outdone themselves.

On the way home James and Maggie told each other of their college plans. James was excited about going to the University of North Carolina at Chapel Hill."James, my plans for college have changed."

"Why?" asked James. "Where are you going?"

"Well you see, Momma is not doing too well now, and is probably going to have another serious operation, so my parents don't want me too far from home."

"Is it real serious?"

"Yes, it is very serious"

"Well, where will you go?"

"Daddy is talking to the Dean of admissions at Peace College in Raleigh, N.C."

"That won't be so bad, we'll be close enough to see each other on the weekends. Are you disappointed?"

"Maybe a little, but I don't want to go to Florida when Momma's health is so uncertain." She paused and then added, "It will be helpful to know you are nearby."

James reminded her, "You remember that I'll be leaving right after graduation to be a counselor at Camp Sea Gull, right?"

"Oh, yes. Where is that?" Maggie asked.

"Down in the eastern part of the state on the Neuse River, right at the mouth of the Pamlico Sound. You could come visit me one weekend," James suggested.

"I don't think I'll have time. I've got a busy summer ahead, but I'll try," Maggie replied.

"Well, you'll write to me then, won't you?"

"Sure, I'll write to you, just send me your address."

He stopped the car in her drive, reached over, and gave her a real long kiss. "And, Maggie can I have a picture of my best girlfriend to take to college with me?" he quickly added.

Maggie felt giddy, but she managed to answer, "I'll work on that this summer."

The next two weeks were uneventful, except for the preparations being made for graduation. Eleven years of schooling was about to end, and graduation was on everyone's mind. Maggie was very excited. Bill and Jake both would be home for her graduation, and, in fact, the whole family would be going, even Jeanie.

The next week the house was filled to capacity again when Bill came home from the Citadel, and Jake returned from traveling. Maggie's mother was happy, because she loved to have all her children home. Sunday came, and they all went to church to hear Maggie sing her solo, "The Sanctus." Her mother and father sat near the front of the church, and a careful observer could have seen them wipe tears from their eyes. "She sings so beautifully," they thought.

The Sunday dining room table was full to over flowing with Annie's dinner of fried chicken, string beans, corn, yams, homemade biscuits and a pineapple upside down cake for dessert. This was as traditional as Annie could have served. She announced, "Maggie, you and Lisa help me clear the table, and the rest of you be ready to leave for graduation services at 4:00."

They all answered, "We'll be ready!"

"We can't miss Maggie's graduation," Bill added.

After the kitchen was cleaned, Maggie went up to her room to get dressed for the graduation ceremony. Maggie slipped on her long white dress and began to fix her hair. Her school had not yet begun to use caps and gowns for graduation. The girls were required to wear long white dresses, and the boys wore navy sport coats and white slacks. They did look like a handsome bunch of kids as they lined up to process down the long aisle of the auditorium to the strains of "Pomp and Circumstance."

A lump swelled in Maggie's throat as she realized that her days as a high-school girl were over tonight, and college was next. She let her mind drift and began to wonder, "What will the future hold? What will college be like? Am I ready to leave home?"

They all went home after graduation services and celebrated with a bowl of punch and a platter of small sandwiches. The day ended with Maggie surrounded by all those whom she loved.

Maggie rolled over Monday morning and saw her diploma sitting on her dressing table; she then realized that she had really graduated from high school. Her summer was already planned, and it was to be a busy one. She wanted to start sewing for her college wardrobe, so she jumped up and started looking through the fashion magazines her mother had bought for her, which gave her ideas for the clothes her mother made.

Jeanie came in the room and begged, "Maggie, please take me to the swimming pool!" Since she had been neglecting Jeanie lately, she agreed to take her. Maggie met James there, and that made the afternoon more enjoyable. When it was time to go home, James offered to take them.

At the house he gave Maggie his camp address, and reminded her that she had promised him a picture to take to school with him.

Maggie agreed, gave him a quick kiss good-bye, and said, "Have a great summer, and I'll see you before you go off to college this fall. I'll try to have a picture for you by then."

"A promise is a promise." James reminded her.

Maggie was excited about her last summer at home and she had big plans for it.

Friday afternoon, Maggie was out in the yard playing with Jeanie and Buck, their dog. Annie came out onto the patio and called to Maggie, "You're wanted on the telephone."

"Who is it?" Maggie asked.

"It sounds like Paul, but I am not sure."

Maggie headed for the house, turned to Jeanie, and said, "Honey, I'll be right back. You go on and throw the ball to Buck."

"Oh, Maggie, you know he doesn't bring it back to me."

"He will if I'm not out here. Try it and see," Maggie told Jeanie as she disappeared into the house.

Maggie took the phone, and when she said hello, she was delighted to hear Paul's voice saying, "Is this my best girlfriend speaking?"

"This is Maggie, if that's who you're talking about."

Paul asked, "How about a date for a drive-in movie? I can use Uncle Gary's car tonight."

"I'd love to go to the movies."

"OK, I'll pick you up at six. We can get a bite to eat and make the 8:00 movie."

"I'll be ready, and Paul, I'm excited you are in Winston."

"Me, too."

For the next three weeks, Paul and Maggie spent their mornings at the park playing tennis, sitting under the spreading oak trees down by the creek that ran through the park, popping into the pharmacy for a mid-morning snack, or just to visit Aunt Estelle.

Their afternoons were usually spent at the club pool, entertaining Jeanie. Some afternoons they baby-sat Paul's cousins, Joe and Jimmy. Sometimes they played games; most of the time it was Monopoly, but when Jeanie wanted to play they got out the Parcheesi board. Lisa liked to play card games best, because she could always win, she being the smart one.

In the evenings Maggie and Paul always dated, walking downtown to the movies, and about twice a week they had a car date. They were really enjoying being together. During the first week, they spent most of their time talking.

Chapter 9

One morning sitting under their favorite oak tree, Maggie asked, "Paul, what have you decided about college?"

"Oh, I was accepted at Clemson into the School of Architecture."

"Wonderful! Why didn't you tell me? I knew you could do it."

"I just received my acceptance the day before I came to Winston, so I haven't had time to tell you."

"I'm so proud of you."

"Yeah, but it's going to be a tough road."

"Don't worry. I know you'll make it. Just think how wonderful it will be to become an architect."

"That will be swell. Now tell me about your plans. You said they were changing."

"Yes, I'm not going to Florida Southern like I first planned. Mother is not well, and she will have to have another operation for cancer, so she wants me to stay close to Winston. Daddy has just gotten me accepted into Peace College in Raleigh. So that's where I'll go."

"Are you disappointed?"

"A little, but I would not be happy that far away from home. I know this is the best for me and my parents."

"I like it because Raleigh is closer to me than Lakeland, Florida."

"Come on, let's go over to the pharmacy and eat some lunch," Maggie said

Paul took Maggie by the hand, pulled her up from the stone bench, gave her a quick kiss, and off they went across the bridge to the pharmacy.

The second Saturday Paul was in town, Maggie planned a picnic to Hanging Rock State Park with her friend Nancy Hanes and her boyfriend Doug Wright. The day had that delicious warmth of the first summer days of June. They all packed their swimsuits and towels, and Maggie took her battery radio. They were off to a day of fun in the sun.

When they arrived, they donned their swimsuits and headed straight for the lake. The water was a little cool but very refreshing. The air was cold on their wet bodies when they got out of the water, so the girls went to the car and put on their cover-ups. The guys were too macho to admit they were cold. Maggie spread out her quilt, and she and Nancy began laying out their picnic lunch. The more they laid out, the hungrier the guys became.

After lunch, they listened to Maggie's radio. Then they decided it was time to pack up and head home.

As they were returning to Winston, Paul said, "Boy, this sure was a great day!"

They all chimed in, "It sure was, and I hope we can do this again!"

After they dropped off Nancy and Doug, Paul drove around awhile, and they talked about going off to college. He told Maggie that he wanted her to come to Clemson one fall weekend to a football game and dance. She eagerly agreed. By then Paul had pulled up under a large oak tree by the park, slipped his arms around her, and kissed her. She knew his kisses were getting more intense, but she never thought he might be falling in love with her. At this stage of her life she wasn't ready to fall in love.

Paul attended church with her on Sunday, then took her home and ate Sunday lunch with her family. Jeanie took Paul into the backyard for a game, or many games of croquet. Maggie joined them after helping her mother do the dishes.

Early the next week, Paul called Maggie to say, "Aunt Estelle and Uncle Gary have rented a cottage next weekend. We are going to Myrtle Beach, and they said I could ask you. Would you like to go?"

"You bet I would!"

"Aunt Estelle said she would call your mother and give her the details, if you wanted to go with us."

"Yes, yes! Please tell Aunt Estelle to call Momma."

In a few days the plans were finalized, and Maggie was busy packing her suitcase to go to Myrtle Beach on Friday. They were to return home on Monday. She danced all around her room when she thought of being at the beach with Paul.

Chapter 9

Once again Maggie was stuck with time moving too slowly, but Friday finally arrived for her trip to Myrtle Beach. The weather was perfect for a trip to the coast. Uncle Gary drove up with the car loaded. Maggie wasn't sure she was going to fit, but everyone moved over, and she wedged herself in between Paul and little Jimmy. Little Joe was in the front seat between his parents. Being crowded wasn't so bad, because Paul could hold her hand and no one would ever notice. The trip was long, but they sang, and played cow poker, and other silly car games. When they arrived at the cottage, Paul and Maggie pitched in and unloaded the car and then took the boys to the beach while Aunt Estelle got everything straightened up inside. As the sun went down, they brought the little boys in and got them ready for dinner. At the dinner table, Aunt Estelle told Paul and Maggie what the rules were to be. They were expected to help with the chores around the cottage when needed, and watch the boys some on the beach. The evenings would be theirs as long as they always told her where they were going, which sounded like a real deal to Paul and Maggie.

The evenings were gorgeous-warm and balmy. The first night they walked on the boardwalk, hand in hand, and then onto the beach with their feet in the warm water. They went to the dance hall the next evening. The band played her kind of music, like "Little Brown Jug," so Maggie got to jitterbug all she wanted to.

Sunday night was clear. A full moon was rising over the ocean, and the sky twinkled with stars above them. Paul suggested that they take a blanket out on the beach and star gaze. Maggie thought this would be a wonderful way to spend their last night at the beach, but she didn't realize how romantic Paul would become.

Lying out there under the stars, Maggie said, "Paul, there's the Big Dipper, there's the Little Dipper, and there's the North Star. Oh, the stars are so beautiful! Don't you just love to lie here and study the stars?"

"Not as much as I love studying you! You're as beautiful as all those stars." He took her into his arms and began kissing her passionately. His hands were exploring her body in ways she found very unsettling. At first she lay there enjoying the excitement she was feeling, but soon she realized this was going somewhere that she was not ready for.

Maggie sat up and suggested, "Let's walk up to the Pavilion and get a cone of ice cream."

Paul reluctantly agreed. They slowly rose from the blanket, folded it and placed it on the walkway to their cottage. They strolled hand in hand to the pavilion, listening to the music as it became louder and louder.

The next day they loaded up and headed back to Winston-Salem. The rest of the week they talked about what life would be like once they left home. Again Paul reminded Maggie that he wanted her to come visit him at Clemson.

"Maggie," Paul said, "Do you have a picture I can have to take to school with me?"

"Paul, I really don't have one I want to give you. I hate my high-school annual picture, but I'm going to have one made, and I promise to send you one by the time you go to college."

"You promise? OK, I'll hold you to that!" Paul replied.

Maggie thought, "Now I need two pictures, and how can I explain to Momma why I need a picture made at a studio? Oh, well. I'll worry about that tomorrow."

The last night Paul was in Winston, they took a walk in the park and just talked. Paul was very amorous, but Maggie kept the situation in check. After Paul left the next morning, Maggie felt a little empty. She really liked Paul and missed him. Then she thought, "But he hasn't grown an inch since I met him. Oh well. I'll give him a little longer."

Chapter 10

It was a little over a week until she was to go to Emily's. Maggie filled her time helping her mother finish the outfits she would take with her to school, looking after her little sister Jeanie, and writing letters to James, Paul, and John.

Maggie and Annie were spending a lot of time together, and Maggie realized that her mother was not feeling well. Maggie found her lying down during the day when she normally did not. She asked, "Momma, are you feeling sick again?"

"No, dear. I just get a little more tired these days," Annie answered.

"Will you and Jeanie be all right if I go to visit Emily?" Maggie asked.

"Now honey, don't you worry. Jeanie and I will be fine, and remember Lisa is beginning to help out a lot when you are gone. Just think, we'll have to be on our own very soon; you'll be going to college in a little over a month."

Maggie had a sinking feeling in her stomach at the thought of being away from her family, and yet, she was excited at the idea of going to college.

Sunday afternoon finally arrived, and the family put Maggie on a bus to Charlotte. She found a seat, wiped a few tears from her eyes, and settled down to read the rest of her book, Little Women, which Uncle Walter had given her to read when she left Charlotte last summer.

Maggie finished the book and began to dream about the upcoming visit. Would John still be interested in her as he had indicated in his letters? She closed her eyes, but before she went to sleep, the bus was pulling into the station. She squinted through the dirty window and made out the figures of John and Emily looking for her. She could not believe Uncle Walter had let the two of them come to meet her. She hoped this meant that he would be a little less strict this summer.

When it came her turn to leave the bus, she waved to Emily and John.

"Here I am!" Maggie shouted.

Emily ran up and hugged her so tightly that she felt she could hardly breathe. John was behind Emily, and when his turn came, he kissed Maggie on the cheek.

"Welcome to Charlotte! Let me have your baggage claim ticket, and I'll get them for you," he said.

"Thank you, John. I'm so happy to be here again. Here's my ticket; I have only one bag. I have the rest in this vanity case I brought with me."

John took the vanity case and ticket from Maggie, and went to secure her other bag. "I'll be back in a sec; don't you two girls go anywhere."

The girls laughed and began exchanging their latest news. When John came back with Maggie's bags, they loaded the car and headed to Emily's house, while Emily and John filled Maggie in on their plans for the week.

"Dave and I have a swim meet Tuesday morning at the pool. We'd like for you and Emily to be there, and of course, we practice every morning, and hope you two will join us for a swim afterwards."

"We'll have to take Lily and Stanley to the park every day that's sunny," Emily announced.

"That's OK by me," Maggie said. "As I recall, we had a lot of fun doing that."

John added, "Count me in! I liked those walks in the park."

They all laughed, knowing he wasn't talking about looking after Lily and Stanley.

Emily anxiously told Maggie that her father had started letting her double car-date, so they could go to the movies with Dave and John. Maggie thought, "This is going to be a great visit."

By now John was rolling into the driveway. Out came Aunt Betty, Lily, and good old Stanley, her pet duck, waddling behind.

Maggie ran and hugged Aunt Betty, kissed Lily, and led the way into the house. John followed the others with Maggie's luggage.

John told the girl's good-bye and added, "I'll see you tonight at the barbecue."

Maggie turned to Emily and asked, "What barbecue?"

Emily explained that her mother had planned a barbecue in the backyard and had invited John and Dave. Maggie thought to herself, "Things have really changed."

"That's so nice of Aunt Betty. How did you manage the relaxed attitude?"

"I don't know. I think Daddy likes and trusts Dave and John. He realizes it could be worse."

"We're going to have a good time, aren't we, Emily?" Maggie mused.

"We plan to."

Emily helped Maggie unpack her bag and change into a pair of shorts and blouse. Several hours later Uncle Walter came home and greeted Maggie fondly.

"Did you read that book I gave you?" Uncle Walter asked her immediately. He was an avid reader and a collector of first-edition books.

Maggie was so happy to be able to honestly say that she had, and that she really enjoyed it very much. Uncle Walter told the girls to hurry and get ready, and come down to help prepare the backyard for the barbecue.

"OK, we'll be down shortly!" They answered.

Everyone was busy having a good time at the barbecue. Uncle Walter was dressed in his chef's apron, puttering with the fire. Maggie and Emily were watching John and Dave set up the badminton set. Lily was playing with Stanley, who waddled around and quacked in delight to have everyone in his backyard. Aunt Betty was still in the kitchen preparing the last-minute dishes.

Aunt Betty had prepared a great barbecue feast of pulled pork with Eastern Carolina vinegar sauce, fresh garden tomatoes, corn on the cob, baked beans and cold, crisp watermelon. The young people ate until they were stuffed, but they all agreed it had been a wonderful way to spend a warm July evening. When the evening was over, the girls walked the boys to the corner, waved goodbye and returned to the backyard to help clean up. They were anxious not to take advantage of Uncle Walter's change of heart.

Monday began with the usual trip to the pool for practice and swimming, but Tuesday there was a swim meet at 9:00. The girls rose early to be there on time, and it seemed strange to put on swimsuits so early in the morning. John won his class in the butterfly stroke, and Dave won first place with a swan dive, which helped their team win the meet. The girls did not get to swim because the meet lasted so long, but they enjoyed the meet and the boys walked them home, which made it OK.

Aunt Betty had made sandwiches for them all and she invited the boys to have lunch with them. After swimming all morning, the boys were famished and eagerly accepted.

Maggie was happy when there was so much going on, but her time in Charlotte was going by so quickly with daily trips to the pool, skating dates, walks in the park with Lily and Stanley, their double dates to movies, and playing Monopoly for hours on rainy days. It was a great time of renewing friendships and having summer romances.

Maggie and John were having a wonderful time getting to know each other all over again, but regretted that their time together was so short. John asked her to come visit him at the University of South Carolina in Columbia for one of the dance weekends, and she gladly accepted the invitation. She promised that as soon as she was at Peace College in Raleigh, she would find a weekend to come. She was excited about having things to look forward to once she was at college.

They promised to write often, and then John asked, "Do you have a picture I can have to take to school with me?"

Maggie thought, "Oh, no, now I need another picture. What am I going to do? I'll have to ask Momma when I get home, but what will she say when I tell her I need three pictures?"

Maggie realized she was lost in thought and quickly answered, "I'll send you one as soon as I get back." She wasn't sure where she would get three pictures - maybe she'd have to get her brother Bill to make one for her. He'd understand why she needed three pictures.

The second week was much like the first, except they kept dreading the time for Maggie to go home. On her last night in Charlotte, the four of them went out to dinner and on to see the movie, "Gone with the Wind." It was making a return appearance, and since none of them had seen it, they all wanted to go. The girls came out wiping their eyes, while the boys laughed at them.

"It's just a movie, girls," John chided.

"I know, but it was so sad," Maggie said.

After a quick trip to the corner drug store for a coke, they strolled hand in hand to the car. The ride home was quiet, with each of them thinking that this was their last night together this summer, and maybe forever, because each was starting a new part of life. Who knew where it would lead?

Maggie broke the silence when she said, "I've had such a wonderful time! I hope we can all get together again."

They all agreed, as John pulled the car up in front of the house. The boys got out and escorted the girls to the door. After a goodnight kiss the girls went inside.

"I'll be here in the morning to take you two to the bus station, and Dave wants to go with us. Is that OK?" John questioned.

"That's fine!" the girls answered in unison, as they closed the front door.

The next morning, bright and early, John and Dave appeared at the door. They took Maggie's bags and placed them in the trunk of the car, while Maggie was saying her good-byes. Uncle Walter presented Maggie with a new book, *Pride and Prejudice*, to read on the way home. She took the book, thanked him, and kissed him good-bye again.

As she got in the car she called back and said, "Thank you for letting me visit you! I've had such a good time these two weeks!"

"Give our love to your family, and tell them we hope to see them soon!" responded Aunt Betty.

John drove off with Maggie waving, and blowing kisses. She was sorry to be leaving, but she focused her sights on home and she was glad to be on her way. She had missed her family, and she was still worried about her mother. At the bus station, John took care of checking her in and checked her bag. She kept her vanity case with her. He was such a gentleman; she was going to miss his pampering. She boarded the bus and seated herself by a window, where she could blow a final kiss to the buddies she was leaving behind. The bus moved out slowly, and now she was on her way to Winston-Salem, and home. Maggie took out her book and read the title of her book, Pride and Prejudice. Uncle Walter would make that choice. She opened the book and began to read.

Chapter 11

The bus rolled into Winston-Salem with a groggy Maggie looking to see who had come to meet her. As she peered through the window she saw Bill waiting to greet her. She was glad to see that he had come, because on the way home, she decided to ask him how to approach Momma about getting a picture made by a studio photographer. Also, if she didn't get anywhere with their mother, she would ask him if he could take one of her. Bill would tease her for a while about why she needed a picture so badly, but in the end, he would help her with her problem. Bill was like that.

As she descended the steps of the bus, Bill came up and gave her a quick kiss on the cheek. He took her vanity case and went in and got her bag. "Come on Sis, I've got to get you home. I've got a date with Anne tonight, and I can't be late."

Maggie hurried on to the car and when Bill got in she immediately poured out her dilemma. "Bill, I need your advice and maybe your help."

"You aren't pregnant are you?"

"Bill! I can't believe you could say that to me!"

"Oh, I was just kidding, but you do seem a little desperate."

"I am desperate. You see, I need three pictures to send to my boyfriends, and I don't know if Momma and Daddy will understand."

"No, and I don't think I understand. Boyfriends! Maggie, you have your senior annual picture; just have that copied, and send them that one."

"Bill, you obviously haven't looked at my picture; even Momma said it was horrible."

"What's wrong with it, sis?"

"I look mad, or sick. I don't know which, but no boy is going to want that on his dresser at college."

"Do you think you can get a better one made? You're the same girl."

"Ha! That's funny, but you haven't answered my question."

"Sis, all you need to do is just ask; all they can do is say no."

"You're a lot of help, big brother."

As Bill wheeled into their drive, he got serious, and said again, "You should just go to Momma and ask. If she says no, well, then I'll try to make you look like Elizabeth Taylor."

Maggie jumped out of the car. Running to the house she called back to Bill, "Thanks, big brother! I love you, even though you make me so mad sometimes! Don't forget to bring my bag."

"Yeah, yeah," mumbled Bill.

The next morning Maggie woke up in her own room with Lisa beside her and it felt good. She rolled over to face the windows and saw it was going to be a rainy day, a good day to unpack her suitcase and put all her stuff away. As she lay there planning her day, Bill stuck his head in the door and said, "Sis, don't forget Miriam is coming by bus Friday. I want you to go with me to meet her, that is, if you'd like to."

"I'd love to go with you. You know, she is my guest. What time does her bus arrive?"

"Three o'clock. We should leave here around two."

"I'll be ready and waiting."

Maggie dressed and went downstairs to fix some breakfast. Everyone else had eaten and gone on with their daily routine. Momma was in the kitchen, so this was a perfect time to approach her with the problem. She entered the kitchen and asked, "Momma, how are you feeling?"

"I'm fine," she said.

Chapter 11

Maggie fixed a bowl of cereal and sat down at the table. "Momma, please sit down with me. I need to ask you something."

"That's fine dear. We haven't had a chance to talk, just you and me, in quite some time," Annie said, as she sat across the table from Maggie. "Tell me what's on your mind."

Maggie gulped and drew a deep breath and blurted out, "I want to have a picture made at a real photography studio." Then she waited for what she knew was coming, and was prepared with her rebuttal.

"OK, honey." She smiled, "Why don't you call Carroll's Studio and make an appointment? I hope it will be better than your high-school picture."

Maggie jumped up, ran around the table, and hugged her mother as tightly as she could and said, "Momma, I love you so much!" She thought, "How could her mother know how much she wanted a new picture made?"

Bill came in and asked, "What's with all this hugging and kissing?"

Maggie ran over, hugged Bill, kissed him, and related, "Momma says I can call Carroll's Studio to make an appointment to have my picture made."

"See, didn't I tell you, to go ask your Momma? She was a girl once, too," Bill teased.

"I beg your pardon, young man; I think I still remember when," their mother retorted.

They all laughed as Maggie left the room.

She went straight to the phone and made an appointment for the following Monday. As she was looking up the number, she realized that Miriam would be visiting for five days, but she couldn't wait, and anyway, Miriam could go with her.

As she hung up the phone, she gave out a little squeal, "Yes!"

Chapter 12

Maggie came back into the kitchen, and her mother said, "Maggie, Wally Smith has been calling you for several days. He asked me to have you call him as soon as you got home."

"OK, Momma, I will in a little while."

"Honey, he sounded a little bit anxious to talk to you. Maybe it's important."

"I'll call him right now."

Maggie went to the den, sat down cross-legged in Ruben's big chair, and dialed the YMCA. Wally was the assistant director of the local YMCA. She and Wally worked together on programs for the Young Peoples Service League at their church. She liked Wally very much, but he was much too old for her to date. Maggie was sure he wanted to talk about the fall programming for the YPSL. He probably had forgotten that she would be off to college and that he would be working with someone else.

The operator at the Y answered, "May I help you?"

"I would like to speak to Mr. Wally Smith, this is Maggie McGee."

"Just a moment, Miss McGee. I'll see if I can find him."

"Hello, Maggie! This is Wally. Where have you been? I've been trying to get you for days," Wally said breathlessly.

"Hi, Wally! I just returned from Charlotte, where I was visiting my cousin Emily."

Chapter 12

"I hope you had a nice trip, but I sure am glad you're home! I do hope you'll be home for a while."

"Yes, I'll be at home now until I leave for college. Why?"

"Well, I was calling because my brother, Tim, is coming next weekend to stay with me until he leaves to go back to college. I was hoping you might like to meet him, and if you have any spare time, I was hoping you could show him around town while I'm busy working."

"I would love to meet your brother, Wally! Just call me when he gets here, and we can make plans to get together."

"That sounds just great! He's due to get here a week from this Saturday, but it might be too late to call. You never know when you're driving. How about if we meet you at church next Sunday morning. You'll be there, won't you?"

"I'll be there, and I'll wait for you two out on the church lawn. I'll be singing in the choir, but at least I can meet Tim before church services."

"Can we go somewhere for lunch after church?" Wally asked.

"I would love to!" Maggie replied.

Maggie went back in the kitchen to tell her mother what Wally wanted. Her mother replied, "When are you going to get ready for college?"

"Oh, I'll be ready." Maggie turned to go up to her room to finish unpacking and putting her clothes in the laundry. The rest of the week was busy with more shopping, and doing the finish work on the school outfits her mother had made. As she looked through her lovely new clothes, she began to fully realize that she was really going away to college and her feelings of excitement were mixed with anxiety. She was definitely going to miss her family.

Chapter 13

Friday was a beautiful day with the skies that legendary Carolina blue color with an occasional white fluffy cloud passing overhead. Maggie was in her dream world, thinking of how wonderful her life was, when Bill brought her back to the real world.

"Maggie, it's time to go to the bus station. I don't want to miss Miriam's bus." Bill called urgently.

Maggie came down the steps two at a time saying, "OK, OK, let's go!"

They jumped in the car and sped off as Annie watched from the kitchen window, shaking her head, "Please Lord, look after them. They are too much for me."

On their way to the station, Maggie asked, "How did you explain to Anne that you would be dating someone else this weekend?"

"Oh, that was easy, Anne left yesterday to work at her church camp. She'll be gone for a month, and she's dating other people at school as well."

"That's almost until she goes back to school, isn't it?"

"Yeah." Bill said a little disgusted. "Now what are the plans for Miriam's visit?"

"Tonight, I planned for you, James, Miriam, and me to go to the movies. That's after we have dinner with the family, of course."

Chapter 13

"Is James back? I thought he was down at Camp Sea Gull," Bill questioned.

"He's home for the weekend, and that makes it real nice that I have someone to date while Miriam is here. Saturday afternoon I've planned a swimming party at the club; Nancy and Doug are coming with three other couples. Sunday we'll go to church and then have lunch at home, because Jake will be home for the weekend."

"That sounds great; I wanted Jake to meet Miriam. Just let me have some time with her alone," Bill added.

"You can make plans for Sunday and Monday nights. I don't have a date for those nights,but remember, I have an appointment Monday afternoon at 2:00 to have my picture taken, and I want Miriam to go with me."

"That's fine, because I'll be at work."

By the time they had their plans worked out, Bill was pulling into a parking space. As they got out of the car, they spied the bus coming in from Charleston.

They ran and waited by the bus until Miriam came through the door. Maggie ran and took her by the hand and said to Bill, "Here, take her ticket and get her bag. Miriam and I will meet you at the car."

"Thanks a lot, but I'm not here as the valet, Maggie. She's my girl, so if you don't mind, I'd like to say hello, and then I'll get her bag!"

"OK, OK, I'll let you have a little kiss, but then let's get going."

On the way to their house, Miriam and Maggie didn't stop chattering until Bill said, "Will you girls slow down a bit and let me talk a little?"

"Sure, we'll listen, but make it quick, because we have a lot more to tell each other," Maggie chided.

Bill told Miriam how glad he was that she was in town, and even though Maggie had made plans to keep her busy, he had plans for them to have some time together. Miriam seemed to be pleased. About that time Bill turned the car into the driveway.

Maggie jumped out, calling to Miriam to follow her, leaving Bill to lug her suitcase up to the upstairs guestroom. Maggie moved her things into the bedroom so she and Miriam could share the guestroom. This left Lisa in their room by herself, but she didn't seem to mind. In fact, she was looking forward to being rid of her messy roommate for a few days.

Bill said good-bye to Miriam, telling her, "I've got to go back to work, but I'll see you at dinner. Maggie has plans for us to go to the movies with James and her after dinner. Isn't that right, Maggie?"

She nodded.

Maggie helped Miriam unpack, and then they sat straddle-legged in the middle of the bed.

"What have you been up to since we were last together?" Maggie asked.

"Not too much. Well, of course graduation, then I got accepted to the College of Charleston. And, oh I won the piano competition I competed in."

"That sounds pretty exciting."

"Now, tell me what you've been doing." Miriam said.

"Graduation, of course. Paul came for three weeks, and then I went to Charlotte to visit my cousin Emily."

"Sounds like you had a busy summer."

Maggie saw that it was almost time for dinner and said to Miriam, "We better get dressed. Bill will be coming home soon, and my date will be arriving at seven. Momma serves dinner at six, so we don't have any time to waste."

The two girls started to decide what they would wear. Laughing and giggling, they dressed in pretty sun-dresses and tied their hair back in ribbons. Each one surveyed the other and decided they were perfectly dressed for a late-summer evening date.

The next morning, the girls slept late and even as they awakened, they lay there in the bed chattering away. Maggie's mother called up the steps, "You girls had better get dressed and come downstairs before you miss breakfast!"

"We'll be down right away," Maggie answered.

"Maggie, remember you promised to play with Jeanie today, and you have your swimming party this afternoon," Annie reminded Maggie.

"Yes, I know Momma. Tell Jeanie that Miriam and I will be out to play with her shortly."

Maggie fixed some cinnamon raisin toast, with a glass of milk. When they had finished and cleaned up the kitchen, they went out to the back-yard, and there was Jeanie standing with croquet mallets poised, ready for them to take their pick. Jeanie's ball was expectantly sitting in front of the first wicket. Jeanie was always happy when Maggie took time to play with her, and Maggie never tired of playing with her little sister. As the game progressed, Buck ran in and out of the course, barking at the colorful balls, and generally making the game more difficult.

When the game was over, Jeanie begged them to play just one more game, but Maggie said, "No, Jeanie. You can come upstairs with Miriam and me while we get dressed for our dates." After they put the croquet set away, Jeanie led the way into the house and bounded upstairs and into the guest room.

Miriam was sweet about Jeanie following them to their room to get dressed, but Maggie had to send Jeanie downstairs when she continued to ask one question after another.

"Where are you going?", asked Jeanie.

"We are going to the club to a swim party," answered Maggie.

"Can I go?"

"No."

"Why?"

"This party is just for us grown-ups."

"You aren't a grown-up."

"Yes, I am!" Maggie was getting a bit irritated at this point.

"Momma says you have a lot of growing up to do," Jeanie went on.

Maggie turned and said, "Jeanie, I think it is time for you to go downstairs and play."

"Why?"

Maggie took Jeanie by the nape of the neck and showed her to the door, "Because I said so!"

Jeanie stopped at the door, waved at Miriam, and said, "Good-bye, I'll see you later!"

Maggie closed the door, turned, and apologized to Miriam for the diatribe, "You see what I have to go through all the time!"

"I think it would be nice to have a little sister," Miriam answered, sounding a little melancholy.

"Yeah, it is fun to have a little sister most of the time," Maggie said. "Well, let's get dressed. The boys will be here in a few minutes."

"Who are you dating for the party?" Miriam asked. "Jake?"

"No, Jake won't get here until late tonight. I have a date with James Ferguson.

He's sort of my boyfriend. We've been dating, off and on, all through high school. He's been away at Camp Sea Gull as a counselor all summer, but he's home for the weekend. Isn't that convenient?"

"Do you like him?" Miriam quizzed.

"I suppose I do. He's lots of fun and pretty good looking, tall, sandy haired, with a dimple in his chin. He doesn't get mad if I date other boys; he always comes back and asks me for dates." Maggie thought awhile and then said, "Yes, I really do like him."

The swimming party at the club was perfect. The sun was warm, but a soft breeze kept it from being a scorcher of an afternoon. They swam, dove, and sunned themselves while listening to each other's summer experiences. There was no hint of how near they all were to having to grow up in the turmoil of war. More and more they overheard talk of war and it loomed over them, like an approaching thunderstorm.

Chapter 13

After the party was over, James took Maggie home, and Bill and Miriam had a few moments alone as they drove back to the house. When they arrived home, Jake was there waiting. He had just gotten back from visiting his grandmother in Florida. Jake had enlisted in the Army Air Corps several weeks before and was to leave sometime after the first of September for basic training.

Later they all crawled into Bill's car, picked up Bonnie, Jake's date, and went out to their favorite eating spot, Charlie's Drive In, on the outskirts of town.

Bill said, "Let's go in and get a booth, so we can see who's here."

They all piled out of the car and crowded into a booth. The boys began asking Jake why he was enlisting.

Jake answered, "Guys, we are going to be at war before long, and I want to be able to choose where I serve."

The talk went on and on about enlisting as opposed to waiting to be drafted. Finally, Maggie interrupted, "Change the subject, please! We're not in the war; it's way on the other side of the globe. It doesn't really affect us."

Miriam and Bonnie agreed, "Yeah, let's change the subject and dance."

Bill got up, went over, and put a nickel in the juke box, and out came Maggie's favorite, "Little Brown Jug" by Glenn Miller's band. They all took to the dance floor and jitterbugged until they were exhausted. The evening had been fun, that is, after Maggie made the boys stop talking about war.

Sunday morning was hot and humid. The girls dressed in their chintz sun dresses, with small bolero jackets. Bill drove them to church, after which they went home and joined the rest of the family around the dining room table for another of Annie's wonderful Sunday dinners.

Ruben began, "Let us pray." They all joined hands to connect the family into a complete circle. "Father, make us truly grateful for each other, all our blessings, and this meal prepared for us by loving hands. Help us to be aware of the needs of others and bring peace to all in this troubled world. This we pray in Christ's name." They all joined him with, "Amen."

Jake squeezed Maggie's hand. Maggie smiled at Jake and thought, "There it is again, Daddy praying for peace. I still don't understand why we are so concerned with what's happening on the other side of the world."

Jake and Maggie double dated with Bill and Miriam Sunday night. The evening was beautiful, clear and warm with a sweet smell of honeysuckle in the air.

They went to a drive-in movie, ate hot dogs, and drank Pepsi. Maggie enjoyed going out with Jake, but when he kissed her, it was like her brother kissing her and it gave her a strange feeling.

Jake asked Maggie, "I hear you are going to have your picture made tomorrow."

"Yes, and I am so excited! I'm going to a real photographer."

"Well, Maggie, since I don't have a steady girlfriend, can I have one of your pictures to take with me when I leave for basic training?"

Maggie laughed, "Jake, sure you can have one." She went on, "You know we aren't girlfriend and boyfriend, don't you?"

"Sure, but we might be, someday."

Maggie laughed again and snuggled up to Jake, like a little sister.

They all went home and went upstairs to their separate bedrooms. It felt odd.

Chapter 14

Maggie opened her eyes and realized, "Today is the day I get my picture made!" She jumped out of the bed and ran to her room, pulling out clothes one at a time, tossing them here and there.

"What's going on?" Lisa asked.

"I'm deciding what to wear when I get my picture made, and today is the day!" Maggie answered.

"Oh, Maggie, you act like that's a big deal."

"It is a big deal. Just wittily you have three boys who want your picture, and see what you say," Maggie said a little irritated.

Maggie grabbed an armload of clothes and went back to the guest room to get Miriam to help her decide what to wear. "Miriam will understand," she thought.

Miriam sat up in bed, rubbing her eyes, "Maggie, what are you doing?"

"I'm trying to pick out the perfect outfit to wear today. I'm having my picture made to give to three boys."

"Are you sure that's a good idea, Maggie?"

"What's wrong with that? They all asked me for one."

"Well, if you can get by with it, I suppose it's OK, but it could be trouble, if you ask me."

"Come on. Get up, and help me decide what I'm going to wear."

Miriam went through the stack of clothes and pulled out a white shark-skin blouse. "I think this will make a good neckline for a picture."

"I like that blouse," Maggie said. "I wear that apple-green skirt with it. I always feel pretty when I put it on. That's it!"

They raced downstairs when her mother called them to breakfast. Bill and Jake were there ready to go to work as soon as they finished breakfast.

"Maggie, don't forget to smile real pretty for the photographer. Just think of all those boys you are making happy," Bill chided.

"Yeah, Maggie, remember I'm one of those boys," Jake added.

"OK. Don't make fun of me. This is a very important day for me," Maggie pleaded, as the boys rose from the table and left for work.

The girls cleaned the kitchen and then went upstairs to prepare for the upcoming appointment. They showered and rolled their hair. Maggie was excited at the thought of having her picture taken by a professional.

They walked to the bus stop, and in a few minutes they boarded the bus for a ride downtown, where the streets were filled with people bustling along, going in and out of shops - their arms laden with purchases. No one paid any attention to the girls, but Maggie wanted to stop each one anyway and tell them that she was on her way to have her picture taken by a real photographer.

Finally they arrived at the entrance of the Carroll Photography Studio. On each side of the entrance were display cases with pictures of brides, babies, families, young men, and lovely young ladies. She paused for a moment, and secretly wondered if he could make her look as good as those other young ladies. She opened the door, and they climbed the stairs.

"May I help you?" asked the receptionist.

"I'm Maggie McGee, and I have an appointment to have my picture taken."

"Have a seat, and I'll tell Mr. Carroll you have arrived," the receptionist said.

Chapter 14

Maggie looked at Miriam and smiled nervously. Mr. Carroll emerged from his office and invited the girls into the studio. Maggie rose to follow him, but Miriam remained seated.

Mr. Carroll motioned to Miriam, "Come on in. You can watch, and maybe that will help put Maggie at ease. Turning to Maggie he said, "Would you like her to come with you?"

"Oh, yes, I certainly would like that."

They entered a room filled with lights of all shapes and sizes. Maggie thought, "It looks pretty stark and unfriendly." Mr. Carroll motioned for them to sit down.

"Now, Maggie, what is this photograph being made for? Is it to be a serious photo or a glamorous one?"

"It's a picture to give to my boyfriends," Maggie said sheepishly.

"Boyfriends? Uhm. Then we need to make you look glamorous, don't we?"

"I would like that."

He called his assistant in and instructed her to put a little touch of make-up on Maggie, while he adjusted the lights.

By now Maggie was so excited that she could hardly sit still. The assistant tried to calm her down, but the time had come to pose for "the picture."

Mr. Carroll posed her on a draped table. "Now Maggie, relax and keep your head up. I'll do the rest." He moved from one side to another, snapping one shot right after another. He would stop and repose her, and then start snapping his camera again. "I think I have taken enough, and I believe I have taken exactly what you want. You can relax now."

He walked them to the outer sitting area and told Maggie, "I'll have your proofs ready next Monday."

The girls left the studio and on the bus ride home, Miriam assured Maggie that her picture was going to be great. When they got home, Maggie admitted that she was pretty exhausted from all the excitement. She was glad Miriam and Bill were going out alone, so she could stay at home. She went to bed early, and didn't even hear Miriam crawl into the bed beside her.

Next morning the girls were up bright and early. Miriam was busy packing her clothes and getting ready to leave. Bill was to pick her up around 11:00 and take her to lunch at the Snack Shack and then on to catch her bus back to Charleston. Maggie and Miriam went downstairs for breakfast.

"This has been a great visit, Maggie. I hope we can stay friends and get together again."

"I certainly plan to stay in touch. I'll write and give you my address as soon as I get to college. Maybe you can come visit me this winter." Maggie asked.

"I think that would be fun. Please write to me."

"I will, I promise." Maggie said.

Bill was there right on the dot of 11:00. Miriam was ready and good-byes were said to all the family. Maggie had to say good-bye to her friend at the house because she had promised her mother that she and Lisa would take Jeanie to the movie, "Dumbo", and Jeanie never forgets. For Miriam and Bill, it gave them a chance to have these last moments alone.

The rest of that week Maggie and her mother made lists of what was left to get ready for her to take to college. With only three weeks left, there was still much to do.

Maggie was sitting on the patio one afternoon when Bill came home from work. He joined her in the swing. He sat there a minute or two and then said, "Maggie, I have decided not to go back to the Citadel this fall."

"Why not? You liked it there, and you made good grades."

"Yeah, I know, but I want to enlist in the Army Air Corps next spring. I can work for Dad until I leave for basic training."

"Oh Bill, Momma will be devastated! Maybe Daddy will understand, but I don't."

"Sis, I don't want to be drafted, and I'm just the kinda guy they're looking for. Please try to understand, and help Momma to accept my decision."

"You know I will try, but it won't be easy."

That evening at dinner, Bill announced to the family that he did not plan to return to the Citadel.

Bill continued about his plan to work with his father until after Christmas, and then in the spring, to enlist in the Army Air Corps to become a pilot. Annie and the girls were very unhappy with the news, but Ruben said, "Bill and I have discussed the situation, and if he wants to get into the Air Corps, this is what he should do."

Maggie whined, forgetting her promise to Bill, "Why? We're not in the war. I don't understand why he and Jake have to be in such a hurry."

"Maggie, you're living in your own world, and you're not paying attention to what is going on elsewhere. In my opinion we will be in the war by Christmas." Ruben continued, "We must help our boys make the right decision for themselves and support them in any way we can."

Maggie listened to her father, but she didn't like what he was saying. She hung her head and said in a low whisper, "I'm sorry Bill. You know I want what is best for you."

Her mother wiped a tear from her eye and added, "Yes, Bill, we all do."

Maggie went upstairs to pack a few more things. Jeanie tried to help, asking one question after another. Lisa offered to help carry the boxes downstairs for her. Maggie felt Lisa was going to miss her also, but yet, she also thought, "Lisa always wanted to have a room to herself anyway."

From then on, life would be different for all of them.

Chapter 15

Saturday, August 14, Wally called to remind Maggie that his brother Tim was due in late that day. He wanted to be sure that she was still planning to meet them at church and have lunch with them afterwards.

"I'm looking forward to meeting your brother and having lunch with you two, Wally," Maggie answered. "I'll meet you in front of the church, just a little before 11:00."

"Sounds fine! See you tomorrow, Maggie!" Wally hung up the phone.

The next morning she rose early to wash and curl her hair, and she spent plenty of time getting ready for church. Ruben called, "Everyone come down here! It's time to leave for church."

Lisa noticed how pretty Maggie looked, and she asked, "Maggie, you sure are pretty this morning. Any particular reason?"

"I've got a date for church and lunch afterwards."

"Who is this one?"

"He's Wally Smith's brother. He's in town visiting Wally for about three weeks. Wally wants me to date him and show him around Winston-Salem. He's never been here before."

"Momma, here she goes, adding another boy to her list!" Lisa teased.

"Leave Maggie alone. She is just helping to entertain a friend's brother while he's visiting," Annie defended Maggie.

Chapter 15

Ruben parked the car, and they all piled out and walked over to where Wally was standing.

Wally extended his hand to Mr. McGee, saying, "So glad to see you and your family this beautiful morning! I would like to introduce you to my brother. Tim, this is Mr. and Mrs. McGee and their family, Lisa, Jeanie, Bill, and Maggie."

Maggie smiled at Tim and thought to herself, "Gee, he's tall...stockily built...he might be a football player...uhm... blond curly hair and the bluest eyes I've ever seen. The next few weeks might turn out to be fun."

Tim smiled back as if to say, "I like you."

Maggie excused herself to join the choir as they began to line up in front of the church. As she turned to go, she said, "I'll meet you right here after church services."

Wally motioned to them, "Come on, we had better get in church before the choir comes."

When the service ended, Maggie told her family good-bye and left with Wally and Tim. Maggie was surprised when they arrived at the car, it was a new Chevrolet, and even more surprised to learn, it belonged to Tim. She had never had a boyfriend who owned a car. All of her other boyfriends had to borrow someone's car. Tim opened the front door and seated Maggie beside him. Wally crawled into the back seat. Maggie felt so grown up as Tim started the engine and asked, "Wally, where we are going?"

"Take a right at the corner and then go straight. We're going to the Robert E. Lee Hotel. They have a wonderful Sunday buffet."

Maggie thought she must be dreaming - out to lunch at the hotel with two good-looking men. She was glad that she had spent so much time getting ready for this day.

Lunch was elegant. The table was laden with every kind of meat, salad, and vegetable dish imaginable. It was displayed with greens, fruits and flowers. There was such a mass of food that it took a long time to go down the line.

They took their time eating their delicious lunch, and finding out about each other.

"Maggie, what are your plans, now that you've finished high school?" Tim asked.

"I'll be going to Peace College in Raleigh in September. I'm going to study music, particularly voice."

"Oh, do you sing?" Tim paused, "I mean sing really well?"

"Does she sing!" Wally said, "I can tell you she has a beautiful voice."

"I sure hope I get to hear you sing while I'm here," Tim added.

"How long do you plan to stay?" Maggie asked.

"I plan to visit Wally until I have to return to school, September third."

"That's great! What are your plans for school?" Maggie said.

"I attend Ohio State University, and I will be entering my junior year. I'm studying law, but don't hold that against me," Tim laughed.

Maggie laughed too. She thought, "I think I like him. He has such a winning smile and a good sense of humor. And he's older than me! And tall!"

"I think we better go," Wally said, "I need to be back at the "Y" before two. Just let me off, and you two can have the afternoon to get better acquainted."

"Sounds good to me! Can you spare me the afternoon, Maggie?" Tim asked.

"That suits me, Tim. I can show you around town."

"Great! Let's go and take this guy back to work. Then we can have some fun!"

They took Wally back to the "Y" and spent the rest of the day cruising around Winston in Tim's green Chevrolet. She took him to the Reynolds Tobacco warehouses where cigarettes were made. She told him that was the largest industry in Winston. Then they drove to Old Salem, got out and walked over the Salem College campus, and up to the Moravian Cemetery where she told Tim about the snowy Moravian Easter Sunrise service she attended in sandals. He laughed and they went on with their tour. She showed him where the early settlement of Salem began, and explained that later another settlement was started nearby and was named Winston. Many years later as the two towns grew, they merged and became known as Winston-Salem. When the tour ended, she smiled at Tim and added. "And that is where I live."

"Very interesting, young lady."

They got back to the car and Tim said, "Where to now?"

She gave him directions to the Country Club. They got out and went to the terrace where they ate a light supper. As they sat there, they made plans for the next week. Tim was anxious to see her as often as possible.

The next morning Maggie awoke to a hot sticky day. She rose, showered, fixed her hair, and went downstairs for breakfast.

"Carroll Studio just called to say your proofs are ready," Annie said.

"Why didn't you tell me? I gotta go get them!"

"Slow down! They just called, and you have all day. Lisa needs some school supplies. Can you take her with you?"

"Sure, if she can be ready real quick."

Annie called to Lisa, telling her to get ready to go to town with Maggie.

Lisa replied, "I'll be ready in 30 minutes."

A half hour later, Maggie and Lisa went out the front door, calling to their mother, "We're going to catch the bus, and we'll be back this afternoon."

"All right, but be careful. Lisa, do you have your list with you?"

"Yes, Momma."

The bus ride to town seemed to take forever for Maggie, but finally they arrived. "I want to go to Carroll's Studio first," Maggie said. "Then we can go shop for your supplies." Lisa agreed, knowing how anxious Maggie was to see her proofs.

At the studio, Maggie opened the door and the receptionist looked up and asked them to have a seat. "Mr. Carroll will be with you in a moment." Maggie was filled with excitement and kept fidgeting, and getting up and down. She was nervous and had a little fear that she might not like her proofs.

"Come on, Maggie, sit down! It's just a picture," Lisa said.

"Oh, Lisa, this picture is very important, and it's got to be good!"

Lisa just stared at Maggie and smiled. She thought, "How could it not be good? Maggie is so pretty!"

Mr. Carroll opened the door and invited the girls into his office, where he had all the proofs spread out on his desk. "Maggie, I think you will like your proofs, or let's say, I think your boyfriends are going to like your picture."

She took one look at the proofs and smiled.

"Maggie," Lisa said, "Your proofs are wonderful. I don't know how you will decide which one to have printed."

"Mr. Carroll, I love my proofs! Thank you so much. This means a lot to me."

Gathering the proofs together, putting them in an envelope, and handing them to Maggie, Mr. Carroll said, "If you can bring them right back in a few days, I'll have them ready for you before you leave for college. You did say you were leaving September sixth, didn't you?"

She took the proofs and said, "Yes, that's right. Thank you very much, Mr. Carroll. I'll have these back to you by Friday.

Turning to her sister she said, "OK, Lisa. Where do you need to go for your supplies?"

"I can get everything I need at The Book Store, and it's just in the next block." She knew Maggie was anxious to get home and show Momma and Daddy her proofs. She had to admit she was a little excited for Maggie about the picture, but she would never let her sister know that.

Chapter 15

The girls boarded the bus home, and all the way home Maggie was trying to decide how she would tell her mother that she needed five pictures. That is, if she gives Jake one. He keeps saying that he wants one to take with him when he leaves to go into the Air Corps. Maggie asked Lisa, "Do you think Momma and Daddy will let me have five pictures made?"

"Five?" Lisa exclaimed, "Who are you giving five pictures to?"

"Well, there is Paul, John, James and Tim," Maggie answered.

"You just met Tim, and that's just four."

"Jake insists he wants one, too. He says he doesn't have a steady girl, and every G.I. needs a pretty girl's picture to carry with him. He says we might fall in love before it's all over. And Tim knows I've had my picture taken, and he has already asked me for one."

"Gee, Maggie, that all sounds so complicated."

"I guess, but I'm keeping it straight."

The bus rounded the curve and their home came into view. Lisa pulled the bell cord, and they picked up their belongings and prepared to get off the bus.

Maggie ran to the house and began calling for her mother as soon as she was inside, "Momma, where are you?"

"I'm fixing dinner. You don't have to holler so loud, do you?"

She entered the kitchen like a small hurricane, "Momma, just look at my proofs. You won't believe what a pretty daughter you have!" She shoved the envelope into her mother's hands.

"Wait a minute, honey. Let me wash my hands first." After drying her hands, Annie took the envelope, and, as she looked through the proofs, she smiled at her daughter. "These are just as pretty as you are, honey. Have you decided which pose you like best?"

Maggie took the proofs, selected the one she liked best, and gave it to her mother. "I think this one is my favorite. What do you think?"

"Yes, I think that's a real good picture of you. How many prints do you think you will want?"

Maggie hemmed and hawed, unable to gather nerve enough to give her mother the actual number.

Annie spoke up and said, "Why don't you get six? At least that will leave one for your father and me to frame and put on our dresser."

She grabbed her mother and gave her a great big hug and kiss. As she turned to go up to her room she called back, "Thank you! I love you!"

"Don't forget to show them to your father when he gets home," Annie called after her.

"I'll be sure to show him what a pretty daughter he has!"

Annie turned back to her stove, shaking her head, and thinking, "She sure makes life interesting."

When her father came in from work that night, Maggie wasted no time in showing him her proofs. He loved them and gave his permission to have six prints made. He didn't understand why she needed that many, but he took his wife's word that she needed six pictures.

The following week was filled with dates with Tim - a movie, dinner at a fancy restaurant, and even a trip to the theater in Greensboro, to see "Madame Butterfly." It seemed funny to be dating someone older who drives his own car and takes her on very sophisticated dates. Maggie decided she liked dating someone who made her feel more grown up.

On their way to Greensboro, Maggie asked, "Why did you decide to study law?"

"Well, it runs in the family; you see my father and my grandfather were lawyers. Wally didn't want to study law so, it was up to me to keep up the family tradition."

"Do you think you will enjoy practicing law?"

"I really do. I like reading and studying, and you do a lot of that in practicing law."

"Will you go into criminal or corporate law?"

"Corporate. That's what my Dad's firm does, so I will join his firm. Even though he is dead, it still bears his name. Now enough about me."

Chapter 15

Tim turned to Maggie and smiled, "I know you are studying music, but how do you plan to use it?"

"I like religious choral music, so I think I might like to lead a church choir and give music lessons, as well."

"I loved hearing you sing in church last Sunday. I think you will make a good choir director."

Tim pulled the car into the parking lot and escorted Maggie into the theater. "Madame Butterfly" was fantastic, and when the chorus began to sing, a desire welled up in her that made her wonder if she wanted to go on stage.

All the way home Maggie sang the songs from the play for Tim.

As he pulled the car to a stop in the driveway, Tim said, "I surely did enjoy the play, and also the encore on the way home."

"I'm sorry, but I couldn't get that music out of my head. I guess you can tell how much I enjoyed the evening."

Tim walked her to the door and gave her a peck on the cheek and said, "Good night, song bird!"

She went to sleep that night humming the songs from the musical and picturing herself on stage.

Friday, she caught the bus to town and went straight to Carroll's Studio. She sat and waited about ten minutes for Mr. Carroll. He was taking pictures of a mother and her beautiful baby. Maggie enjoyed watching the mother come from the studio with her new baby. "They looked so sweet," she thought to herself, "That's what I hope is in my future! I guess I'd rather be a mother than be on stage."

Mr. Carroll escorted the pair to the door and said, "Good-bye, Mrs. Tyler. Your proofs will be ready next week. We'll call you to let you know when they're ready."

Mr. Carroll turned to Maggie, "Good morning, Miss McGee! Are you ready to order your pictures?

"I sure am," she said enthusiastically.

He opened the door to his office and ushered Maggie in. "Now Maggie, let's see which pose you selected."

She pulled out the pose she liked best and gave it to Mr. Carroll.

"I thought you would like that one. What sizes do you need, and how many do you want?"

"I want six copies of five by sevens," Maggie said sheepishly.

"Six? My, we have a lot of boyfriends, don't we?"

"One is for my Momma and Daddy."

"It's good that you are not leaving them out. Would you like any of these tinted?"

"No, I don't think so."

"Well, may I suggest we do them in sepia tone. It will show your auburn hair better."

"Oh, yes, I would like that."

Mr. Carroll was busy making notes on the selected proof. He looked up at Maggie and asked, "Now when do you need these?"

"I leave for college September sixth, and I would like to have them before then. I need to mail several, and it would be nice to get that done before I leave for school."

"What about if I have them ready for you on September fourth?"

"That will be perfect!"

Mr. Carroll smiled at Maggie and asked, "Now, how many mailers will you need?"

"Three," she replied with a timid smile.

"I think I have all the information I need. You may pick these up September fourth, Miss McGee."

Maggie thanked him profusely, and left his office walking on air.

Chapter 16

Saturday morning Maggie rose early and packed a picnic for Tim and herself. She had planned a trip to Hanging Rock State Park. She packed her swimsuit, a cover-up and a blanket for their picnic. Tim pulled into the drive right at 10:00, jumped out of the car and literally ran to the door. Maggie was ready. Tim picked up the basket and blanket and reached for Maggie's hand to lead her to the car.

"Momma, Tim and I are going. We'll be home by seven." She called back to her mother.

"OK, honey. Have fun, but do be careful."

"We will."

The day was an unusual August day - not too humid, but hot enough to make the lake inviting, with a gentle breeze stirring that made sitting by the lake pleasant. They found a nice, secluded place to spread their blanket. Tim wanted to know what she had packed in the basket. Out came southern fried chicken, deviled eggs, ham biscuits, and a piece of chocolate cake big enough for the two of them.

He could not believe his eyes. "Did you fix all of this?"

"I packed the picnic, but Momma did the cooking; I'm afraid I can't cook."

He seemed a little bit disappointed, but, he thought, "She's got everything else, and she can always learn to cook."

They lay on the quilt in the filtered sun and talked. Tim rose up and before Maggie knew what was happening, he had gathered her into his arms and kissed her one time after another. Maggie's head was spinning as she felt his tongue slip into her mouth. His kisses were almost demanding. She felt an excitement and pleasure that she had never felt before. Suddenly she realized that if she didn't stop Tim, there would be no going back, and she was not ready to give herself to him, or anyone else, until her wedding night.

Maggie broke away and announced, "I think we had better start packing the picnic in the basket and head back to the car. It's time to start for home."

"Please, Maggie, can't we just stay a little longer?"

"I think you know why we can't stay any longer."

Tim protested for a bit, but he knew that she was right, so he began helping to pack the car, and in a few minutes, they were on the road home.

They arrived home on time, and they spent the rest of the evening in the double swing on the patio. Despite that moment of tension between them, it had been a wonderful day, and as they sat there, they held hands and made plans to see each other every day the next week.

Sunday they met at church, but they could not sit together because Maggie was singing with the choir and had a small solo part in the anthem. Tim was delighted to hear her sing. Her voice was clear as a bell, and it gave him the shivers to hear her hit those high notes. After church he hugged her and told her how thrilled he was to have heard her sing. They headed to her house where they were all to have another of her mother's wonderful Sunday dinners. Tim felt honored to be included.

Tim could not believe that he was sitting around this family table surrounded by smiling faces and infectious laughter. Everyone was talking, and it seemed that no one was listening. He was used to a table of only three - his mother, his brother and himself. His father had died when he was very young.

The table was surrounded by people whose lives were changing. Bill, who was home until spring when he planned to enlist in the Army Air Corps, sat next to Jake, who was leaving the same day as Maggie. Jake was getting ready to leave for basic training. Maggie and Tim were next, and then little Jeanie sat next to Tim, of whom she had become very fond. She took every opportunity to sit beside him. Next there was Lisa and then Momma and Daddy. It was a full dining room, and a real feast was placed on the table.

Her father asked everyone to hold hands for the blessing. Everyone joined hands and bowed their heads. "Father, we are truly thankful for this meal and our many other blessings. Make us ever mindful of your love and open our hearts to the needs of all of those around us. Bring peace to this troubled world. This we pray in Christ's name and for his sake. Amen."

At once, Bill piped up with, "Pass the chicken!"

Momma shot a disapproving look at Bill, and everyone else laughed. The feast had begun.

When dinner was over and the kitchen had been cleaned, all the family gathered in the recreation room to play their new game, Monopoly. The game lasted all afternoon and into the early evening with much arguing and laughing. As soon as the game was over, Maggie and Tim excused themselves and took a long walk in the park under the star-studded sky.

Tim's final week passed too quickly. The days were filled with packing and finishing a few last-minute mending projects, but Maggie always reserved the evenings for dates with Tim.

One of the highlights of the week was when Tim took her to a concert of the North Carolina Symphony. It was held at the Reynolds Auditorium, which was close enough to her house that they could walk. After the concert, as they were walking home, Tim asked, "What was your favorite piece they played?"

Maggie strolled along thinking, "Well, I think my favorite was "Londonderry Air", by Frederick Weatherly, better known as "O'Danny Boy."

"Boy you sure are smart to know all that."

"Oh, Tim I loved the whole concert really. Thank you for a wonderful evening."

With that she turned around and kissed him.

The weekend was fast approaching, and Tim wanted to plan a special evening for their last night together. Friday night he announced to Maggie that he was taking her to the Robert E. Lee Roof Garden for dinner Saturday night. Then he would meet her for church Sunday and would leave from there to drive home. He had to be back at school the first of the next week.

As she dressed for her Saturday night date, she could not help but remember her date with Paul at the very same place. He had been just a boy, and she was hardly past playing dolls. They had been young, acting so grown up. Now she was going there again with a very grown young man, and she hoped she could be a little more sophisticated.

When she heard Tim's car drive in the driveway, she couldn't help peeping out of her bedroom window. There he was, a handsome, blond, curly-haired young man dressed in a navy blazer and white duck pants. Her heart flipped, and she wondered if she was dressed properly to complement this handsome "older" man.

At the restaurant, Tim tipped the head waiter and asked for a table near the dance floor and also near the outside balcony. They were ushered to the best table in the restaurant. Tim seated Maggie and then seated himself as close to her as he could get. Maggie felt like a princess.

Tim smiled at her for what seemed like an eternity and said, "Maggie, you look so beautiful tonight. I hope it's because you're with me." He went on, "Did you make your dress?"

She answered, "Yes, I made this dress, and I wore it specially for our last night together."

He took her hand and kissed it. He asked, "May I have this dance, Miss McGee?"

She stood and he immediately took her in his arms and swept her onto the dance floor to the strains of "Night and Day, you are the One." Tim danced Maggie out to the balcony and held her in his arms as they stood there enjoying the glow from the town below, and the warm evening breeze. He turned her to him and gave her a long lingering kiss. They stood there for a long time before returning to their table. Maggie felt a bit flushed, and was beginning to wonder where their relationship might lead. During the meal, Tim asked her to be sure to write to him regularly. He pulled out a piece of paper, wrote down his address, and then he asked for hers. She told him he would have to wait until she was at college, and then she would send it. He took her hand again, looked at her, and said, "Maggie, you promise?"

She smiled back at him and answered, "I promise!" She tucked his address into her tiny beaded purse.

"May I come to Winston during the Christmas holidays? Tim asked.

"That would be nice."

"And may I have a date for New Year's Eve?"

Maggie hesitated wondering what else might happen between now and then, but said, "Usually, someone plans a party. Would that be all right with you?"

"Whatever you plan to do will be fine with me. I just want to celebrate the New Year with you," Tim replied.

"You can count on that."

He led her to the dance floor for one final dance. The band was playing "Star Dust," and that was always the signal for the last dance of the evening.

Tim held Maggie's hand all the way home. When he took her to the door he put his arms around her and kissed her as if he never wanted to stop. Maggie gently pushed him away and said, "Tim, it's time for me to go in. I do have a curfew."

Tim turned to leave saying, "I'll see you at church in the morning at 10:30."

"I'll be there. Good night, Tim. Thank you for a memorable evening."

Sunday morning, Tim was waiting when Maggie arrived. They stood and talked and greeted friends while they waited to enter the church. Her parents arrived, and Jeanie ran and grabbed Tim's hand. She looked at Maggie and asked, "Can I sit with you and Tim?"

Before Maggie could answer, Tim said, "Sure you can, little one. You can't sit between us though."

The three of them went in and were seated with the rest of the family.

All during church Maggie thought, "He's leaving as soon as we get out of church. It's going to be mighty lonely without his constant attention. But, then I'll be going to school this week, and everything will be different. I like Tim a lot, but then there's John, Paul, and James. Really, I like them all." She didn't get much from church that day; her mind was too preoccupied.

After church they lingered a while talking to friends, and then he led Maggie to his car. "Let me take you home. Then I must get on the road back to Ohio."

She got in beside him, and they held hands all the way to the house.

Tim said, "By the way, I know you had a picture made, but you haven't given one to me. May I have one?"

"They aren't ready yet. I'll have to send you one."

"Please do. I know I won't forget how pretty you are, but it will be nice to have one to remind me."

He pulled the car into the drive, and the two of them sat there not knowing what to say. Maggie broke the silence, "Tim do you have time to have lunch with the family?"

"No, Maggie, I had better get some miles behind me before I eat something. If I eat your mother's good Sunday dinner now, I would get too sleepy to drive. But, thank you for asking."

Maggie reached over, gave him a quick kiss, and said, "I'd better get out so you can be on your way."

He pulled her to him and insisted, "I want a better kiss than that to remember." He kissed her long and hard and then let her go. She crawled out of the car, blew him a kiss, and he was on his way.

Monday morning Maggie rose early. Her first thoughts were of Tim and how much fun they had together. She began missing him, but then she remembered her pictures needed to be picked up, and James had called to say he was home, and wanted to come over that evening. Maggie loved to keep busy, so this was fine with her.

When she went down to the breakfast-room, she found Bill having his breakfast before going to work.

"Sis, what are you doing up so early?" He asked.

"I've got to go downtown to pick up my pictures. They are ready today."

"Do you want me to pick them up for you? I'm going to town to get some office supplies for Daddy. I can run them right back to you."

"Bill, that is just wonderful, because I have so much to do! That would be a big help!"

Several hours later Bill returned with the pictures and commented, "Sis, they sure are pretty. If I weren't your brother, I'd be begging for one of them, too."

About that time Jake came in and saw the picture. He reminded Maggie that she had promised him one.

"You sure you want one and are not just being nice?"

"I told you, you're my only girl, and I need a picture to talk to when I'm lonely."

"OK, here take one, but you be sure to look after it, and bring it back."

"Jake," Bill said, "If you want me to take you to the bus station, you need to be ready when I come home for lunch at 12:00, and I'll take you then."

"You're leaving today?" Maggie asked.

"Yes, I have to be in Raleigh by 6:00. They'll load us up then, and take us to Fort Bragg for basic training," Jake replied.

"I still don't understand your hurry to enlist."

"I'm afraid you will soon enough, Maggie." He kissed her and headed upstairs.

"See you at twelve, buddy," said Bill.

Maggie went straight to her room and wrote letters to John and Paul to put in the mailers with her pictures. She signed each picture, "All my love, Maggie." She sealed the envelopes and placed them on the library table downstairs. She asked Bill to mail them for her when he returned to the office.

James had gone on a trip with his parents as soon as he finished at Camp Sea Gull, so this was the first time she had seen James since the weekend back in July. Even though they had not seen each other much all summer, he still kept in close touch, and asked to see her when he got back. He was headed to the UNC at Chapel Hill, and that was close enough to Peace that they planned to see each other often.

That night James was looking mighty handsome. His tan set off his dark curly hair, making him even more handsome than she remembered. As they sat down in the booth at the Snack Shack, Maggie said, "James, you sure do look handsome tonight! Working at the camp this summer sure is becoming to you."

"Thanks, I had a good summer, but it's mighty good to be home. I sure did miss seeing you. It will be nice to have you close enough so we can see each other occasionally."

Maggie thought, "What a difference dating James is, as opposed to Tim. I'm not sure who I like the best. I feel more like myself sitting here with James. He kisses more like the high-school boys, not like Tim's passionate kisses."

James suggested that they take a drive out in the nearby country before going home. Maggie seated herself close to him and squeezed his arm, murmuring, "I really have missed you this summer."

James smiled at her and began to drive.

When they were back at the house, James reminded Maggie that she had promised him a picture. "Did you have it taken?"

"I sure did," she replied. "If you are sure that you want one, I have one for you."

"Go get it right now! I want to see it!"

She ran upstairs and picked up another picture. That was the fourth one, and one was for her parents. She had only one more in case she met someone at college. "Oh, well, I can have some more made, if I need to," she thought.

She came back down to the den and handed the photo to James.

"Gee, Maggie. You are beautiful, and your picture shows it! I'll be proud to set this on my dresser at school. I'll call you as soon as I get settled, and give you my address. Let's plan to get together for a weekend soon."

She told James she was looking forward to being able to see him. It would be good to have someone from home nearby. James rose to leave, and Maggie followed him to the door. He kissed her and said, "I'll be calling you real soon."

The next day she would leave for college. She was all packed and ready, but she was not sure she was ready emotionally for the big change that was coming.

Chapter 17

Maggie arrived at Peace College early on September 6th to an overcast morning that matched her mood. She was elated at the prospect of attending college, but a sadness hung over her about leaving home for the first time. But as her father drove up Fayetteville Street, the majestic main building of Peace College was hidden by huge stately oak trees, which lined a long brick walkway. The giant white columns rose four stories, making the entrance seem imposing. She felt as if she were entering the era of "Gone with the Wind."

Her parents moved her into the suite of rooms in East Dormitory. The suite was on the second floor, which consisted of two bedrooms connected by a private bath. Maggie would share her room with Franny Cramer and Nancy Hanes, her friend from Winston-Salem. Their room had three beds and three desks on one side of the room and a double dresser and a single dresser on the other side. Each girl had her own closet. The adjoining room had two beds, two desks, two closets, and a double dresser which Mary Forester and Lilly Watson shared. Nancy arrived about an hour later than Maggie, and the two girls were silly with excitement, eagerly anticipating meeting the three other girls with whom they would be sharing this suite.

Jeanie and Lisa helped with the lighter boxes. Jeanie wanted to open the boxes, while Lisa was bent on making Maggie's section of the room neat. The last things to be unpacked were the boyfriend pictures. Maggie proudly set the pictures of James, Paul, Jake, and John on her side of the dresser, which she shared with Nancy.

Chapter 17

Later that day, Franny Cramer, a pretty girl with flowing copper-red hair and green eyes, burst in the door with her entourage - a maid and a chauffeur lugged in boxes and heavy suitcases. Mrs. Cramer followed, bringing in a bag of Franny's favorite snacks. Franny announced that she was to be their suitemate. Maggie looked at Nancy as if to say, "This should be interesting." Before the day ended, Mary, a slender girl with dark brown hair and eyes to match, and Lilly, a tall giant of a girl with a head full of blonde curls and blue eyes, moved into the next room to complete their suite. The five of them made an odd assortment of college girls, each from different backgrounds, and each with her own special redeeming features.

They spent the day unpacking and attending college events for new students. The day flew by and before they knew it, it was time for Ruben and Annie to leave, and Maggie was beginning to dread the moment. Hugs and kisses and a few tears were exchanged, and before Maggie realized it, she was alone with all these strangers, except for her friend, Nancy. She was feeling grateful that she and Nancy had decided to room together.

That first night when Maggie crawled into bed, she thought, "What a collection of girls I have to share my living space with! A spoiled, little rich girl, a girl right out of the country, a giant of a girl with very little that seems attractive, and my good friend Nancy, who tends to be a little stand-offish, and then there is me."

As she went to sleep, she thought of what her mother had told her, "Maggie, part of going off to school is to continue your education, but equally important is to teach you to get along with all kinds of people."

Maggie's last thought was, "This is bound to teach me that."

The next few weeks, Maggie settled into the routine of classes and getting used to the rules of a girl's school. She had to dress like a lady every evening for dinner, which meant that she had to don a dress or suit, with heels and hose. Whenever they left the campus, all students were required to wear dresses or suits, shoes with heels, hose, hat, and gloves. In other words a Peace girl had to always present herself as a lady wherever she was seen. By the end of the first week, Maggie realized that checking her mail box was the highlight of her day. Within the next week, she received a letter from Paul:

Sept. 10, 1941

Dearest Maggie,

School has begun here at Clemson, and I am settling in rapidly. The routine is interesting, and my course work doesn't appear to be too difficult. I like my roommate, Joe Masters; who comes from Charlotte. He says he went to high school with your cousin Emily. It is really a small world, isn't it? I seem to be drawn to North Carolinians.

Maggie, I received your picture today, and I love it! As I sit and look at it, I can almost hear your infectious giggle, and it makes me miss you even more than I ever thought I could. It seems like such a long time since we were together.

I would really like for you to come to Clemson for our homecoming football game and the dance. It's the weekend after Thanksgiving, November28th. Let me know if you can come, as soon as possible, so I can reserve a place for you to stay. I am told there is a bed and breakfast nearby, where a lot of the girls stay on weekends. I will try to get you a room there. Maggie, every time I look at your picture I remember that night on the beach, when I held you in my arms under the moonlit sky. I will be dreaming of you and feeling your lips on mine again. Write me soon.

All my love,

Paul

Maggie sat there on her bed dreaming of her spending the weekend at Clemson. She squeezed her knees up to her chest and let out a squeal. Franny came in the door and said, "What's going on with you?"

"Paul has asked me to Clemson for a football game and dance the weekend after Thanksgiving."

"Are you going?"

Chapter 17

"I have to call Momma and see if she thinks it is all right for me to go."

Maggie immediately reached for the phone and called her mother to see if it would be all right to plan a trip to Clemson the last of November for Paul's homecoming weekend. When her mother gave her consent, Maggie added, "Oh, Momma, you'll have to write the Dean and give your permission for me to leave the campus that weekend.

"Yes, Honey, I'll do that tonight after I talk with your father."

"Thanks, Momma. I gotta go now. Bye!"

"Wait a minute Maggie! I want to know how you like school," her mother insisted.

"Momma, it's great! I'm getting to sing a lot, and you know how I love to sing. I think I'm doing well in all of my classes. Momma, I've got to go now. It's time for dinner, and you know I have to get dressed like a lady." All the time she carried on this conversation, she was pulling on her first stocking.

"Bye, honey. Study hard, and I mean the books and not the boys," Annie added.

"Bye, Momma," said Maggie as she pulled on her second stocking, while holding the phone with her chin.

The other girls filed out of the room, and Nancy called back to Maggie, "You had better get off that phone and get to the dining room. You don't want to start off being late your first month."

"OK. I'm right behind you."

When all the girls were back in the suite after dinner, Maggie got out her stationery, sat cross legged on her bed, and began to write to Paul.

Lilly asked, "Who are you writing to tonight?"

I'm answering a letter from Paul. He has invited me to homecoming weekend at Clemson in November. He wants an answer as soon as I can let him know, so he can find a place for me to stay." Maggie went on, "I can't believe I'm going to Clemson for a ballgame and a dance!"

"Which one is he?" Mary asked as she waved her arm toward the gallery on Maggie's dresser.

She jumped off the bed and showed Paul's picture to each girl, one at a time.

"He's good looking," said Franny.

"Yeah, but he's a little too short to suit me," Maggie said.

They all laughed, and someone said, "You can't have everything!"

A week went by, with another letter from Paul, but as yet she had not heard from John. While a far more serious young man than Paul, John was equally as good looking, and taller.

By the end of September she had received three letters from Paul, but not a word had she heard from John. Maggie began to worry that he had not received her last letter and her picture. She was afraid he might be angry with her. She decided to wait another few days, and if she did not get a letter, she would write him again. The weekend passed, then Monday came and went without a letter.

When Maggie checked her mail box Tuesday, she was elated to finally find a letter from John. She ran to East Dorm, bounded up the stairs two at a time, popped into her room, and jumped on her bed sitting cross legged, as she liked to do. She ripped open John's letter and began to read:

Sept. 25, 1941

Dear Maggie,

I do hope you will forgive me for taking so long to write to you, but when I first arrived my schedule was all screwed up. It has taken all this time getting into all the courses I needed to take. Now that classes have started, I think I am going to like college life. I hope you are enjoying being a college girl.

Maggie, I am going to be in Raleigh the last week of October, and I hope you will be available. USC will be participating in a swimming and diving competitions with NC State that weekend. I would like to have dates Friday and Saturday nights, and it would be great if you would attend the meet on Saturday. I will write to you later when I can send you my schedule. Of course, I want you to cheer for me, and not some State boy. Ha!

My folks came to see me this past weekend, and brought me my mail. In it was a much-anticipated letter from you, and that beautiful picture you sent. I was proud to put it on my desk, where I look at it while I study. The guys that wander in and out of my room tease me that I don't deserve such a beauty. I agree with them, but I don't let them know.

Maggie, I have really missed you these past weeks, and I do hope I can see you when I come to Raleigh. Write soon, I'll be waiting to hear.

It's been a long time between kisses.

Love you,

John

Immediately, Maggie pulled out her box of stationery and began to write John that she would love to see him the last weekend of October. Yes, he could have dates Friday and Saturday. Yes, she would attend the meet, and yes, she would cheer for him - she didn't know many state boys anyway! As she finished the letter and was stuffing it in its envelope, Mary came in.

"Who are you writing to now?" Mary asked.

"I'm writing to John. He's coming to Raleigh the last of October and wants me to date him Friday and Saturday nights," Maggie answered.

"Which one is he?"

"He's the dark-haired one that's standing by a swimming pool."

"Oh, he's the good-looking one, isn't he?"

"Yeah, and he's tall too."

"Maggie, which of the boys is your favorite?" Mary asked.

"I like them all, Mary," Maggie answered.

"You'd better watch out, or you'll lose them all."

"They'll never find out, and I'm not old enough to get serious."

Mary left the room shaking her head. She didn't understand Maggie.

The month of October passed so quickly along with the deep red color in the huge oaks on the front lawn of the campus. Maggie's mail box continued to yield a flood of letters. One was from Jake, who had finished basic training and was being sent to Kelly Field in San Antonio, Texas, for his pre-flight training. Jake wrote that he enjoyed her letters and loved her picture. He asked her to keep writing, because at this time, she was still his only girl friend. Maggie sat right down and answered Jake's letter. She really missed him, but only in the way she missed her brother Bill.

Another letter was from James, who was in college at UNC, in Chapel Hill. His letter was mostly about getting into the swing of college life, but he did ask her if she would be home during the Thanksgiving holidays and if he could see her. He said, "I really have been missing you, and I have something to ask you when I see you over the holidays."

Maggie was peeved that he left her hanging. "What is he going to ask?" she wondered. "And why does he have to wait?"

John arrived in Raleigh, the last weekend of October, and Maggie and he spent every minute possible together. John found dating at Peace a little odd, but he managed a kiss every time the chaperone left the porch or turned her head. Saturday morning, Maggie took a taxi to NC State, where she met John and attended the swim meet. It was exciting, especially because John won the diving competition. After the meet, they spent the afternoon walking at Pullen Park, and talking about their experiences with college life. The weekend left Maggie thinking that John might be her favorite boyfriend.

The first weekend of November John was throwing a few things in a duffle bag. He was going with a carload of his new-found college friends to the annual USC vs. Clemson football game. It was a typical fall day with a light wind rustling the golden leaves from one place to another. John bounded out of his dorm and jumped into the car with his buddies. Off they went with their USC banner flapping in the wind and their spirits flying high.

John had planned to spend the weekend with his high-school buddy, Joe Masters, who was now attending Clemson. He and Joe planned to meet after the game because they would be sitting on opposite sides of the field. The girls on John's side were wearing corsages of white chrysanthemums tied with crimson and black ribbons. The girls with the orange chrysanthemums tied with orange ribbons were headed to the other side of the field. Watching the parade of lovely girls all dressed up in their fall outfits made him wish for Maggie.

The game was exciting. Clemson was up 14 to 7 going into the last quarter, but in the very last minute of the game USC scored. John held his breath when the kicker lined up to try for the extra point. The ball was kicked, and it soared up- up- and through the crossbars, and as it cleared the goal post the whistle blew signaling the end of the game. John let out a yell, along with all the other USC fans. A tie is better than a loss, especially when he was staying in the dorm with the "enemy."

After the game, John made his way to the east entrance of the stadium, where he found Joe there waiting for him. They threw their arms around each other and headed to Joe's dormitory to freshen up before they met the other guys at a local joint.

They caught up with each other's lives all the way to the dorm and when they arrived there, Joe said, "Come on in, John. My room is on the second floor."

Joe stopped at his dorm door and told John, "Enter my home away from home, if you can find room to walk!"

John squeezed his way into the room and just when Joe was ready to introduce John to his roommate, Paul Stark, John stopped dead still. He pointed to Maggie's picture on one of the study desks and exclaimed angrily, "I've got one just like that one! Who does that belong to?"

Paul moved right over in front of John and said, "That's my girl!" Paul was so angry, he was about to swing at John.

The boys in the room held them apart and someone said, "Don't take it out on each other. That girl is stringing you both along. You ought to be mad at *her*!"

The two cooled off, and Paul said, "I bet she didn't sign yours, 'All my love, Maggie.' Did she?"

"You wanna bet?" John replied.

Joe figured it was time to get John out of there and let Paul lick his wounds. As they walked down the hall, John unloaded his disappointment on Joe. "I really liked Maggie, and I thought she and I had something special."

"Come on John, I know you're hurt, but you're not ready to get serious about a girl. You'll meet lots of cute girls at college. Let's go meet the guys and go get something to eat, I'm starving."

"Me too!"

Five days later, Maggie checked her mail box and found she had a letter from Paul. It seemed a little thick and a little peculiar in how it felt. She didn't have any idea what Paul was sending to her. As usual she raced to her room and assumed her position on her bed. She ripped open the envelope, and out spilled her picture torn into bits. Obviously something was very wrong. But what? Tears formed in her dark-brown eyes. What had she done?

Nov. 15, 1941

Maggie,

I don't know how to tell you that my heart is torn into pieces just like your picture. I can't believe that you were giving away your picture like it was a calling card. At least you can't use this one to break another guy's heart.

We're finished.

Paul

Chapter 17

Maggie was totally confused. What had happened to make Paul so angry? She thought he could have at least told her what she had done wrong. She started to write to him, but he was so emphatic when he wrote, "We're finished." She put down the pen and decided there was nothing she could say unless she knew what had brought this on. She sat there putting the pieces of her picture together and wondering if she could ever make things right with Paul.

She told her roommates about Paul's letter, and that she didn't know why he was so angry.

"Maggie, I warned you," Mary said.

Five days later, Maggie was still trying to figure out what had happened to make Paul so angry, but it became crystal clear when she received a letter from John with her picture in it. Maggie thought, "At least he didn't tear it into pieces." She slowly unfolded John's letter, almost afraid to read what he had to say.

Nov. 21, 1941

Dear Maggie,

What do you think I saw on another guy's dresser, when I went to the USC vs. Clemson football game? Yes, this beautiful picture that I am returning to you. His picture was also signed, 'All my love, Maggie.' Paul was very angry and hurt, and he tried to take it out on me. I realize we are too young to get serious, but I liked thinking of you as my girl. Maybe we will meet again someday, when you grow up.

John

Maggie sat in the middle of her bed with hot tears running down her cheeks. She never dreamed it was possible for the two of them to meet, and find out they had the same picture. She realized that she should not have signed their pictures, "All my love, Maggie." As she was sitting there facing the predicament she had caused, she remembered what her mother had said to her:

"Maggie, be careful with your actions, or you might break some young man's heart."

Maggie was still sitting there as each of her suitemates came into their room. They were all sad for her, but secretly they felt she had been playing carelessly with these boys. Now Maggie knew she had, too. She wanted to call her mother but decided it was only a matter of a few days before she would go home for Thanksgiving, so she would wait and tell her then.

James called to ask for a date that Saturday night. She was happy to hear from him. She had been feeling sorry for herself the past few days, so she put away John's and Paul's pictures. Her dresser looked empty. She had decided not to write either one since she felt they would never forgive her. She admitted to herself that she could give no excuse except being a foolish girl playing at collecting boyfriends. She made herself a promise, "I won't be that irresponsible again!"

It was good to see James that Saturday night. They went to the movies with Nancy and her new boyfriend Joe. As they walked back to Peace, Maggie and James caught each other up on their high-school buddies. James told her of several of their classmates who had already enlisted. He told her he was planning to enter the Navy as soon as the school year was over.

Maggie was puzzled, and she asked him, "Why are all of you boys enlisting before you have to? We aren't at war yet."

"No, but we will be very soon, and most of us don't want to be drafted."

"Let's stop by the drug store before we walk back to Peace," Maggie suggested.

Everyone agreed.

Seated at a large booth in the corner, they ordered four milkshakes, and talked of the upcoming football game between UNC and State. Maggie was going with James, sitting on the UNC side, and Nancy was attending the game with Joe, sitting on the NC State side. This made for lively conversation, but they kept it very civil.

Chapter 17

As they neared Peace, James asked Maggie if she would like to ride home with him when he left for Thanksgiving.

"Have you got a car?" Maggie asked.

"My parents brought me one of our cars this past weekend, to keep until the end of the school year."

"That's wonderful! I'll have to check it out with my parents. They will have to call the Dean and give their permission for me to leave the campus with you in a car," she explained.

"Why do you have to do that?" James asked.

"Well, you see, my parents gave a list to the Dean of those who I can leave the campus with alone, and specially if I am leaving in a car. Your name was not put on the list because you didn't have a car when we first came to school. So, now if I leave un-chaperoned with you or anyone else, you have to be approved by my parents."

"I guess I understand. Just be sure and get me approved, and call me when it's all worked out. When can you leave on Wednesday?"

"My last class is at 11:00, so I can be ready as soon as I get out of that class at noon."

"That'll work. I can leave Chapel Hill at 12:00, and I'll come straight here to pick you up. Then we can get something to eat."

They arrived at the long, oak-covered walk up to the front door of Peace. James took Maggie in his arms and gave her one last kiss, before she entered the inter sanctum. She giggled and pushed him away, saying, "You'll get me kicked out of here if you don't watch out!"

They went up the long walkway hand in hand, smiling at each other. It had been a good night.

Wednesday morning, before Thanksgiving, Maggie was up and packed before the suite started to stir. She was anxious to get home and talk to her mother.

By 1:00, they were leaving Peace, heading west to Winston-Salem. They found a little burger place along the highway, and got a bite to eat.

Maggie was very excited as they turned into the drive around 4:00. Jeanie came running out to the car with her mother right behind her. Annie thanked James for bringing Maggie home and offered him some cookies that she and Jeanie had just baked.

"I better get on home," he said. "My parents worry about me when I'm driving on the highway."

"I can certainly understand how they feel. Here are a few to take with you," Annie said.

James had taken her bags from the car and said, "I'll take them in for you."

"No, we'll take them in," Maggie said, as she kissed him on the cheek and waved to him saying, "Go on and get home so you don't worry your parents."

As James backed the car out of the drive, he stuck his head out of the window and called out to Maggie, "I'll pick you up about 2:00 Sunday afternoon. OK?"

"I'll be ready!" As she turned to pick up her bag, she saw that her mother was carrying the large one and Jeanie was struggling with the small one. She ran to Jeanie, hugged her, and said, "That's too big for you. Let me help you with it."

When Maggie was inside, she took her bags upstairs, opened them, and took out her picture - the one that had been returned by John. There was her writing "All my love Maggie." She came back downstairs and said to her mother, "Momma, I need to talk."

Jeanie was all over Maggie wanting her to play. Her mother saw the distressed look on Maggie's face and said to Lisa, "Take Jeanie downstairs and play with her so I can talk to Maggie."

Lisa grabbed Jeanie's hand and said, "OK, brat! Let's go play with your dolls!"

"Momma, Lisa called me a brat. I'm not, am I?"

"No, you aren't, honey. Lisa didn't mean that. You two go on now. Maggie and I'll come down there in a minute."

Chapter 17

As they left the room, Annie turned to Maggie and asked, "What's the matter? Why are you putting that picture in our picture frame and taking ours out?"

"Momma, you won't believe what happened to me!"

"No, not unless you tell me."

"A couple of weeks ago, John - you remember John, don't you?"

"Yes, he's your friend from Charlotte, isn't he?"

"Not any more."

"What happened?"

"Several weekends ago, USC was playing a football game at Clemson. John went and he was planning to spend the night in the dorm room with a high-school buddy from Charlotte, but his buddy turned out to be Paul Stark's roommate. John went in to their dorm room and saw my picture and must have said right out that he had one just like it. The next week Paul wrote me and I received my picture, torn into bits with an angry letter, saying we are finished.'"

"I knew something had happened, because I talked to Aunt Estelle and she asked why you two had broken up. I told her I didn't know, but I supposed I'd find out when you came home for Thanksgiving. Where did that picture come from?"

"I didn't finish my sad story. Paul didn't tell me what happened. He just said that I must be giving out my pictures like calling cards. About a week later, I received a letter from John, telling me the same story. He sent this one back to me, and said maybe we would meet again after I grew up. They were both mad at me but they were more hurt that I had signed them both, 'All My Love, Maggie.' I realize now that was wrong, so I'm putting this one that I signed into your frame. I will always love you two, but I will never give anyone, 'All my Love', until I meet my prince."

"I think that's a very good idea, but don't beat yourself up too badly. I found out yesterday from Aunt Estelle, that Paul has a new girlfriend, and he is bringing her to their family's Thanksgiving Day dinner."

"He didn't hurt very long, did he?"

"I think you learned a good lesson from this and now you can put all that behind you. Just be more careful of how you treat your relationships. Be honest, dear, and no one will get hurt. Now go get unpacked and get ready for dinner. Your father will be home early. He's anxious to see you. He has missed having you around."

Maggie went over to her mother and hugged her as tightly as she could, "I love you so much. How could I get along without you?"

"Just don't try."

She went up to her bedroom, straight to her desk, sat down, and pulled a red-satin stationery box from her bottom right drawer. She sat there a moment looking at it. Then she opened the box, and placed the unsigned picture in it with her last picture. She thought to herself. "I've promised one to Tim, which I will give to him when he comes after Christmas. That leaves me only one left, and that one is reserved for my true love, as soon as he comes along. Tim might be my prince; time will tell. My prince may still be out there somewhere. I promise I will be more careful, playing this courting game."

She returned the box to its drawer, closed it, and proceeded back downstairs to see her father.

Chapter 18

Maggie ran up to her father and hugged and kissed him, "Hi, Daddy! I'm so glad to be home and see you and the family again!"

Thanksgiving Day was a beautiful, southern fall day. Everything was brown and golden, the sun was shining, and a little wind stirred the leaves all around. The nip in the air made it perfect for Maggie to wear one of her new fall outfits. She rolled over and thought of all the things she was thankful for — her home, her family, and the lessons she had just learned. She rose, dressed, and went downstairs to help her mother with their Thanksgiving dinner. She was excited to learn that Jake had arrived late in the night. She did not realize he would be home. That was one more thing to add to her list of things to be thankful for.

Promptly at 2:00 the family assembled around the dining room table. As they reached for each other's hands, Maggie thought, "How wonderful it is to have everyone home for Thanksgiving!"

They bowed their heads, and Ruben prayed, "Heavenly Father, please bless this home, this family, and all those families who are gathered together in thy name. Make us all truly thankful on this special Thanksgiving Day. We pray for peace to come to the whole wide world. This we ask in Christ's name and for his sake."

"Amen," everyone joined in agreeing with every word Ruben had spoken.

Conversations bounced back and forth around the table like a ping pong ball.

Bill told everyone that he planned to enlist in the Army Air Corps in the spring. Jake talked about his basic training and that he was on a week's leave. He was being sent to Kelly Field in San Antonio, Texas, to start his pre-flight training. Jeanie had started kindergarten and was quick to show everyone her first attempts at writing and her art work. Everyone oohed and aahed, which pleased her immensely. Maggie felt a lump in her throat when she saw how her little Jeanie was growing up. Then Jake asked Lisa what she was doing.

Annie interrupted and said, "Lisa has just been inducted into the Honor Society with the highest grades in her class! We are so proud of her!"

"And Lisa has her first real boyfriend," Bill teased.

Maggie turned to Lisa and asked, "Is that really so, Lisa?"

"Yes, but you don't have to make a big deal out of it," Lisa blushed.

"Oh, Lisa, I am so happy for you! Its so much fun! Maybe I can give you some tips on boyfriends."

Everyone laughed, and Ruben said, "Maggie you had better tend to your own dating. I think Lisa will do fine on her own."

She was a little hurt, but she didn't pursue the subject any further.

After dessert was served and they finished their coffee, they scattered to different parts of the house - the den sofa, the rec room sofa, and the back yard for a croquet game with Jeanie. Maggie and Lisa helped their mother clear the table and clean the kitchen.

It had been a wonderful family gathering.

As Maggie came out of the kitchen, she met Jake coming out of the den. He asked her if she was dating James over the weekend. She said no, that James had gone with his family to his grandmother's and would not get back until late Saturday. She went on to say that James was picking her up Sunday at 2:00 to take her back to Peace.

Jake grabbed her and with a quick kiss said, "OK, you are dating me until we leave on Sunday. Let's start tonight by going to the movies."

Chapter 18

Maggie smiled at Jake and said, "Suits me. What time do you want me to be ready?"

"Be ready at five. I'll see what Bill is doing. We might double date with him and his date. Is it still Anne?"

"As far as I know, they're still going together, but you had better check with him."

As she turned to go to her room, she blew him a kiss and said, "I'll be ready at five."

Maggie burst into her bedroom and began to put her things away. Lisa had been real sweet and had not taken over any of Maggie's areas. Lisa walked in and said, "Hi, Sis!" Maggie turned and looked at Lisa. She had grown taller, and at thirteen she was becoming a beautiful girl. Her hair had turned so dark that it looked black and it fell in soft curls around her shoulders. Maggie went over to her sister and hugged her. This time she really wanted to let her know how glad she was to see her.

The weekend flew by, and everyone was very happy to be together. Friday night they all played Monopoly, and Lisa was glad she had a new boyfriend, Allan, to join the group. The rec room was filled with waves of laughter.

Their parents sat upstairs in their sitting room listening.

Annie said to Ruben, "How I wish we could keep them here safe and happy, just like they are right now."

Ruben looked up from the newspaper and smiled at Annie as he said, "Honey, that's not the way life is supposed to be. We are here to nurture them as they grow, but we must let them go and find their own way."

Annie sighed and said, "I know you're right, but it's so nice to hear them all together downstairs having such a good time. Next year there's no telling where they all will be."

"Don't worry, Annie, we'll just put them into God's hands and pray that he will take care of them." Ruben hugged her close to him, consoling her.

She smiled and continued picking up the mess that everyone had strewn around the house.

On Sunday morning, the family was getting ready for church and Annie was a little sad. Ruben asked, "What's the matter Annie?"

"This afternoon Maggie goes back to college. Jake leaves for Texas. This house is going to feel so empty again, and you know what a worrier I am. You know I'm afraid of flying, so that makes me worry more about Jake." She went on and on.

Ruben took her by the hand and said, "Come on, let's go to church, and leave the worrying to God."

They all piled into the car and went off to church. That afternoon, James came by to pick up Maggie. As they left, their young faces were a mixture of sadness and happiness - emotions of leaving their family combined with the eager anticipation of getting back to their lives at school.

Chapter 19

Maggie was happy to be back at Peace, although she missed her family, especially Jeanie. Classes had begun, and she was enjoying her voice lessons and singing with the chorus. They practiced every day for the performance to be given the night before Christmas vacation.

Maggie and James dated every weekend. The second weekend James came was December 7th and it was a warm and sunny day in Raleigh. All the Peace girls and their dates were strolling out on the front campus or sitting under one of the big oaks. It was late in the afternoon, about time for the dates to leave the campus, when several girls came out of the front door screaming, "The Japanese have bombed Pearl Harbor!"

Everyone was shocked and turned to each other, "Where's Pearl Harbor? I thought we were worrying about Germany not Japan."

They all began to file into the front hall of Peace to listen to the radio. It slowly began to dawn on everyone that their lives were suddenly changed. The boys began talking about enlisting. As the boys began to leave, the mood of the day, which had been so invigorating, had now become very somber.

Maggie and James walked hand in hand to the front gate, without saying a word. James broke the silence. "Well, Maggie, I guess this means I will be enlisting in the Navy at the end of the school year."

Maggie turned to him with glassy eyes, reached up, kissed him, and answered, "I know."

James left with all the other young men who were there that fateful Sunday, December 7, 1941.

The next few weeks passed very slowly as there was a melancholy feeling among the girls at Peace. The usual, happy-go-lucky chatter that normally permeated the dorm was replaced by sobering conversations. All the talk among the girls was about what would happen to their boyfriends and brothers, and possibly even their fathers. Not much studying was done, and the professors didn't even expect much, for most of the class discussions were about the news coming in on the radio.

Life, as they knew it, had change.

Chapter 20

Maggie was busy packing to go home for Christmas. She should have been filled with the excitement of the season to come, but she could not get Pearl Harbor out of her mind and what it would mean to her life. It was all anyone could talk about. The radio was constantly reporting news from the Pacific, and war had been declared on Germany and Japan. That's all the young men were thinking about. Maggie was very confused and scared. She wanted to be home with her family right now. She felt her father could explain this situation to her.

James came and picked her up. The trip home was a quiet one, as they were lost in their thoughts. It was good to have James to look after her, but by next year he would be God knows where.

James pulled up in front of Maggie's house, and Maggie jumped out and ran inside. She ran into her mother's arms and began to cry. She couldn't help herself.

"Maggie, what's the matter? You haven't lost another boyfriend, have you?" her mother said.

"Momma, no. Haven't you heard about Pearl Harbor?" Maggie answered, as she wiped her tears.

"Of course, honey, but we must keep our chins up and face what we must."

"But Momma, all the boys talk about is going into the service, and going to fight." Maggie went on and on, "Daddy won't have to go, will he?"

"No, honey, your daddy won't have to go, he's too old," her mother consoled her.

James came in the front door bringing Maggie's bags. "Hello, Mrs. McGee."

"Hello, James. Won't you come in? I'll fix you and Maggie some cocoa. It's beginning to get cold outside."

"No, thank you, Mrs. McGee. I had best be going on home. You know my mother always worries until she sees me drive in."

"I know how that is. Mothers are like that. They can't help it. Thank you for bringing Maggie home. I hope we'll see you during the holidays," Mrs. McGee said as she left to take Maggie's bags upstairs.

"Maggie!" James said. "I have to go now, but I'll call you tonight so we can make some plans. I'll be leaving after Christmas to go to Virginia to visit my father's family. We'll be returning the day before the break is over, so I can take you back to school."

"That will be wonderful! James, there's a youth dance at the Club the Tuesday before Christmas. Would you like to take me?" Maggie moved closer to James, looking up at him, and smiling expectantly.

James grabbed her, kissed her, and said, "You bet I would! It's a date! Now I gotta go."

As she ran upstairs, she thought, "How lucky can I be?" Tim had just written her to say that he would be in Winston-Salem visiting his brother Wally on December 28th and asked her to go to the Roof Garden to celebrate New Year's Eve. He reminded her that he had not received a picture. She said to herself, "No problem! You'll get that for your Christmas present." The holidays were working out just right. Tim was coming to town just as James was leaving.

Maggie was putting her things away when Lisa walked in.

"Hi, Lisa! Come on in. I'll have things straightened up before you know it."

"Don't worry. I'll help you, then we can talk."

Chapter 20

They talked for over an hour about school and boyfriends, the impending war crisis, and then dumb things like hair styles, and the latest fashions. Maggie thought to herself, "Lisa is definitely growing up." She really enjoyed talking girl talk with her not-so-little sister.

Jeanie ran into the room and flung herself on Maggie's lap. They hugged and hugged.

"Where were you when I got home, little one?" Maggie asked her.

"I was at my dancing class. I can dance, Maggie! You want me to show you?"

"You bet I do." She noticed how cute Jeanie looked in her little tutu.

Jeanie began to turn in circles and made cute little curtsies.

Jeanie stopped suddenly and said, "Oh, Momma said it's time to come down for dinner."

"OK, you go on downstairs. We'll be right down."

As Maggie came down the stairs she saw her father coming from the kitchen. She ran to him, hugged him, and said through her tears, "Oh, Daddy, I'm so glad you're old."

"Look here, young lady. What brought that on?" Daddy asked.

"All the boys are talking about going to war, and I was afraid you might have to go, but Momma said you were too old to fight in the war."

"She said that, did she?" Daddy turned and directed a fake scowl at his wife.

"Yes, I did say that, and don't make light of the situation. Maggie is very upset with all the war talk. It's very serious for all of us. Jake is already gone, and Bill plans to enlist in the Air Corps after Christmas. This is just the beginning. We all will be affected."

Now her father became serious, as they all sat down for dinner. "Before I ask the blessing on this wonderful meal, I want to comment on the world situation, and how it may affect this family. As you all know, after the attack on Pearl Harbor, we declared war on the Japanese and Germans on December 9th. This means all our healthy, young men will either enlist or be drafted into some branch of service. Jake is in Texas training to fly big bombers. Bill plans to enlist in the Air Corps. That leaves just us old men and you girls. What can we do?" He paused and looked around at each of the family. "Well, we must do anything we can to help the war effort, but most of all we have to keep our chins up - no crying - and make our men's jobs as easy as we possibly can. They have much to face, and we must not burden them with our problems. So let's all put a smile on our faces and get to work to help our young men in their duty to our country."

After Ruben's eloquent blessing, a hush fell over the table. Slowly the chatter around the table returned to the news of the day. Maggie told them what she had been doing at Peace, especially the concert the chorus gave before she came home. She told them that she sang two solos, "O Holy Night" and "I Wonder as I Wander."

Her father smiled and said, "I wish Momma and I could have been there; I know you sang beautifully."

Bill chimed in and said, "I don't. It's been nice not having to listen to her howling all the time!" He turned and winked at Maggie, who turned and stuck out her tongue at him.

Chapter 20

"Well, Ruben, things are back to normal," Momma slipped her hand over and patted his hand.

"Girls, your daddy and Bill are going to put up the Christmas tree tonight, and in the morning we're going to decorate the tree and the house. It's time to get some tinsel and glitter strewn around."

Chapter 21

The next morning was December 18, 1941, barely over a week after Pearl Harbor, but Maggie still could not put it out of her mind. It seemed to invade her every thought. This beautiful winter morning, it seemed so strange when she heard her mother call, "Girls, get up and come to breakfast! We have a big day's work to do. The Christmas tree is waiting to be decorated."

Lisa popped out of bed and threw on her clothes, but Maggie just rolled over and pulled the covers over her head. She didn't feel like decorating a Christmas tree. She didn't want to think about making merry and glittering up the house.

Lisa pulled her covers off and said, "Get up, you lazy thing, Momma needs us to help."

Maggie sat up in bed, yanked the covers back, and shouted, "I can't get into the spirit. Don't you realize what is happening to our lives?"

Lisa said in a very calm voice, "Maggie, didn't you hear what Daddy said? We girls have to do everything we can to make life normal, so the boys can do their duty."

As she got out of bed, Maggie looked at Lisa, and began to get dressed for the day. She thought to herself, "Lisa has always been more grown up than I ever was at her age and she's right - life has to go on, that's what the boys are fighting for. She smiled at Lisa and said, "You're right, Sis. I'll be right down."

Chapter 21

As she went downstairs, she heard Jeanie squealing with delight as she opened a box of ornaments for the tree. How could she not want to be a part of this day? They had to live as normally as possible.

Everyone was around the breakfast table when Maggie arrived.

Bill said, "Well, princess, did you decide to get up?"

"Shut up! Don't spoil this day for me!"

Her mother spoke sternly, admonishing them to be civil to each other.

After breakfast was over, Ruben and Bill left for work, and the girls decorated the house. By the time the men came home from work, the house had been transformed into a magical wonderland. Now it was time to begin the Christmas baking and present wrapping. Everyone was busy, and without knowing it, Maggie had forgotten about Pearl Harbor.

Tuesday, Maggie woke up and realized that this was the day James was taking her to the Club dance. She busied herself deciding what to wear and how she would wear her hair. Lisa walked into their room, Maggie looked up, and asked, "Lisa, help me decide how to wear my hair to the Club dance tonight."

"Let me put your hair up. I have two pretty clips we can put in it. I think you would look great with your hair swept up."

"Oh, that sounds wonderful! I would love for you to fix my hair!"

Maggie thought, "This is so nice having a sister who will help you when you need her. It's as if she has turned into a good friend." She smiled, kissed Lisa, and said, "Thanks, you're great!"

When Maggie went downstairs in her royal-blue ball gown with her hair piled on top of her head adorned with two lovely hair clips, Bill whistled and said, "Gee, you look great! How did you manage that?"

"Lisa fixed my hair. Doesn't it look wonderful?"

Everyone agreed that Maggie looked lovely.

The door bell rang, and Bill went to the door, opened it, and said, "Come in James! Maggie's ready, and she sure looks great."

Maggie picked up her wrap and was ready to go. She quickly kissed James and said, "Let's go, before Bill thinks of something mean to say."

"Goodnight Mr. and Mrs. McGee," James said. "I'll have her home by twelve thirty."

They both smiled and said, "Have a good time."

The family attended late-night services on Christmas Eve, and on Christmas morning they opened their presents. Jeanie was so happy and excited that it infected everyone.

Christmas afternoon James came by to bring Maggie her Christmas present, a picture of him with Maggie at graduation. He also came to tell her good-bye, for he was leaving the next morning to visit his father's family in Virginia. He assured her that he would be back in Winston in time to take her back to school in January.

Maggie would miss James, but she was a little relieved to know she wouldn't have to juggle dates between him and Tim. This juggling game was beginning to make her nervous.

Chapter 22

On December 28th, Maggie was anticipating Tim's arrival. The phone rang, and when she picked it up she heard his voice.

"Good morning, pretty girl! May I come out to see you, and maybe take you to lunch?" He sounded excited.

"Yes, you may, Tim! I'll be anxiously awaiting your arrival."

"Just go to your window and watch. I'll be there before you know it."

"I'll be ready."

She could not believe how excited she was at the thought of seeing Tim again. She ran, combed her hair, and put on fresh lipstick. She picked up Tim's Christmas present and went back downstairs to wait for him.

As she watched, Tim swung his car into their driveway and jumped out as soon as the car stopped. Maggie opened the door, and there he was as handsome as ever. He stepped inside and swept Maggie into his arms and kissed her until she was breathless.

Maggie stepped back and smiled at Tim. "Merry Christmas!" she said. "Come into the house!"

She ushered him into the den to exchange their gifts. Maggie opened her box, a beautiful gold locket. "Oh, Tim. I love it. Thank you. Now, here's yours."

He took the ribbon off carefully and began to unwrap the paper. His eyes were smiling as he unveiled Maggie's picture in a lovely silver frame. He sat there for a long while just staring and smiling at the picture.

"Say something," said Maggie. "Do you like it, or do you hate it?"

He turned to her and said, "It's beautiful, and I love it!" With that he pulled her to him and kissed her.

"Let's go get some lunch," Tim said. "We have some catching up to do."

They rode around for a while, holding hands. Finally they decided to stop at a small local barbecue place. They went in and found a booth in the back corner. They slipped in, and sat side by side. A few minutes passed before either one spoke a word.

"Do you know how glad I am to be sitting here with you Maggie? I've thought of nothing else the past few weeks."

Maggie smiled and leaned close to him as she answered, "I'm awfully glad to see you again, too!"

Their conversation covered all the news of their activities since they were last together, but since Pearl Harbor there seemed to be no way to avoid the subject of war. "Maggie, you realize don't you, that I will probably be drafted before the end of this school year? Some of my classmates have already enlisted, and some have already been drafted." Tim went on, "So I know I will be lucky if I get to finish my junior year."

Maggie felt the tears welling in her eyes, but she remembered what her father had said. She quickly smiled and said, "I'll write to you, so you won't forget me."

"Fat chance I could forget you, Maggie!" Tim laughed as he retorted.

They were enjoying the afternoon when she looked at her watch and said, "Tim, I've got to go home! I'm taking Jeanie to her dancing lesson at 4:00."

Tim asked for the check and turned to Maggie, "May I take you and Jeanie?"

"That will be nice, but you'll have to sit and wait an hour while Jeanie takes her lesson."

"I can handle that. Another hour with you would be welcomed." He took her hand and said, "Let's go!"

When they arrived at her house, Maggie went in to get Jeanie. There she was in her pink tutu with her hair tied up in pink ribbons. "Jeanie, you look so cute! Who fixed your hair?"

"Lisa," Jeanie answered as she twirled around.

"You may make a good hairdresser, Lisa," Maggie chided.

Lisa just smiled.

"Here, let's get your coat on. Tim is in the car waiting to take us to your dancing lesson."

Jeanie backed up to Maggie, and Maggie slipped a white fur-trimmed coat on her. She thought, "She looks like a little doll." She grabbed Jeanie's hand and called out to their mother, "Momma, I have Jeanie, and Tim and I are taking her to dancing. We'll be home after that."

"Thank you both."

Several hours later, Tim walked Maggie and Jeanie to the door, where Mrs. McGee met them. She asked Tim if he would like to join the family for dinner, which of course he was delighted to do. Jeanie began to jump up and down. She grabbed Tim's hand and ushered him into the family room to see the drawings she had done that day.

Bill was very nice to Tim through dinner. Maggie was relieved that he didn't tease her about her boyfriends. The subject of entering the military service was very much on their minds, and it dominated the conversation. When Tim left that night, he kissed Maggie and told her what a wonderful day it had been. He asked if he could see her on Tuesday. Maggie said, "Yes, anytime after lunch."

"I'll pick you up about 2:00, if that's all right," Tim said, as he went to his car. Maggie blew him a kiss and closed the door.

She closed her eyes and thought, "He really is a nice guy. I think I could fall for him." With that she raced upstairs and went to bed.

The next few days passed swiftly and as pleasantly as the world events would allow. Before Maggie knew it, it was New Year's Eve, and she was dressing to go with Tim, Wally, and Wally's girlfriend, to have dinner and celebrate at the Roof Garden on top of the Robert E. Lee Hotel.

They pulled up to the hotel where the valet came out to meet them, opened the door, and she stepped out taking Tim's hand. She was thinking about the last time she had come to this elegant hotel, to dine and dance. She was a little scared then, but oh, so excited. Now she felt a sense of being all grown-up, stepping into this enchanting place, with Tim. As they entered the lobby of the hotel, the beauty of it all decorated for the season, sent shivers over Maggie. She squeezed Tim's hand, looked up at him, and smiled.

The evening was cold and as they entered the Roof Garden restaurant, snow began to fall outside. Every one in the restaurant seemed to have left Pearl Harbor, and all it meant behind for this evening of celebration. Tim and Maggie danced and celebrated until it was now January 1st, 1942

Tim left January 3rd to go back to Ohio State. It was sad to say goodbye, for she had enjoyed his company. She spent the weekend with the family, going to church and talking over the things that were to come - such as Maggie's eighteenth birthday, Bill's enlisting in the Air Corps, and the family's summer plans.

Sunday afternoon, James drove up in front of the house to take Maggie back to college. She felt a little sad, because she wasn't sure when Bill would be leaving, and whether she would get to see him before he left. Reuben put her bags in the car and gave her a great big hug and kiss and said, "Work hard, and make Momma and me proud."

Maggie stooped down, picked up Jeanie, and gave her a big hug and kiss. Putting her down, Maggie jumped into the car, blew everyone another kiss, and off she and James drove.

Chapter 23

Maggie was glad to be back at college. As she entered her suite, all the girls began talking at once. "How were your holidays? Who did you date? What neat things did you get?" The questions went on and on, and Maggie was relieved to see that being home for the holidays had helped everyone return to normal. When the questions were all answered, they began unpacking and getting ready to return to the routine of their classes.

James called a few days later from UNC to tell her that he would not be able to come over very often. "My grades were not what they should be, and I have to study and get them up so I can finish this school year, and then I'll enlist in the Navy. If I don't, I'll be drafted."

"I understand." Maggie answered.

James added, "I'll take you home for Easter. Don't forget the Spring Germans dance here the last weekend of April. I'll reserve a room for you where the other girls are staying."

"Oh, James, you know I won't forget the Spring Germans dance weekend! It's much too important for me to forget. I'm already excited! You're so good to me! Now go and do your studying, but keep in touch!"

"OK, Maggie. I'll call you soon."

When Maggie hung up, she thought, "Life is going to be pretty boring the rest of this school year. James was my last chance for a steady date, and now he won't be coming often. I'll have to be looking around for date possibilities."

That Friday afternoon her first opportunity came. Maggie, her roommate Franny, and three other girls decided to go downtown shopping. Later on in the afternoon, the girls stopped at Perkins Drug and Soda Shop for some refreshments. They took a round table at the back, and before they ordered, a group of guys from the SAE Fraternity came over to the table.

"Hi, Franny, can we fellows join you girls?" Joe asked.

"Of course," the girls answered all as one.

Joe pulled up a chair close to Maggie and said. "I'm Joe Adams."

"Joe, this is Maggie McGee," Franny said.

The rest of the guys sat down and began introducing themselves.

Joe and Maggie found it easy to talk, and before the afternoon was over, Joe had asked her to the movies.

As the girls were leaving, Joe said, "I'll see you at six tomorrow night."

Maggie called back, "I'll be ready!"

"Did Joe ask you for a date?" asked Franny.

"Yes, and I think I like him."

"You should. He's real popular, and he's the President of the SAE Fraternity."

"Hmmm."

Saturday night Joe arrived right on time, and the evening proved to be very enjoyable.

The following week, Maggie received letters from Jake and Tim.

Jake wrote that he was being transferred to Coleman Field, Texas, where he would be flying PT-17's for more pre-flight training. He wrote that he missed everyone, especially Maggie.

Tim's letter stated that he was back in school, doing very well. He still was expecting to be drafted anytime, but he was hoping to finish his junior year. He thanked her again for her picture and said that he loved having it on his dresser to remind him of how much fun they had had when he was in Winston at Christmas.

It was Friday morning, January 16, 1942 — Maggie's 18th birthday, and her family called first thing in the morning to sing "Happy Birthday" to her! It seemed odd not to be home for her eighteenth birthday with all her family, but she thought, "This is growing up, I suppose." James also called to wish her a happy birthday and to apologize that he could not come over.

Coincidentally, Maggie had a date with Joe again that Friday. When he found out it was her birthday, he asked to take her out for dinner and a movie. When he came to pick Maggie up, she said, "I'm sorry, I can't go with you in your car. We'll have to walk."

"You've got to be kidding!"

"No, I can't leave the campus in your car unless my parents give permission to the college."

"Well, OK, I guess we'll walk, but get your parent's to put me on the list."

Later, as they were returning home, Joe asked Maggie to a dance at his fraternity house the next Saturday.

"Joe, I would love to go with you, but I'll have to get my parents to get your name on that list before I can leave campus alone with you."

"Can you get it done by Saturday?"

"Sure, I'll call Momma tonight and tell her to call the Dean," she assured him.

As soon as she went to her room, she called and told her mother about meeting Joe Adams. She went on to say that she had been dating him every weekend for several weeks. Then she pleaded, "Momma, I need you to call the Dean and put Joe on the list of boys I can leave the campus with alone."

"Are you sure he is a nice boy, Maggie?"

"Yes, Mother. He's asked me to go to a dance at his fraternity house next Saturday night."

"I'll have to ask your father about that."

"Oh, Momma, please say I can go. I really do like Joe. He's the president of the fraternity, and he is so good looking."

"Maggie, I'll talk to your father tonight, and I'll call you in the morning. I will call the Dean, if Daddy thinks it is all right for you to go with Joe in his car. Don't worry. I'll try to convince him that it is OK."

When she returned from her 8:00 class the next morning, her mother had called and left a message with Mary. "Your mom called and said your dad agreed to your going to the dance, and she will call the Dean today," Mary told her.

Maggie jumped up and down, saying, "Momma and Daddy, I love you! I love you!"

She immediately called and left a message with Joe's roommate that everything was arranged. She would be ready at 6:00 Saturday night.

She had a wonderful time at her first fraternity dance, and she really was beginning to like Joe. She had not known what to expect at a Fraternity Dance, but she found all his brothers very nice and each made sure she was having a good time.

By the end of January, she still hadn't heard from James, and she was thinking how much she missed talking to him. Just then the phone rang, and it was James. "Maggie, I'm calling to see if you could go to a movie next Friday night?"

"That would be so nice! I've missed seeing you," Maggie replied.

"I'm having to study all the time to keep my grades up. I miss my weekends, but I don't have a choice. I'll see you Friday around 5:00. How about dinner and a movie?"

"That sounds great! I'll look forward to seeing you."

January had not been as bad as Maggie had expected, but February looked pretty dismal. Except for dates with Joe on the weekends, she didn't see much to look forward to.

Chapter 23

The days were gray and cold. Her mother called around the middle of the month to say that Bill had enlisted and would be going to basic training in a couple of weeks. Her mother cried, and then Maggie cried. As she hung up, she thought, "This is really happening - Jake has already gone, now Bill." She knew that before the end of the school year all of her male friends would be serving somewhere. Her spirits were turning gray, just like the world outside.

She sat straddle legged on her bed preparing to write a letter to Jake, when Mary came in, "Maggie, have you signed up to go to the square dance?"

"What square dance?"

"Obviously you haven't. There's going to be a square dance here at Peace."

"When? I didn't think they would let us dance."

"They let us square dance; that way we can't get too close to the boys. The dance will be Saturday on Valentine's day,"

"I can't go then. Joe has asked me to the Sweetheart Dinner and Dance at his Frat House."

"Gee, Maggie, Joe has become a steady thing with you. How did you manage that? Do you like him?"

"Well, we were both without someone to date, and yes, I do like him."

"What happened to James, did you two break up?"

"No, James is trying to keep his grades up so he can finish his freshman year. If he doesn't, he might flunk out, and then he'd get drafted. He wants to enlist in the Navy as soon as school is out. That means he has to study extra hard, which means weekends are out for dating. We write to each other, and he calls me every weekend. I do miss seeing him."

"Are you in love with him?"

"Sometimes I think so, but then I meet someone like Joe, and I'm not real sure. James and I have dated for so long, it's hard to know how I feel about him."

Mary rose to go to her room, "Oh, Maggie, you make things so complicated."

Maggie sat there for a long time and wondered, "Do I complicate life, or is life just complicated?" She shook her head, and thought to herself, "Oh, well, what does it matter?" and resumed her writing.

Chapter 24

The morning after the square dance, Maggie and Mary were going to breakfast, when Maggie asked, "How was the dance?"

"It was lots of fun, and I met some really cute boys from State. How was your date last night?"

"Exciting."

"Maggie, do you remember a boy named Fred who I was dating before Christmas?" Mary asked.

"Sure, what happened to him?"

"I don't know. We just drifted apart. He called me yesterday and asked me to the spring dance at State."

"When is that?" Maggie asked.

"March 14th."

As they seated themselves at the table, Maggie suddenly realized that she was hungry. They always served special treats on Sunday morning, which she enjoyed.

As they sat there eating, she told Mary that she was planning to go home the next weekend to see Bill, before he left for Fort Bragg for basic training. She wasn't alone. Many of the girls were going home weekends now to see a family member or a friend off before their training.

Despite the anticipation of her trip home, before she knew it she was on the long bus trip home. She still could not believe how fast her world was changing.

When she arrived home, she entered a house filled with the most delicious smells. Obviously her mother had been busy baking all of Bill's favorite foods. She went straight to the kitchen and asked, "So, when will Bill be home?"

"He and your father should be coming in about 5:00," Annie answered.

"I'll go upstairs and change my clothes and be right back down to set the table."

"That would be a real big help."

"Where are Lisa and Jeanie?" Maggie inquired.

"Lisa took Jeanie to her music lesson. They should be coming in any minute."

As she was descending the stairs, Maggie heard Jeanie bursting in the front door calling for her. "Maggie!"

"Here I am, right here!"

Lisa and Jeanie came up and they greeted each other warmly. Jeanie plopped herself on Maggie's bed, and Lisa immediately said, "Jeanie, get off that bed! Look what a mess you are making of it."

Annie called for some help in the kitchen. "You girls come on down! The boys have just driven in, and I need the table set."

As Ruben and Bill came in the back door, Maggie didn't know whom to hug first. In the end she ran to Bill and gave him a bear hug.

"Hey, Sis, what's that for? I'm not headed for the war yet!"

"Oh, be serious Bill. I'm just glad to see you."

When they all were seated for dinner, Bill told the family what time he was leaving for Fort Bragg. A silence came over them all until Bill came out with, "Don't get sad on me. This isn't the end of me. I'll be home to pester all of you before you know it!"

Everyone laughed and began talking as usual.

Sunday morning they all rose and met at the breakfast table ready to go to church.

Chapter 24

After church they went together to the Country Club for lunch. When they returned home, Ruben took Maggie and Bill to the bus station. Bill boarded a bus to Fort Bragg, and Maggie boarded the bus to return to Raleigh. She waved a tearful good-bye to Bill. As she watched his bus pull out, she wondered how long it would be until they were all together again. The trip back to Peace that Sunday afternoon was long and lonely.

Back at school, she checked her mail on the way to her room. She found a letter from Tim, but decided to go up and unpack before opening it.

When she came into the room, Franny told her that she had received two phone calls, one from Joe and the other from James. They both wanted her to call them when she came in.

"Thanks, Franny."

"You don't sound very excited. I'd be real excited if two guys were calling me."

"I know, but this has been an upsetting weekend. My brother Bill is leaving this week to join the Army Air Corps, and my mother did not look well."

"Maybe your mother was just sad over your brother leaving?"

"I'm sure that was some of it, but Momma's health is not good these days. I'm real worried. It seems she is going to have to have a hysterectomy if she doesn't improve."

"I'm so sorry, Maggie. Come on in and get comfortable. Make your calls and read that letter you have there. I'm sure you'll feel better." Franny went on, "It's almost dinner time too, so get on the phone and cheer up."

After Maggie called Joe and James, she sat on her bed and opened Tim's letter. His letters were always fun to read because he related funny stories from his classes in trial law. Most of his letter was about how they had been assured that they would finish their junior year, even if they were drafted before the year ended. He was sure he would be going to basic training before May. This did not help to lift Maggie's spirits. Tim wrote how he missed her, and how much her picture meant to him, and how her smiling face lit up his day every morning.

Maggie was suddenly brought back to the real world when Nancy, her best friend and suitemate said, "Come on, Maggie! Let's go get some dinner!"

The next week, Maggie's mother called and told her that Bill had reported to Fort Bragg for basic training. She was also surprised to receive another letter from Tim, saying he was to report to Fort Bragg for basic training April 1st. He wrote that from all he could find out, he would be there about three months. If it were possible, he would try to get a weekend pass and come to see her. She quickly wrote him that she hoped that he might secure a pass. She seemed to be spending a lot of her time writing letters - Jake, Bill, now Tim and soon James.

On Saturday the 14th, the suite was all a dither with Mary, Franny and Nancy all dressing to go to the Spring Dance at State, and Maggie getting ready for a date with Joe to go to the movies.

"Does someone have an extra pair of hose? All of mine have runs in them," Nancy called out.

"Here, I have an extra pair," Franny answered, as she handed the stockings to Nancy.

Mary stuck her head in their door and asked, "I need a necklace to wear with this blue dress. Can any of you help me?"

Maggie showed her a necklace of blue glass beads, and Franny took out a string of pearls and offered them to Mary. In the end she chose Nancy's gold choker with a moonstone center.

Finally, they were all dressed and looking beautiful.

As each date arrived, a knock came on the door saying, "Miss McGee, your date is waiting in the parlor." And on and on until each of the girls were on their way to the parlor.

The next morning, like most Sunday mornings, the talk was all about the previous night's events. This particular morning Mary monopolized the conversation. Right after she arrived at the dance, a fellow named Ken Winters, whom she had met at the square dance several weeks before at Peace, broke in on her for a dance. Mary thought Ken was cute. The best part was that Ken's roommate had seen Mary speak to Ken and asked Ken to introduce them. Ken danced Mary over to the stag line and introduced her to his roommate, Jack Sims. Mary was obviously excited, as she went on and on. "Jack was so good looking, and he wants to date me some more! I can't wait to hear from him!"

Jack called Mary the next week and asked, "I'd like to come to see you Sunday afternoon. Is that OK with you?" Before Mary could accept, Jack went on to say, "I'd also like to bring my roommate Ken Winters with me. Do you think you can find him a date?"

Without even hesitating, Mary accepted and assured Jack that she would find Ken a date. Actually she knew that Maggie had turned down a date with Joe to study for her harmony class exam, but she was sure she could talk Maggie into doing this favor for her.

When Mary approached her, Maggie was furious that Mary had assumed she would date Ken. She said, "Suppose Joe finds out that I turned down a date with him to study, and then he finds out I went on a date with someone else?"

Mary said, "He won't find out, and it's just a Sunday afternoon date. Please do me this favor."

Maggie walked off without answering Mary.

Maggie dated Joe Saturday night, but she did not tell him about Mary wanting her to blind-date Ken Winters. He wouldn't understand. Joe asked again about coming to see her on Sunday afternoon, and Maggie again declined because she had to study for an exam. When Joe left, he kissed her and said, "OK, I'll see you next Saturday night."

Maggie turned to go in, blew him a kiss, and said, "See you next Saturday night."

Sunday morning Mary was still bugging Maggie to just do her this one big favor. Maggie refused to even discuss it. They had become such good friends, but Maggie really needed to study, and she did not want to take a chance that Joe would find out that she had dated someone else that Sunday afternoon. She was well aware that things can happen when you least expect it.

Sunday afternoon the knock came to the suite door. "Miss Forester and Miss McGee, your dates are in the front parlor."

"I told you I am not dating your friend's friend, and that's it!" Maggie steamed.

"But Maggie, I couldn't find anyone else to date Ken, and you know how much this means to me."

As Mary left, she said, "Don't let me down. Please!"

Franny and Nancy did not know whose side to take, but they knew that Mary really wanted to see Jack. Before they could convince Maggie to go down for this blind date, over the intercom the Dean's voice came booming, "Miss McGee, you have a date on the front lawn!"

Silently, Maggie brushed her beautiful auburn hair, freshened up her lips, and left the room without saying a word.

When Maggie arrived on the front lawn, she spotted Mary and her new-found friend deep in conversation, and there sitting nearby on a bench under the big oak tree was a very lonely-looking guy.

Mary turned and saw Maggie coming toward them. She ran and grabbed Maggie's hand, looking very relieved. She led Maggie over to her friends and said, "Maggie, this is Jack Sims and his roommate Ken Winters. Guys, this is Maggie McGee."

From that point on, the afternoon was very pleasant.Maggie and Ken strolled down the long front walk and up and down Fayetteville Street. During their walk, conversation came very easily, and by the time they returned to the campus, they knew the necessary details about each other. Ken asked if he could call her and come over for another date.

Maggie thought this over for a few minutes, and realized that I do like him a lot. Then she answered, "Yes, I would like that."

When they returned to Mary and Jack, Mary was relieved to see that Maggie and Ken were both smiling. She thought the date must have gone pretty well. Maybe Maggie would speak to her again.

Chapter 24

Soon the bell rang, signaling that the dates were over and that the fellows must leave the campus. Maggie hated those bells. They made her feel as if she were in grade school, but she had to admit that they kept her on schedule and kept her from being late and getting more of those darn demerits. Soon after she came to Peace, she learned to avoid those demerits, because, if you received enough of them, you were confined to the campus.

She and Mary returned to their room, and half-way there Maggie broke the silence to say, "I really am glad I met your friends; I just hope that Joe doesn't find out!"

Mary took her hand and squeezed it, "Thanks for helping me out. I hope Joe doesn't find out, too." She asked eagerly, "Did you like Ken?"

"I did, and he asked if he could call me for a date. I hope he will."

All the next week Maggie found herself hoping that Ken would call, but by the end of the week, there had been no word from either Ken or Jack.

Friday afternoon Mary came into Maggie's room. "Have you heard from Ken?"

"No, I was going to ask if you had heard from Jack." Maggie added, "Does Jack have our room phone number?"

"No. When he called before, he used the Peace phone system. I thought you might have given our number to Ken."

"He didn't ask, and I didn't want to presume to give it to him. You know what calling Peace means, don't you?"

"Yes, they might give up trying to reach us, since it is so hard to get through."

Later that afternoon, a telegram arrived and Maggie opened it, expecting some terrible news. It read, "Tried calling - stop - Tired trying- stop- Please call us. Signed Ken and Jack."

Maggie ran into Mary's room and showed her the telegram. They wasted no time in calling the boys. Maggie was surprised at how excited she was to hear Ken's voice, and before she knew it, they had arranged a date that very night.

"Be sure to give Ken our phone number," Mary called to Maggie from the door as she left to go to dinner. "You had better get off that phone, or you'll be late."

"I'm coming! Don't leave me!" Maggie told Ken good-bye and that she would see him at 7:00. As the girls went down the hall to dinner, they were chattering with excitement.

Maggie's weekends were now full again, as she found herself trying to fit in dates with Joe and Ken. The second weekend after meeting Ken, Joe went out of town, and she dated Ken the entire weekend. They stayed on campus most of the time. Their favorite spots were the swing on the upstairs porch, off the Main Parlor, and strolling on the front campus and up and down Fayetteville Street.

The second weekend, when Ken came over for a Friday-night date, they were sitting in the swing holding hands and watching the fireflies flitting in and out of the old oak trees. Ken surprised Maggie when he asked her to attend the Engineer's Brawl the next weekend, April 11th.

Maggie hesitated, and then answered, "I'm so sorry Ken, but I have a date for the dance. But, I really thank you for asking."

"Break it."

"You know I can't do that, but you can dance with me once or twice," Maggie smiled, as she answered him.

Just then the bell rang to signal that only ten minutes remained to walk all dates to the door or the front gate. She chose to walk Ken to the front gate, because he could give her a kiss without one of the chaperones giving her a disapproving look.

On Monday Maggie received a letter from Tim telling her that he had been drafted and had to report to Fort Bragg by April 15th. She sat right down and wrote back. She reminded him to be sure to send her his address as soon as he was settled into his new Army life.

Chapter 24

Friday night Ken came over as usual. Maggie found it more and more difficult to find time to date Joe, because she enjoyed her dates more with Ken.

As Ken left that evening, he kissed her and said, "I'll see you at the dance, and don't forget to save a dance for me."

Maggie laughed and blew him a kiss as he walked off down Fayetteville Street. She turned around to walk back to the dorm and just smiled to herself.

Chapter 25

Maggie rose later than usual the day of the Engineer's Brawl. After breakfast she proceeded to wash her hair and lay out her new ball gown. Joe would be calling for her at 5:00 to take her out to dinner and then on to the dance.

This was the first gown that her mother had not made for her, or been involved with because she wasn't feeling well. Instead Maggie had taken her suitemates with her shopping to Lord and Taylor's to buy her first store-bought gown. She had wished that her mother could be there with her, but that was not possible.

Maggie had tried on several dresses with no luck, until the sales woman brought out a dress made of emerald-green taffeta, with a dropped waist line and a spray of yellow roses down the skirt.

"Oh, Maggie, you must try that one on," Nancy said.

All the girls loved it, the decision was easy from there on. Maggie left the store hugging her new gown in her arms.

All day Saturday, the girls helped prepare for the big night ahead. Maggie decided to fix her hair in an upswept style to be more elegant, just as Lisa had fixed her hair at Christmas. Finally she was ready to slip on the dress.

"What kind of jewelry are you going to wear, Maggie?" Franny asked.

She turned to her dresser, pulled out a pendant with a large jade stone, and showed the girls. "I'm planning to wear this necklace my father brought me from New York City for my 18th birthday."

Chapter 25

There was a chorus of oohs and aahs from the girls that indicated their approval. Maggie was all dressed and getting a little anxious to get started. Soon, a knock came at the door, and when it was opened a girl announced, "Miss McGee, your date is waiting in the parlor."

She waved to the girls and said, "I'll see all of you at the dance!"

The Interfraternity Council
OF
N.C. State College
PRESENTS
THE
Final Dances
OF 1942

They walked outside to Joe's car, and Maggie slipped in as he came around and got behind the steering wheel. He reached over and kissed Maggie and said, "Gee, you sure do look glamorous this evening, young lady!"

Maggie smiled and moved over as close to him as she could.

After a nice drive to the gymnasium, she and Joe entered the dance. Ken was there at the entrance and smiled widely as he said, "Hi, Maggie!"

"Who was that guy?" Joe asked.

"That was Ken Winters. You know, the boy who came to Peace with Jack Sims when Jack wanted to date my suitemate, but was afraid to come to Peace alone. I don't know why boys are afraid of us Peace girls. Do you?" Maggie said coyly.

"Yeah, I do." Joe hugged her tightly and smiled. "So that's the guy you dated after you refused to let me come to see you. You had to study, as I remember."

"Joe, I explained all that to you. Mary put me in an impossible position. Let's not talk about it any more. I'm ready to dance."

Joe swept her out on the dance floor. They danced the first dance, and then it began to happen. Some strange guy would break in on Maggie, and after a few steps, Ken was there, taking her into his arms and dancing all across the dance floor. Every time Joe broke in on Maggie, another strange guy would break in on her, and then, there was Ken again. This went on all through the dance until the last dance. Joe came to rescue Maggie, and they let him have the last dance. Maggie had obviously enjoyed the attention, but Joe was irate.

"Maggie, I thought this Ken guy was just a blind date," Joe queried testily.

"He was. I've only known him a couple of weeks."

"Well, he acted as if he brought you to the dance, and you didn't seem to mind all his attention."

"What was I supposed to do - refuse to dance with him?"

Joe found Maggie's wrap, and led her sullenly to his car.

Joe closed her door and went around. As he closed his door and started the car, he blurted out, "Maggie, are you dating this guy Ken?"

"I have dated him a few times, but only when you were out of town or hadn't asked for a date," she answered, sounding a little bit irritated.

Joe pulled into the drive at Peace College and sat silently for a few minutes. "Maggie, I don't want you to date Ken any more."

"Joe, I can't promise that. After all, you and I have never talked about going steady."

"That's what I'm talking about now."

"I can't promise that, Joe. This year is almost over, and you are graduating. Who knows where you might go? I think we should just go on the way we have been going, and not complicate our relationship."

By now Joe was out of the car and coming around to open her door. They walked side by side to the front door without saying a word. Joe gave her a quick kiss and said, "Maggie, I need to think about us. Maybe I'll call you soon."

As she slipped through the huge front doors, she thought, "I know I won't hear from Joe again." She climbed the stairs to her room thinking about what a wonderful time she had at the dance, but Joe had ruined it all by demanding that she not date Ken again. After all, she thought, "He had no right to ask that of me." She knew she wanted to date Ken again more than she wanted to see Joe again. Joe said she had to make a choice, so she'd make her choice. "It's going to be Ken."

When Maggie entered her room, all the other girls had already arrived. There was a constant chattering about all the fun they had at the dance.

Franny looked at Maggie and asked, "What's wrong, Maggie? I know you had a good time, because you were the belle of the ball. Why are you so glum?"

"Joe and I just broke up, I think."

"Why?" Nancy asked.

"He asked me not to date Ken anymore."

"He hasn't asked you to go steady, has he?" Nancy quizzed her.

"He did tonight, if I wouldn't date Ken again."

"What did you tell him?" Franny asked.

"I told him I didn't think we should start going steady right now, because he graduates soon, and who knows where he will be going? I am not ready to promise that I'll just date him for the next few weeks, and that made him mad. So he left saying maybe he would call me."

The girls all agreed that she had been right not to promise to go steady just so Joe would continue dating her for the next few weeks. Maggie felt a little better, as she drifted off to sleep.

Maggie ended up being right about Joe - he never called again.

Chapter 26

Sunday after church, Ken called to ask if he could come over that afternoon. Maggie's spirits lifted, and she told him that she would love to see him. While sitting out under one of the big oaks, Maggie told Ken how angry Joe was after the dance the night before, and that she probably would never hear from him again.

"I'm sorry if I made him mad. All I wanted to do was to make sure you had a good time, and that I danced with you as often as I could."

"Well, I did have a good time."

"When are you leaving for Easter holidays?"

"Thursday afternoon, and we come back on Monday."

"I'm going to miss seeing you, you know?"

"I'll miss you, too, Ken."

The bell sounded, and it was time to walk Ken to the front gate and kiss him good-bye until after Easter.

That week was monopolized with completing a paper that she had to turn in before she left, and her afternoons and evenings were filled with choral rehearsals for their spring concert.

Thursday after lunch, James drove up in the drive, and Maggie was waiting for him. She was anxious to get home for a few days.

She and James talked all the way to Winston, catching up on what had happened to them since they were last together. James was pleased that his grades had improved, and that he would be allowed to finish his freshman year. He also told her that he had enlisted in the Navy and would leave for basic training as soon as the school year was over.

Maggie shocked James when she told him about her big decision about not returning to Peace in the fall.

"Why did you decide to do that?"

"My mother's health isn't good, and with the war on, my father's office helpers are being drafted, or are leaving to work in war jobs. He needs office help very badly. I've decided to enroll at Salem College to continue my voice training, and also to enroll in a business school to take bookkeeping and secretarial courses."

"I think that makes sense, Maggie." James said when she finished. "Boy, our lives are really changing, aren't they?"

"They really are. And there isn't much we can do about it." When Maggie looked up, she saw that they were pulling into her driveway. She jumped out and ran as she saw her mother and Jeanie coming out the front door.

Jeanie ran into Maggie's arms, saying, "Come in, Maggie, and hear me play the piano!" She called back to James, "You can come hear me too, if you want to!"

"No, I had better be going home. I'll hear you the next time I come over to see Maggie. OK?"

James, turned to Maggie and asked, "May I see you tomorrow night?"

"Yes, that will be fine."

Easter time was always Maggie's favorite time of year, but this Easter was beginning to seem a little sad. Annie told her that Bill had written that he was being sent to Santa Ana, California, to begin pre-flight training. Jake was still in Waco, Texas, flying B-13s.

Tim called Maggie from Fort Bragg to wish her a happy Easter and to tell her that he had started his basic training. He said he wasn't sure if he could get a weekend pass to come to see her, but he was going to try and would let her know.

With James leaving for basic training when school was over, that only left Ken. Maggie worried that it wouldn't be too long before he would be drafted or would enlist.

Easter morning the sun was shining and the day was going to be beautiful. When she looked out the window, she felt like singing, "Welcome Happy Morning, age to age shall say." When she came down to breakfast, a corsage of orchids lay on the table. She opened the card and was surprised to read, "Have a Happy Easter, Love Ken."

"Who is the corsage from?" Lisa asked as she entered the kitchen.

"Ken Winters."

"Who is he?" Lisa questioned, astonished that there was another new guy in Maggie's life.

"You haven't met him yet, but I hope you will soon. I met him on a blind date at Peace, and we have been dating ever since."

Jeanie ran in, saw the flowers, and asked, "Can I have one?"

"No, those were sent to Maggie from one of her boyfriends," her mother replied.

The family arrived at church and filed into their usual pew. Maggie thought, "This is where I need to be." To her delight, the church service opened with the singing of her favorite hymn, "Welcome Happy Morning." All seemed right with the world, as she stood beside her parents, singing her heart out, "age to age shall say."

James met her after church and asked if he might come over that evening and take her to a movie. She was happy to say, "Yes, I would love to go to the movies with you."

When he took her home after the movie, they strolled slowly to the door not wanting to say goodnight. James kissed her more passionately than he had ever done before, catching Maggie by surprise.

James said, "I do hope when I go into the service you will write to me often. I'm really going to miss seeing you."

"You know I will write often and keep you informed about what is going on at home," Maggie assured him.

He kissed her once again, and said, "I'll pick you up around 10:00 in the morning to go back to school."

"I'll be ready," Maggie answered, as she closed the door behind her.

Chapter 27

Maggie was unpacking her bags, contemplating her last days at Peace. She had told her parents that she was thinking of staying at home next fall and not returning to school. They were excited about her enrolling at Salem College to continue her voice training and going to the local business college, but they wanted to know what had prompted her to make such a decision. Maggie explained that she knew her father needed help in his office, and she hoped that she could work there with him. Also, she knew her mother's health was not good, and she could be at home to help with little Jeanie, and take some strain off of her mother. They told her how proud they were of her, and just how much help that would be for both of them, at this time.

She knew that she was making the right decision, but it made her sad to think that she was leaving her friends in a month or so. While she was deep in thought, the phone rang. Being the only one in the suite, she answered it, and it was Ken.

"I was calling to see if you were back at school, and to ask if I might come over tomorrow afternoon and play some tennis. I have something I want to tell you."

"Sure, I would love to see you, and I have something to tell you, too."

Maggie rose early Tuesday. She was excited at the thought of seeing Ken again. She was beginning to realize how much she missed him. She realized more and more that her feelings for Ken were different from her feelings for any of her other boyfriends.

Chapter 27

She was standing in front of Peace, waiting for him when he arrived. Her heart turned a flip when she saw him come through the gates. She thought, "I wonder what he has to tell me?" He walked up and took her hand as he gave her a quick kiss.

They strolled over toward the tennis courts, but before they started playing, they sat down under a big oak tree to talk.

"Ken, what did you have to tell me? I can't wait any longer."

"You may wish we had waited."

"Go on now, you are scaring me."

"Well, while I was home I got my parent's permission to join the ROTC."

"What's that?"

"It's a college program called the Reserve Officer Training Corps."

"That means you enlisted in the Army, doesn't it?"

"Yeah, but I would be drafted if I didn't join something, and this gets me in with some training, not just as a buck private. Enough about me. What did you have to tell me?"

"While I was home, I decided not to return to Peace next fall."

"Why?"

"Daddy needs help desperately in his office, and I can help him, plus my mother is not well at all, and she needs me at home. I'll be going to Salem for my music, and to a business college to take business courses."

"It sounds like you've thought this through. I approve, except that you'll be in Winston-Salem instead of Raleigh. But, who knows? I may not be back in Raleigh either."

"Oh, don't talk like that, Ken!"

Maggie leaned against Ken as he put his arms around her and said, "Let's play some tennis."

The rest of the afternoon, Maggie and Ken put aside the upcoming changes in their lives and just enjoyed the warm sunny weather and played a few games of tennis. They had fun despite the war, and Maggie was pleased that she even beat Ken in one game. She no longer just batted the ball back over the net - she had become a real tennis player.

During those last few weeks at Peace, they dated every chance they found, and Maggie felt comforted that they had promised to see each other as often as possible when Maggie was back in Winston.

Chapter 28

The next few weeks raced along, and Maggie was amazed when it was already time to pack her bags for the Spring Germans weekend in Chapel Hill.

Saturday morning May 9th, Maggie awoke all excited. James picked her up at 12:00, took her to lunch, and drove on to Chapel Hill to attend the dance. He dropped her off at the Carolina Inn around 3:00, where she was sharing a room with three other girls from Peace.

As James was leaving, he called back to her, "Call me if you need anything! I'll be back at six."

"I'll be fine," she waved to him, "and I'll be ready."

She went inside to her room. She immediately shook out the wrinkles in her gown and hung it up. It was the same gown she had worn to the Engineer's Brawl. She hoped she would have as much fun at this dance as she did at the Brawl.

James picked her up promptly, and he could not believe how beautiful she looked. He took her by the hand and led her to his car. As they settled into the car and headed for a restaurant, James said, "Maggie, I can't believe how grown-up you look. You're positively beautiful!"

She smiled, "It's just because you haven't seen me so dressed up for so long."

"I know. It has been a long time."

The evening was wonderful. The gym was decorated like a spring garden and also smelled like one. All of James's fraternity brothers danced with her too. Maggie loved to dance, so the evening was a success in every way.

After the dance, they walked slowly to the car, and James drove out to the outer edge of Chapel Hill and slowed down until he found a nice quiet parking place. James slipped over until he was close to Maggie. She turned and smiled.

"We have some serious talking to do," James said, as he drew her to him and kissed her passionately.

Before Maggie could answer, he went on, "Maggie, I enlisted in the Navy this week. I have to report for basic training June 15th."

Maggie's eyes filled with tears, "Oh, James, I was hoping it would not be so soon."

"You knew I planned to enlist as soon as this year was over, didn't you?"

"Yes, but I hoped you might not have to leave until the end of the summer, maybe."

He kissed her again long and hard. He sat back and startled Maggie by saying, "Maggie, I want you to wear my fraternity pin while I'm away."

Maggie was so caught off guard that she didn't know what to say, and suddenly he had pinned his fraternity pin on her dress. He took her into his arms and kissed her as if he didn't ever want to let her go.

They sat there silently in the moonlight with their minds awash in thought — Maggie wondering how to break it to James that she didn't want to wear his fraternity pin, and James wondering why she wasn't reacting better.

Soon James started the car and drove slowly back to the Inn. He walked Maggie to the door and kissed her goodnight.

Maggie whispered, "I had a wonderful time, James."

Chapter 28

When she entered the room, the other girls were just coming in. They all were excited and related to each other how much fun they had had. Maggie chimed in, but she did not let on how troubled she really was.

She took off her dress, and removed James' fraternity pin. She was so surprised when he pinned it on her dress that she was at a loss for words. She sat there and stared at it. Knowing this usually meant, "engaged to be engaged," she knew she could not let James go on thinking that their relationship was this serious.

She crawled into bed and lay there for hours rehearsing what to say to James. She wanted to remain friends, even special friends. But she wasn't ready to let him think it meant, "engaged to be engaged." Maybe she would wear it for a little while and then give it back to him. "It might be fun to wear a guy's fraternity pin," she thought. Suddenly she remembered what her mother had told her, "Be honest Maggie, or you might break some young man's heart." She finally fell asleep determined to return James's pin to him in the morning.

She was up and ready when James came to pick her up for breakfast. They walked down Franklin Street and went into a small café. James ushered her to the booth in the back of the café, and Maggie slipped in. She was nervous and wanted to get this over with in a hurry. She knew this would probably mean the end of their relationship, and another picture would be returned, but she had to set things right between them. She was thinking, "after all, I have met Ken, and he is beginning to be real special to me."

James sat down, snapped his fingers, and said, "Wake up! What has you in such a trance?"

"Sit down James, I have something I need to say to you."

"This sounds serious."

"It is serious." She took his hands, and placed his pin in them. "James, I cannot accept your fraternity pin. I am very honored that you gave it to me, but with our future so uncertain, I can't let you go off thinking that our relationship is any more than it has always been."

"Maggie, I didn't expect any more of you than that you would be my girl and write to me while I'm gone. You know that it means so much to me to have my best girl friend write to me."

"James, I'll write to you as often as I can. I promise. It won't take your fraternity pin to make me write to the best friend I've ever had."

James slipped the pin into his pocket. Maggie thought, "He looked a little relieved." They laughed and talked all through breakfast and then walked back to the car hand in hand.

She breathed a sigh of relief when she slipped into the front seat. "At least it didn't end our friendship," she thought. "Maybe I won't get his picture back."

On the way back to Peace, James asked Maggie, "When are you going home? I'll be glad to take you."

"Thanks, James, but my father is coming to take me home."

"When will that be?"

"Friday, May 29th. When will you be home?"

"The next Saturday. I'll call you when I get there."

As she stepped out of the car, she thought, "Oh boy, we are back to normal!" She turned and kissed James saying, "It was a wonderful weekend, James. Thanks, and I'll look forward to seeing you in Winston."

James crawled into his car and drove off. Maggie walked slowly up the stairs to her suite. She thought to herself, "Momma would be proud of me. I was honest with James and myself."

When she opened the door to her room, all her suitemates were gathered around and Nancy asked, "Tell us about your weekend, did any thing special happen?"

"No, it was just a wonderful dance with a special friend."

"Oh, shucks, you usually have something exciting happen," Lily blurted out.

With that they all filed out of their suite down to the dining room.

Chapter 29

In mid May, 1942, Maggie received letters from Tim and Jake. Tim wrote that he might get a weekend pass at the end of June, before going to Texas for tank school, and Jake was finishing up his training in B-13s in Waco, Texas. It seemed so much of her time these days was spent writing letters - not that she minded, in fact, she loved keeping in touch with each of them, but it constantly kept her mind on the fact that her friends were preparing to go to war.

The last week of school she told all her friends that she would not be back the following fall. It was a sad time for all of them, but she knew that she was making the right decision. Ken had come over to see her on her last night at Peace. He promised to come to Winston as often as he could. That night when he kissed her good-bye, she knew in her heart that he was someone very special to her.

Friday morning Ruben came with his station wagon to move her home. The thought of being back at home with her family actually made Maggie feel relieved. When they rolled in the driveway, there was her mother, Lisa, and Jeanie coming out into the yard to greet her. She was out of the car and running over to them in no time. She knew this was where she needed to be.

The summer of 1942 Maggie worked in Ruben's office, helped her mother around the house, looked after Jeanie, and wrote letters. Her mailing list seemed to grow. She was writing to her brother Bill, Jake, Tim, and now James, who had left for boot camp at The Great Lakes Training Center near Chicago. Ken was her only local boyfriend left, and he was half a state away. He came to see her about every other weekend, but that left many other evenings to fill. She and Nancy kept each other company. They saw every movie that came to town, but Nancy would be returning to Peace in the fall, and Maggie wondered what she would do then.

Her father owned a group of gas stations, so the work in his office consisted of checking the reports that came in from each service station and recording them in the ledger book. Then she had to scan all the gas-rationing stamps that were sent in to find the counterfeit ones, which was very important. You had to stay on top of the number of counterfeit stamps showing up, because your quota of gasoline, to replace what you sold, was based on the stamps you turned into the government. You were only allowed a percentage of your quota to be counterfeit. She used a black light that showed up the counterfeit stamps. The job was long and boring, but it had to be done, and as yet, she didn't know how to do much more.

Tim arrived the last weekend of June to visit with his brother, Wally. He called Maggie and asked her out Friday and Saturday nights. She was glad to see him, and they spent as much time as they could together. Tim was on his way to Fort Hood to gunnery school, and ultimately he would be assigned to a tank division. Tim did not seem very happy about being in the Army, but neither did many of the other boys she knew. Sunday morning they met at church, and afterwards, she and Tim joined Wally for lunch, after which they took Tim to the bus station to catch the bus to Austin, TX.

Chapter 29

"Tim," Maggie said, as the bus rolled in, "I hope you will write to me and tell me everything you are doing in the Army."

"I will try to write as often as I can," replied Tim, "but I've been told very clearly that we will never be allowed to reveal details that could help the enemy if the mail were intercepted. And, when I do write from overseas, it will have to be one of those V-mails, which is very small, so I don't know how to tell you very much."

"Can you keep a journal?"

"What do you mean?"

"A pocket journal and keep a record of all your adventures in it? The details could wait until you get back."

"That could work," said Tim, brightening. I'll keep it vague enough to protect us all, but enough information that will jog my memory later."

Tim gave Maggie a long, solemn hug before boarding his bus. Glancing back one last time, he smiled bravely, turned, and filed into the bus.

While driving Maggie home, Wally said, "Tim seemed pretty low. I don't think he is acclimating to Army life very well."

"Yes, I noticed that, so I suggested he keep a journal, which may help him feel more connected to home, but I don't know."

"I don't either, but I sure hope so."

They drove home in silence, but as Maggie was getting out of the car Wally said, "Maggie, thanks for being such a support to Tim."

"Your welcome, Wally, but it's no problem. I like Tim and I'll write to him often, don't worry."

Monday morning Maggie was back at work, checking reports again. This week would be no different from the last. Wednesday afternoon, while Ruben played a game of golf, she took Jeanie to the club to swim. Golf was Ruben's one hobby, and he tried not to let anything cause him to miss his weekly relaxation.

The other afternoons and evenings Maggie was at the sewing machine, helping her mother make dresses for Jeanie. Sometimes she helped teach Lisa how to sew. This wasn't a chore, for she loved to sew almost as much as she loved to sing.

She looked forward to the weekends when Ken came to visit. The family had grown fond of him, especially Jeanie, who thought he was coming to see her, because he spent so much time playing games with her and listening to her play the piano. Ken always shared Sunday with the family, going to church and afterwards enjoying Annie's wonderful Sunday dinner. Maggie's mother was finally beginning to regain her health, so life at the McGee house was getting back to normal.

Her mother moved Maggie into the guestroom, because it was time for Lisa to start back to school, and Maggie's schedule no longer matched a school girl's schedule. She missed Lisa, but it was nice to have her own room. By the middle of August, Maggie had enrolled in both Salem College and Collier's Business College.

Ken came the last weekend of August and told Maggie that he would be going back to State the next week. He was not sure for how long, but at least he could start his junior year.

As the leaves began to blaze in autumn colors and drift to the ground, they created myriad patterns on their lawn. Maggie sat outside and her mind drifted as she thought about her brother and friends...

Bill was still in Santa Ana, training to be a pilot. Jake was beginning advanced pilot training at Waco Air Force Base, Texas. Tim was at Fort Hood, Texas, training as a gunner in tanks. James was being sent to New London, Connecticut, to begin his training as a member of a submarine crew. As Maggie finished answering their letters, she thought, "How far they all are from the lives they each had planned."

With so many young service men traveling from base to base, and far away from home, families were encouraged to pick them up on the weekends and give them a good meal for a little touch of home.

The McGee family decided that this was something they could do. Ruben would go to the bus station on Sundays to bring three or four young soldiers home with him for Annie's Sunday dinner and a bit of family fun in the afternoon. Ruben returned the grateful young men late in the afternoon and sent them on their way.

Maggie took over most of the entertaining, and as they were leaving, they all left their addresses, asking her if she would write to them. She felt this was something she could do. Some replied once or twice, others wrote for months and months, and then the letters stopped. This always worried her, because she never knew what might have happened to them.

Maggie's letter writing consumed even a greater portion of her time now, but she thought if she could cheer them up a little, she was glad to spend her time writing to them. They all said mail call was the high point of every day. Her letters were scattered all over the world - Africa, France, England, and the Pacific.

When she finished her letter to Ken, she was grateful that he was no further away from Winston-Salem than Raleigh, but for how long, she dared not think.

Ken had arranged for Maggie to attend a dance at State that fall, and Maggie was thrilled to be going to Raleigh to attend a college dance again. She was also excited about the coming weekend because not only had she not seen Ken in a couple of weeks, but she also planned to visit her friends at Peace, especially Nancy.

Chapter 30

Maggie's days were quite different now. It was the first of October, and instead of fun with friends, choral practices, dates and dances, she found herself busy working with her father in the mornings and going to classes in the afternoons. When she came home, there was always Jeanie begging her to play, and there were always more and more letters to write and read. She came home one afternoon to find two letters from Tim that must have been backed up.

Sept. 12, 1942

Dearest Maggie,

I have just completed my training as a tank gunner, and will soon be leaving Texas to become part of the 1st Armored Corps under the command of General George S. Patton. I do not know where we are being sent, or what our destination will be. When I get my next orders, I will try to write and tell you where I am, if I can. How they picked this six foot-two guy to be a turret gunner, I will never know. I get a little claustrophobic sometimes, but I guess I could be a foot soldier, and that would be worse.

Maggie, I sure wish I could see you one more time before I ship out, but I understand they need troops overseas right now, so I don't know if I will get a leave any time soon. They are pretty secretive about where we are going. I must admit to you that I am pretty scared about this whole war business. Sometimes I feel like I won't make it back home.

I look at your picture every day, and that gives me something to hold onto and to fight for. Please keep your letters coming. I live from one letter to the next.

Sweetie, taps just blew, so, it's time to close down and hit the sack. It sure will feel good tonight, because we've been packing up all our gear. I feel we will be moving out of this place any day now.

Love as always, Tim

Maggie sat in her room, and read the letter over and over. She worried that he was getting too serious; after all, they had only dated a total of four weeks. Of course, she had written him regularly during this time. She didn't think she had led him on in any way, but she certainly did not want to hurt him. She had learned her lesson on that score. She went on to the next letter.

Dear Maggie, *October 16, 1942*

Life is pretty boring here, so I haven't much to write to you about, except how much I miss you, and I wish I could walk off and find you, and hold you in my arms again. I'll have to dream about that for a while.

No one tells us anything about what we are here for, but it must be something big. I dread the thoughts of having to go to war, because I still have this bad feeling I won't be one of the boys coming home. There is nothing to talk about with the guys, except those girls we're leaving behind. It doesn't help to listen to them; it just makes me miss you even more.

You might not hear from me for the next few weeks, but know that I am thinking of you. Please write to me often, that's the only thing I have to look forward to in the future.

All my love, Tim

Maggie was troubled when she read his letters, because she felt he was definitely getting too serious, and there were those words again, All my love. She knew them well, for they had caused her a great deal of heartache and disappointment. She did not like to think that she had hurt someone with her flippant use of words. Or was it that Tim was just lonely and needed to think of her in this way. Either way, she decided to wait two weeks or so before she answered his letters.

When she finally sat down to write to Tim, she didn't know how to start. He obviously was dreaming of a future with her. How could she be honest and tell him that she liked him very much, but that was as far as it went now? She didn't want to tell him that she had met someone else with whom she might be falling in love, not when he was in the war and felt so desperately lonely and hopeless. She began to write:

Dear Tim, *October 29, 1942*

I received your letters and was very happy to hear from you. I know it must be rather unsettling to be packed up ready to go somewhere and not know where. It is hard for us here at home to realize what you must be going through.

Every night I pray that all you boys will be kept safe and return home to us soon.

I am well into my classes at Salem College. I am enjoying my voice lessons. It helps to sing when the world seems to be tumbling upside down. I don't think I'll ever be a good secretary or bookkeeper, but at least I am learning enough to be a big help to Daddy in his office. I'm glad this office work is temporary, just until the war is over and Daddy's help returns. Balancing books, taking dictation and typing letters is not how I see my future. At least for now, I feel like I am doing my part.

Jeanie just came into the room and wanted to say Hi to you. She misses you. Bill has been sent to Harlingen, Texas, to attend gunnery school. His ears ruptured in the flight simulator, and that washed him out of pilot training. He was here on a three-day pass on his way to Texas. He was pretty upset about having to leave pilot training, but he is dealing with it.

Momma had to return to the hospital for a serious operation. Lisa and I have been keeping house and sharing the duties of looking after Jean-

ie. She misses Momma and Daddy terribly. Daddy is gone most of the time, at work, or at the hospital. I do hope Momma will be home soon.

Tim, I anxiously await your next letter. Try not to think negative thoughts. There is always hope. I will continue to pray for your safe return. I promise to write to you often. Tomorrow will be a brighter day.

Love, Maggie

Soon after the first of the year, Maggie received three V-Mail letters from Tim, all at one time. She opened them and arranged them according to their dates.

Dear Maggie, *November 30, 1942*

Here I am in a lay up area, with plenty of time to write and think of you. Andy Brown, my best buddy and I were wounded, not enough to get sent home, shucks, but we needed some medical attention. We were first sent to a field hospital, and now we in a lay up facility. It's pretty nice but since my wound was in my leg, I can't get around too good. I got some shrapnel in my right leg, which the medics removed and now it just needs to heal. Andy received a wound in his left arm, but it is now healing real well. He even played a little ping-pong yesterday, which made him feel pretty darn good.

We are expecting to be reassigned to another group very soon now. We both hope we will be assigned together, that will make being over here a little less lonely.

I received one of your letters yesterday and it sure did lift my spirits. Please keep them coming. We GI's live for mail call.

It's lights out now, so I better finish my letter, so I can get it in the mail in the morning.

I miss you. You can't believe how slowly the time goes over here.

Love as always,Tim

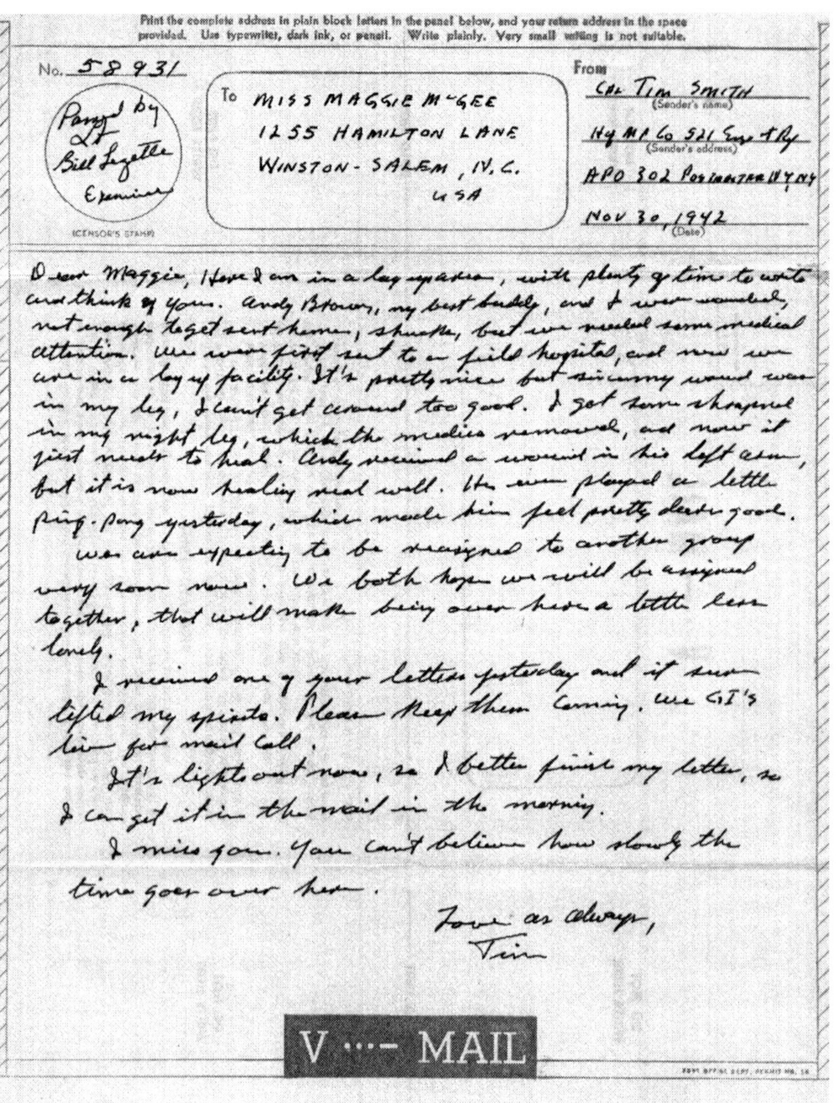

Print the complete address in plain block letters in the panel below, and your return address in the space provided. Use typewriter, dark ink, or pencil. Write plainly. Very small writing is not suitable.

No. 58931

Passed by Lt Bill Legatte Examiner
(CENSOR'S STAMP)

To MISS MAGGIE McGEE
1255 HAMILTON LANE
WINSTON-SALEM, N.C.
USA

From
Cpl Tim Smith
(Sender's name)
Hq MP Co 521 Engr ? Rg
(Sender's address)
APO 302 Postmaster NY NY
NOV 30, 1942
(Date)

Dear Maggie, Here I am in a lay-up area, with plenty of time to write and think of you. Andy Brown, my best buddy, and I were wounded, not enough to get sent home, shucks, but we needed some medical attention. We were first sent to a field hospital, and now we are in a lay up facility. It's pretty nice but since my wound was in my leg, I can't get around too good. I got some shrapnel in my right leg, which the medics removed, and now it just needs to heal. Andy received a wound in his left arm, but it is now healing real well. He even played a little ping-pong yesterday, which made him feel pretty darn good.

We are expecting to be reassigned to another group very soon now. We both hope we will be assigned together, that will make being over here a little less lonely.

I received one of your letters yesterday and it sure lifted my spirits. Please keep them coming. We GI's live for mail call.

It's lights out now, so I better finish my letter, so I can get it in the mail in the morning.

I miss you. You can't believe how slowly the time goes over here.

Love as always,
Tim

V ···– MAIL

Chapter 30

Maggie took a sip of water, and opened the next V-mail letter dated December 11, 1942.

Dear Maggie, *Dec.11, 1942*

Here I am still at the lay-up area. I am now able to go all over the area, even though I still am limping. Andy has begun calling me, "crip." I don't really mind it; he seems to enjoy it, that is calling me that. I hope this is the worst thing that happens to me, but I still have a dogging feeling that I won't be coming home. Andy gets mad when I say that, so I keep my thoughts to myself.

It's December, but it does not feel like soon it will be Christmas. I won't be able to send you a present, but you know I'll be thinking of you and wishing you a Merry Christmas.

Sorry I have to close now. It's time to go to the mess hall and eat that mess. I'm kidding. It's not all that bad, but it's not like that fried chicken and chocolate cake of your mother's. I dream of those wonderful days in Winston.

I'll write again as soon as I can. I'll be leaving here soon, and that means it will be harder to find time to write. Please keep writing.

All my love,

Tim

Maggie folded Tim's second letter. She sat there feeling very nervous, "He's getting too close to saying he's in love with me." More and more, she knew she was very close to being in love with Ken. How could she ever write to Tim and tell him she's found someone else?

She sat there staring at his third letter, afraid to begin reading, for it began, "Dearest Maggie."

Dearest Maggie, December 25,1942

This morning when I awoke, I heard Christmas carols being played. How funny it seemed to be so far away from home and hear singing of peace and love to the world. It's hard to feel joy when the world explodes around you.

Forgive me for boring you with my negative thoughts. I do wish you a wonderful Christmas. How I wish I were there with you and the McGee family.

Andy and I were talking about our girl friends last night. His girl's name is Betty Moser. We were making plans to get our girls together when, and if, we make it back. If you are stuck in a place like this, you sure are lucky to have a buddy like Andy.

I dream of the day when I can be back in the old US of A. I'll be heading straight to Winston and take you in my arms. I love reading your letters, please keep them coming. Merry Christmas, my love.

I love you,

Tim

Then she knew she had to write to Tim and let him know she was seeing someone else. She could not let him dream any longer that she was waiting for him. She wanted to keep writing to him, because she really liked Tim, but she knew she didn't love him. And she had met Ken and was growing more and more fond of him. Of course, she had not known Ken very long either. So, who knew what might happen?

Her thoughts were broken by her mother's voice calling up the stairs "Maggie, it's time for dinner, your father is home."

Maggie gathered up the three V-Mail letters from Tim and headed down the steps to join the family for dinner. When she entered the dining room, her father was already sitting at the head of the table unfolding his napkin, as if he could hardly wait to say grace and begin eating. She rushed right to his side, and started showing him the V-Mails she had received.

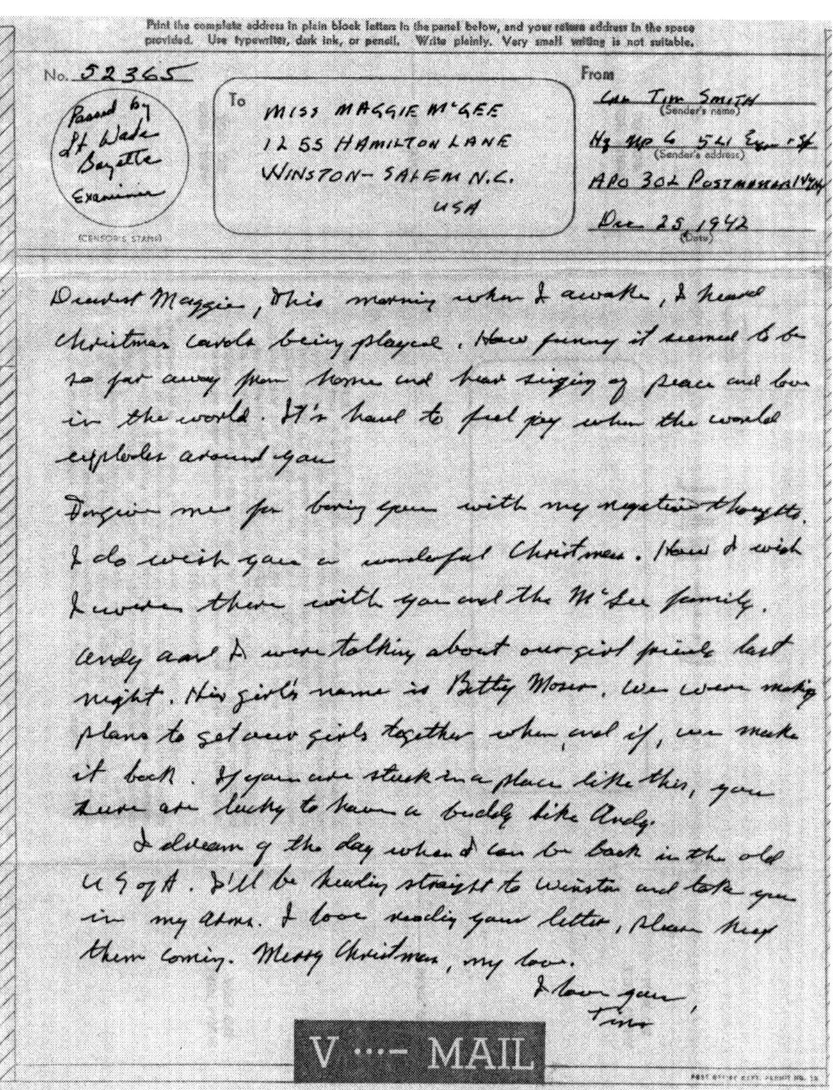

Print the complete address in plain block letters in the panel below, and your return address in the space provided. Use typewriter, dark ink, or pencil. Write plainly. Very small writing is not suitable.

No. 52365

Passed by
Lt Wade
Bayette
Examiner

(CENSOR'S STAMP)

To
MISS MAGGIE McGEE
1255 HAMILTON LANE
WINSTON-SALEM N.C.
USA

From
Cpl Tim Smith
(Sender's name)
Hq Co 6 541 Engr
(Sender's address)
APO 302 Postmaster
Dec 25, 1942
(Date)

Dearest Maggie, This morning when I awoke, I heard Christmas carols being played. How funny it seemed to be so far away from home and hear singing of peace and love in the world. It's hard to feel joy when the world explodes around you.

Forgive me for boring you with my negative thoughts. I do wish you a wonderful Christmas. How I wish I were there with you and the McGee family.

Andy and I were talking about our girl friends last night. His girl's name is Betty Moser. We were making plans to get our girls together when, and if, we make it back. If you are stuck in a place like this, you sure are lucky to have a buddy like Andy.

I dream of the day when I can be back in the old USofA. I'll be heading straight to Winston and take you in my arms. I love reading your letters, please keep them coming. Merry Christmas, my love.

I love you,
Tim

V ···– MAIL

"Maggie, sit down and let you father say the blessing, so we can all eat. That can wait until dinner is over," her mother implored.

"Sorry Momma. It can wait."

After dinner her father took the three V-Mails in his hand. "Yes, this is an interesting new invention being used by the Army that I was just reading about recently in the newspaper. These letters may be written on those stationary blanks, and when mailed they are sent to a central location, microfilmed, then flown to the U.S. and printed out on these little letters. This apparently is saving time and also many tons of mail having to be shipped on much needed ships. Thousands of letters can be microfilmed and flown home much faster. This makes the soldiers receive their mail in weeks instead of months. I understand you can also write letter by V-Mail, Maggie. You should go by the stationary shop and see if they have the blanks in stock. The letters limit what you can write but the guys will receive them sooner."

She went and hugged her father's neck whispering, "I don't know if I want someone filming my mail, but thanks for explaining them. You are so smart, that's why I love you so much." With that she picked up her tiny letters and fled upstairs.

Her father turned to Annie and said, "It takes so little to impress her."

Annie smiled and went into the kitchen.

Chapter 31

During December, 1942, Jake had been home in Winston-Salem, on a month's leave after receiving his pilot's wings. It was very good to have him home, but Maggie wished he could have stayed through Christmas. He left on the 20th to report to Lockbourne AF Base in Columbus, Ohio, for transitional training in B-17s.

The December skies were cold and gray, and all the leaves had fallen from the trees. Maggie was out in the yard raking the leaves and generally getting the yard ready for the holidays. Jeanie was helping her, so she said, wallowing in the leaf piles and strewing them about.

Finally Maggie yelled, "Jeanie, stop jumping in my pile of leaves! You're spreading them out as fast as I rake them! Go in the house and bother Lisa!"

Jeanie stopped playing and headed for the house sobbing. Maggie realized that she was a bit irritated this morning, but not at Jeanie. She ran to catch Jeanie, hugged her, and begged, "Come on, you and I are going to play in the leaves. I'm so sorry I was short with you. I have a lot on my mind."

Jeanie smiled, and for the next hour she and Maggie piled the leaves high, and then ran through them, scattering them back where they came from. Maggie thought, "This is the way life is supposed to be, but this is not the way life is in 1942."

When Jeanie was exhausted, she and Maggie went into the house. Lisa and her mother were turning the house into a fairyland.

The tree was lit and decorated; the stairs were heavy with garlands. The dining room was decorated with icy snow like sculptures. White tapers were on the table encircled with boughs of dark-green holly, covered with the brightest red berries.

"Come on girls," Annie said. "Help us finish the decorating."

Jeanie was quick to dive in and help, but Maggie excused herself and went upstairs.

As she mounted the stairs, her sad thoughts returned. "Tim and all those boys overseas are fighting, and they won't even know it's Christmas. Jake is getting his last training before going overseas. James is in submarine school. Bill is still in gunnery school and won't be coming home." She began to feel sorry for herself, but then she realized there were millions of families going through the same situation. Maggie lay down on her bed and closed her eyes. "Jeanie and Christmas," she said to herself. "We have to carry on for the children's sake. Isn't that what the boys are fighting for?"

She popped up and headed downstairs to help put the final touches on the decorations. Annie smiled at her as if she knew what was troubling Maggie, and down deep inside she felt the same.

On Friday, the week before Christmas, the phone rang, and Maggie heard her mother say, "Yes, Wally, Maggie is here. I'll tell her you're calling. I hope you are doing well, and I hope you have a Merry Christmas." She handed Maggie the phone, saying, "Here, Maggie. It's Wally."

"Wally, how are you? It's been a long time since I've heard from you. What do you hear from Tim?"

"Not much, and not very often. You know he's fighting in Africa? He seems very depressed and despondent in his letters, and Mother worries about him constantly. Have you heard from him lately?"

"Last week I had three short V-Mail letters. He sounded down. He was at a field hospital recuperating from his leg injuries," Maggie answered.

"Yeah, I know he was wounded, and that didn't help Mother's state of mind. I really am worried about her. Maggie, Mother will be in town visiting me for the holidays, and she'd like to meet you. I hope I'm not being too presumptuous," Wally added.

"No, not at all, Wally. I'd love to meet your mother. Why not bring her over around 4:00 Sunday afternoon?"

"Four will be fine, but she wants to come by herself. Is that OK?" Wally asked.

"That's fine, but be sure she knows the way."

"I will. It's been good talking to you Maggie; I hope to see you soon," Wally said.

As Maggie replaced the phone, she thought, "How odd it was that Mrs. Smith wants to come by herself," but she didn't dwell on it long. She went straight and told her mother about Wally's request.

"Why would Mrs. Smith want to meet me, and come by herself?" Maggie asked.

"Maggie dear, I'm sure Tim has spoken of you often, and she just wants to meet you. Don't worry; just be your sweet self. I'm sure she misses Tim, and wants to talk to anyone he is staying in touch with."

"Momma, will you be here when she comes? I'm a little nervous."

"Sure honey. You can count on me."

Late Sunday afternoon came, and Maggie found she was a bit anxious, but she supposed that Mrs. Smith just wanted to get to know her. As her mother said, she was sure Tim had written his mother about how much he cared for Maggie.

The door bell rang, and Maggie's heart jumped into her throat.

"I'll get it," said Annie.

"Come in, Mrs. Smith. I'm Annie McGee, Maggie's mother. Maggie is in the sunroom, and if you'll follow me, we'll join her there."

Mrs. Smith said, "I'm so happy to meet you. I hope this is not an imposition on your family. Tim was very anxious for me to meet Maggie."

"No indeed, Mrs. Smith! We are so happy to meet Tim's mother. We enjoyed the visits he made here last summer."

Maggie was waiting impatiently in the sunroom. Annie escorted Mrs. Smith into the room and introduced her to her daughter. Maggie greeted her, extended her hand, and asked Mrs. Smith to sit beside her on the sofa.

They began with small talk, such as how her trip was and whether she drove or came by train or bus. Then they finished with idle talk about the weather. Finally the conversation turned to Tim, his latest stay at the field hospital, and his subsequent return to the fighting. It was obviously painful for Mrs. Smith to talk about her son.

Annie rose and excused herself, saying that she had promised to play ping-pong with Jeanie in the recreation room. She explained that her husband, Ruben, had taken Lisa, their other daughter, to the church for Young People Service League, and they would be gone for several hours, so the house was quiet for a while.

Mrs. Smith and Maggie exchanged news of Tim, and she and Maggie discussed their concern for Tim's depressed or despondent state of mind.

At that very moment, Mrs. Smith reached into her purse and brought out a box. It was obviously an old, dusty, ring box. She turned to Maggie, and said, "Maggie, dear, Tim asked me to bring this ring to you. Tim hopes you will wear it. It would lift his spirits so much! This ring was his grandmother's, and it was given to him to give to the girl of his choice."

Maggie turned away; she could not believe what was happening. She worried, "Have I done anything, or said anything to bring this about?" She really didn't think so, but here was Tim's poor mother, bearing the most beautiful ring

Maggie had ever seen, pleading for her to accept and wear it. Maggie opened her mouth to reply, but nothing came out. A tear trickled down her cheek as she turned to Mrs. Smith. She tried, again, to think of the right words to say, but, again, nothing would come.

Tim's mother slowly closed the box, returned it to her purse, and said, "Maybe it's best if Tim gives it to you himself." She stood up, gently kissed Maggie, and excused herself.

Maggie managed to say, "Mrs. Smith, I am so happy to have met you. You were so sweet to come." By now Maggie had recovered, and added, "Yes, maybe it would be best for Tim to ask me personally."

"Yes, I really think that's best," Mrs. Smith said as she turned, and left.

Maggie closed the door behind Mrs. Smith and headed straight to her bedroom. She was relieved that Lisa was not home. She flung herself on her bed and cried until she could cry no more. She searched her heart for any reason why Tim might think that she would accept a ring. She got out his letters, untied them, and read each one carefully. Yes, he professed he loved her, but at no time had he mentioned marriage. Once he had asked her to wait for him, but she had not responded to that question.

She gathered up his letters and marched downstairs to find her mother, who could help her sort this out. Maggie barged right into the family room and said, "Jeanie, go upstairs, and play something! I need to talk to Momma!"

"Why?" Jeanie asked.

Annie saw that Maggie was distraught and told Jeanie she could go get some cookies from the cookie jar. She didn't finish the sentence before Jeanie ran up the stairs as fast as her little legs could carry her.

Annie went over to her daughter and comforted her in her arms as Maggie's tears flowed again. "Come over here on the sofa beside me, and tell me what Mrs. Smith said to you. Has something happened to Tim?"

"No, Momma, Tim's all right, but you can't imagine what she asked me to do. She wanted me to take his grandmother's diamond ring, and...

and... I can't believe this is happening! Momma, I promise you, I have not given Tim any reason to think that I would accept a ring. I mean a great, big, diamond ring." She had cried so much that her cries were reduced to sobbing so heavily that it made it difficult for Annie to understand her.

"Now Maggie, calm down, so we can talk this situation over."

Maggie shoved Tim's letters into her mother's hands, and pleaded, "Take these letters, and read each one. Then tell me if you think I should have expected this to happen. I hope I didn't lead him on."

Annie proceeded to read Tim's letters, while Maggie sat beside her, clinging to her like a frightened child. When Annie finished, she turned to Maggie, brushing Maggie's lovely auburn hair away from her face. She began to relate to her what she thought was going on.

"Maggie, I read nothing in Tim's letters that shows anything but a scared young man thrown in the middle of a terrible war. He's scared, depressed, and reaching out for something to hang onto — some reason to endure the horrors of war. That's what you have become for him."

Maggie began to calm down, and her cries were little more than pitiful sighs. Annie continued, "I met a very frightened mother upstairs who was willing to do anything for her son to keep him determined to come home. She saw that possibility in you, Maggie. A worried mother will do anything to help her son endure whatever he must endure."

"What should I do? I can't keep on writing to Tim after this."

"Yes, you must keep writing newsy and encouraging letters," Annie counseled.

"Should I mention the ring, and his mother's visit?"

"No. If Mrs. Smith wants him to know what happened, let her write him about her visit." She went on to say, "Be a good friend, and try to lift his spirits without giving him any false hope. I know it won't be easy, but I know you can do it. Now go upstairs, wash your face, and dab your eyes with a cold wash cloth. Then come back down, and join the family for dinner. Tomorrow is Christmas Eve, and this house must be happy, even though our hearts are heavy."

Chapter 31

Christmas came, the family pulled together and had a happy celebration. Jeanie helped to keep them all smiling, for she was thrilled with all her gifts, especially the ones from Santa Claus. Everything was wondrous to her. Maggie was glad when Christmas was over, and she hoped that another year would bring peace to the world and the safe return of all her friends and loved ones.

Christmas night her parents had all their relatives over for a light supper and their annual Christmas singing. Joy and peace seemed far away this year, but then, she remembered what she told Tim, "There's always hope." She began to sing with all the others, "Joy to the World, the Savior reigns."

News from Bill was not good. Since he had washed out of pilot training, he had been terribly disappointed. The only good part was that he had been given a ten-day leave. He was on his way to Charleston and would be home for Maggie's nineteenth birthday.

January 16, 1943, and Maggie was turning 19. She was thrilled that her birthday celebration involved her whole family, including Bill. Ken came and spent the weekend, making it even more special. With Bill home, the house was filled with his irritating teasing, and Maggie loved it, but she didn't let Bill know. She and Ken double dated with Bill and his new girlfriend Molly Barnes. Maggie had never met Molly before, but they became good friends right away. It seemed so good to have the house full again, but the feeling didn't last very long. When Bill left, the house was suddenly quiet and very empty.

The next few months passed slowly for Maggie, with only a few letters from Tim. He wrote that he was in intense fighting with not much time to write. His letters were still gloomy, but there was no hint that his mother had written him about her visit to Maggie. She was still writing Tim only when she felt it was appropriate, because, by now, her feelings toward Ken were changing from like to love. She followed her mother's suggestion and kept her letters to Tim newsy and encouraging, but it was a struggle for Maggie to find the right words.

She listened to the grim news every night to keep up with what was going on in North Africa. By early March U.S. troops seemed to be getting the upper hand. Every night she prayed that the war would soon be over.

Life in Winston-Salem was pretty lonesome, and Maggie had fallen into a boring routine. One of the highlights of her life was that her Mother's health was gradually improving, but Maggie was still mainly caring for Jeanie. She stayed busy riding the city bus, taking Jeanie to kindergarten, dance lessons, and piano lessons.

Maggie looked forward to all her letters, so she could keep up with where her friends were. Ken was now first on her list. Tim wrote that he and Andy had been reassigned to another tank group. His leg had healed, leaving him with only a slight limp. He wrote saying he hoped that she wouldn't mind.

Jake wrote that he had flown to England, where he was taking some advanced training. He liked England, but it was cold and dreary.

Bill was settled in at Charleston, S.C. continuing in gunnery school.

In her last letter from James, he wrote that he was enjoying his training as a submarine crewman. He was still in New London, Connecticut, but he was expecting to get a furlough before being assigned to a ship. He would be coming home on his way to the west coast, and he would write her as soon as he knew the exact date. He hoped that she would be there and that they could spend some time together.

James came home the last week of April on furlough. He looked very good, and they had a wonderful time. He told her he was being assigned to submarine duty. James made her promise she would write, because her letters meant so much to him. He said she kept him up on all that was going on in Winston. Maggie promised, and James left the next day.

One day while Maggie was sewing she realized, "It's the last of April, and I've not heard from Tim in over a month." She tried to call his brother Wally, but the receptionist at the "Y" told her that he had been drafted and that they had no address for him. She kept thinking of Tim and his ominous words, "I don't think I'll be coming home." She desperately wanted to hear from him soon.

Chapter 31

Ken came the last weekend in May, and when he left that Sunday night, Maggie knew that she was in love with him. She decided that she must write to Tim and tell him that she had fallen in love. When she sat down to write the letter, she began to cry. She didn't want to hurt Tim with a "Dear John" letter, but she felt it was dishonest not to tell him the truth. She assured him that she would continue writing to him, but she wanted him to know she was in love with someone else. She read the letter over and over through her tears. She finally put it in an envelope and sealed it.

Chapter 32

Awakening on the morning of May 3rd, Maggie looked out her window and saw the dogwoods in bloom and tulips waving their heads back and forth as the gentle breeze passed by. The world was so beautiful and serene, yet she had a very unsettled feeling. She had not heard from Tim in two months. Later that morning the phone rang.

She picked it up, "Hello."

"Maggie, this is Wally. How are you?"

"I'm fine, but where are you, and how are you?"

"I'm in Winston, visiting a few friends since I'm home on leave before being shipped over to the Pacific. You know I'm in the Army now, don't you?"

"I just found that out a few days ago when I called the "Y" to ask if you had heard from Tim lately."

"That's why I'm calling you. I've got bad news about Tim. He was killed in Africa when his tank was hit."

There was a long silence.

"Did you hear me? Tim was killed," Wally said, holding back his emotions.

"Yes, Wally, I heard you. I just don't know what to say. How is your mother?"

"She's pretty broken up."

"Will his body be sent home for a funeral?"

"No, he will be buried in Africa for the time being. We can have his body brought home later, if we choose." Wally hurried on, "I would like to come by to see you, Maggie. I have a letter his best buddy, Andy Brown, wrote to Mother. He gives details of their last day together. Mother thought that you might like to read it."

"I certainly would love to know more. It was weird how he was so sure he would not make it home."

"Yes, it was. I'll be there in about an hour, if that is OK."

"I'll be looking for you."

Maggie couldn't sit down. She walked from window to window until she saw Wally pull into the drive. She raced out the door to greet him, and at that moment the tears began to flow. Seeing Wally made Tim's death real.

She quickly wiped them away. "Wally, come on in the house. You sure are looking fit these days."

"The Army has a way of doing that to a guy."

As they settled on the couch, Maggie reached over and hugged Wally. "I'm so sorry."

"I know." He hugged her back.

"I won't tell you how Tim died. It's best if you read this letter from Andy."

He pulled the letter out, handed it to Maggie. She continued to dry her eyes, and read.

April 20, 1943

Dear Mrs. Smith,

I am Andy Brown. I am now in a hospital recovering from the loss of my right leg. I would have written sooner, but it has taken me some time to get myself together. Tim and I were best buddies every since we entered the Army. This is a very difficult letter to write, but I would want Tim to write to my mother if it had been me that was killed. I only lost a leg, Tim lost his life for his country. You should be very proud of him. He did his duty and then some.

On New Year's Day, Tim and I were assigned to a new tank group. The fighting had been fierce, and we were fighting our way toward Tunisia.

March 20th was a beautiful day, and if we had not been standing behind our big guns, which were there only for us to kill the enemy, our spirits would have been soaring. We surveyed the world around us, and I thought, "today will be like every other day since we landed on African soil. I'll either be aiming this thing before me to kill the Germans before they kill me; or I'll be out there scouring the smoking ruins for our dead and wounded, strewn about over this desolate land that we have just claimed."

Before we knew it, the skies were filled with enemy planes, and orders came for us to move out and engage the enemy. General Patton's voice boomed out over the area, "GOOD LUCK BOYS, GIVE 'EM HELL!" Our tank rumbled on, and on, and on. The world seemed to be exploding all around us. Our heads ached for just one moment of silence, but that was not to be. We watched the planes flying overhead dropping their bombs on our buddies' tanks, and trucks. We saw jeeps as they flew up in the air and landed upside down like a pile of rubble. Other planes were flying low, strafing the guys on foot. Tim said to me, "This really must be what Hell is like." At that moment a bomb hit our tank. I heard my buddy scream, "WE'RE HIT! GET THE HELL OUT OF HERE!" There was a chorus of moans and cries, but before I could decide if I could move, there was silence. Not silence like we wished for, but the silence of the dead.

I called out, "Is anybody alive?"

Tim answered weakly. "I'm up here in the turret. I'm alive, but not for long. I've been hit bad in my head, and I have a hole blown in my stomach, gushing blood. Go on. Take cover. The Germans will be back, and I know I can't make it."

I got up on his turret, pulled Tim out, dragging my mangled leg. "Come on, you have to help me. You don't want to die here, do you? I know I don't."

Chapter 32

"Hell, no!" Tim grunted.

Tim fell to the ground, and lay there as if he were dead. I crawled to his side and pulled him under the shelter of an overturned truck. I took off his shirt and stuffed it in his stomach wound. I had to try to stop the blood from draining the life out of him. Just then the Nazi planes were back, starting another strafing run. Tim lay there, half propped up between the wheels of the truck, and watched the world go mad. He tried to raise his head, but could not find the strength. He said, "Andy, go on. I'm dying. You can't help me."

"Hang on, buddy. I'm going to find help. I'll be back for you. Don't go anywhere. You hear me?" I told Tim.

"Sure," Tim only managed a whisper.

I looked back at him. He knew his war was over. He reached into his pocket, and pulled out his picture of Maggie, and stared at it for one long, last look. I heard him whisper, "Maggie, I wanted to come home to you, but that won't happen now. I love you." His voice, weaker still, "Have a good life."

We heard the roar of more planes. He managed to raise his head and open his eyes long enough to realize they were allied planes, and the Nazis were retreating. He managed a weak salute and his head slumped.

Tim found his peace.

His hand relaxed and Maggie's picture fell to the ground. Maggie's photo lay there until a hot desert breeze began to stir, picking it up, and tumbling it across the nearly deserted battlefield. I didn't try to go after it. I was trying to find a medic for Tim. I rescued his journal.

As I was returning with help, trucks, tanks, and jeeps rumbled by and soldiers hurried to save the wounded, and to get ready for the next offensive. A dust devil blew by, and swirled Maggie's picture high into the air. When the breeze gave out, it dropped the picture into a dead bush, and it caught there as if Maggie were watching the rescuers.

Before I could retrieve it, a soldier racing back to his position spotted the picture. He put on his brakes, jumped out and grabbed it. He dusted it off on his pants and looked at it as if to say, "What's a beautiful girl like you doing in a hell hole like this?" He kissed the picture, folded it, and placed it in his pocket. He buttoned the pocket, and patted it tenderly as he jumped back into his jeep and drove off. I am so sorry to have to write this letter, but I hope it is of some consolation. I miss Tim terribly.

Your son's buddy in war,

Andy Brown

Maggie let the letter drop to her lap, she looked up at Wally and said, "Oh, Wally, it must have been just awful for Tim, he was such a gentle person."

"Maggie, he did what we all have to do. I know he was scared, but, hell, we are all scared." Wally rose and took Maggie by the hand, "This war must be over soon."

As she folded the letter and placed it in its envelope, she said, "I pray for peace every night." Maggie returned the letter to Wally, reached up and gave him a kiss on his cheek.

"No, Maggie, Mother insisted that you should have Andy's letter, and Tim's journal," Wally said.

Maggie took the letter, and said, "I'll write to your mother and thank her for thinking of me."

As Wally went out the door, Maggie waved farewell to both him and indirectly, to Tim Smith.

Chapter 33

May arrived, and the dogwoods were in their glory. The azaleas, tulips and jonquils were in full bloom and the world was like a garden. Maggie thought, "How can the world be so beautiful when it is at war?" She rose that morning, feeling that she needed to talk to her mother about Tim.

"Momma, I had just written Tim about Ken. I felt I had to."

"When did you write him?"

"Last week, he will never receive it."

"Good," her mother said as she hugged Maggie. With that Maggie began to cry and ran to her room.

Annie let her go, because she knew she needed some time alone. Tim was the first real casualty of war that Maggie had to face.

Maggie went to her dresser and sat down. Slowly she opened the bottom drawer and took out Tim's letters. She sat there and reread them. She thought his letters were filled with negative thoughts. She hoped her letters and the journal writing she suggested had made him feel more connected to home. She put his letters in their envelopes, and tied them all up with a red ribbon, replacing them in the bottom of the drawer, where she kept the letters from all her friends. On top of Tim's letters she put a red-satin quilted box containing special keepsakes and her last picture.

Several weeks later, Maggie came home from work and lying on the front hall table was a letter addressed to Miss Maggie McGee. She did not recognize the handwriting. As she picked it up, she read the return address - Sgt. Andrew Brown, Walter Reed Hospital,

Washington, D.C. She wondered why he was writing to her, but she was anxious to find out, so she sat down on the bottom step of the stairs, opened the envelope, and out fell a small journal. She noticed how stained and dirty it was, and realized it was Tim's journal. She took out a letter from Andy and read it.

Dear Maggie, *May 12, 1943*

I am Andy Brown. I was Tim's best buddy from the day we entered the service to the day that he was killed in Africa. I am at Walter Reed Hospital recuperating from having my leg removed. It was so mangled when our tank was hit that they could not save it. It was removed just above my knee. I know I am lucky. I will be going home, but Tim lost his life. I will never forget him. He was a great friend.

I will be going home next week to let my stump heal and then I will return to be fitted with a prosthesis.

I am sending you Tim's journal, which I found in his pocket. He was keeping it to give to you. He stopped writing when the fighting became so intense. We didn't have time to eat or sleep, so there was little time to sit and write, only an occasional letter home. I also wrote to his mother telling her about our last day together, and how brave Tim was at the end. He was thinking of you. Perhaps she can share it with you.

I hope you will write to me sometime. Tim and I wanted to get our best girls together. I would like for you to meet my girl friend, Betty.

I will send you my address when I get settled.

Sincerely, Andy

She picked up the journal and began to read:

October 5, 1942

My buddy, Andy and I, and a trainload of fellow soldiers, are leaving Texas on a train with the shades drawn so no one can tell that there are troops inside. No one knows where we are heading. The sun is high in the sky, and the humidity is unbearable. It seems we are heading east, we're guessing Newport News, Virginia - a staging area for troops going overseas. Can't tell anyone where we are headed. I wrote to Maggie today.

October 7, 1942

When we arrived, it seemed the whole world was made up of soldiers, tanks, jeeps, trucks, and all the equipment needed to make a hell of a difference wherever we are sent.

November 1, 1942

We've been on ship board for about three weeks, and the only thing I know is that I keep hearing the code name TORCH. It means nothing to me, but I feel we will soon learn what it means.

November 8, 1942

Orders were being shouted all around us. Obviously this was moving day. The loudspeaker said, "WE WILL LAND AT FEDALA IN FRENCH MOROCCO, ENGAGE THE GERMANS SOON AS YOU GO ASHORE. THEN HEAD TO CASABLANCA FROM THE NORTH. GOOD LUCK MEN, GIVE 'EM HELL. We're on a small boat heading to shore.

November 11, 1942

We made the landing along with all our equipment, and there was a scramble for everyone to man his positions. The wheels rolled on and on, and for two days there has been little resistance. There was some shelling in the harbor, and German planes dropped a lot of bombs. I hope my grueling training - those 36 hours stints in the tank turret - has prepared me for what is coming. Tensions are mounting among the troops, but we know we were trained by the best, General George S. Patton.

November 12, 1942

We are under heavy fire. Sky is black overhead with enemy planes, horizon lit with flashes from enemy guns; planes are coming down in flames. It looks like hell.

November 19, 1942

Days on end, there's no relief. How will anyone survive this?

November 25, 1942

Today our tank sustained a direct hit. Some of our crew didn't survive, but Andy and I were lucky - maybe. Andy was hit in his left arm, and I have shrapnel in my right leg. We are now in a field hospital. They'll patch us up, and we'll be back fighting before we know it. Our tank was destroyed, so we'll be reassigned.

January 1, 1943

It's New Year's Day although it doesn't feel like it and Andy and I are assigned to a new tank group. The fighting has been fierce, as we fight our way toward Tunisia.

March 20th

There hasn't been time to write, but today is a beautiful day. If I wasn't standing behind this gun, I would think it's a day for a picnic with Maggie. But it's another day of kill the Germans or be killed. Oh, my God, what's that? The skies are becoming black with enemy planes

Chapter 33

That was the end of Tim's journal. Maggie was stunned as she thought back to her letters from Tim at that time. It was different reading his journal - like she was going through it with him. As she closed the ledger, she realized the stains on the book were possibly Tim's blood.

Maggie sat quietly sobbing on the bottom step when Annie came in the front door. "Maggie, what's the matter?"

Maggie handed the letter and journal to her mother and said, "This is Tim's journal and a letter from Andy Brown, Tim's buddy. Read them, you'll see what's happening to our boys."

Annie sat down, cradled Maggie in her arms, and just let her cry it all out.

When Annie had finished reading, Maggie took the letter and journal from her and went to her room.

There she opened the drawer to her desk, untied Tim's letters, added the journal and Andy's letter, and then slowly retied the packet and returned it to the drawer.

"How could anyone endure what Tim had gone through?" she thought.

Chapter 34

At the end of May, Ken called. When she heard his voice her heart leapt into her throat. If she had any doubt as to whether she loved Ken, the feeling she had right now proved that he was definitely her prince.

"It's wonderful to hear your voice," she said.

"I can't talk but a minute. I'm on my way to morning drill. I can get a three-day pass this weekend. I'd like to come to Winston to see you, if that is OK with you."

"Ok? That would be simply wonderful. When will you be here?"

"My bus will get in at eight Thursday evening."

"I'll meet you at the bus station. I'm so excited! I can't wait!"

"Honey, I gotta go and let these other guys use the phone. I'll see you Thursday! I love you!"

Maggie stood there hugging the phone, not wanting to hang up.

Annie came into the room and asked, "Who was that on the phone, Maggie?"

"It was Ken, and he's got a three-day pass. I'm meeting him at the bus station at eight Thursday night. I hope Daddy will let me take the car to meet him."

"I think I can persuade him. I think it's essential driving."

"Oh Momma, you're the greatest mom in the whole, wide world!"

Annie smiled and walked into the kitchen to fix lunch. "It is so good to see her happy," she thought. "Oh, how she is growing up! I think I see a young woman in love."

The next three days dragged on slowly. Maggie sat at her desk daydreaming most of the days away. Her father came into the office and found her sitting idle, with her mind a million miles away. "Maggie, have you finished those reports I asked for this morning?"

"No, Daddy, but I'll get right on them and have them ready in no time."

"I'm going to have to have a talk with this Ken guy. He's ruining the best secretary I ever had."

"Oh, Daddy, don't tease him too much. I really like him."

"That's pretty evident. Now get to work."

Thursday morning, Maggie took special care to fix her hair and select the right outfit to wear. She went to work, but after lunch she had to look after Jeanie.

When she brought Jeanie home from her dance lesson, she said, "I'm going upstairs to freshen up, and then I'm going to the bus station to meet Ken."

"Can I go with you, Maggie?" Jeanie begged.

"No, honey. Ken and I might not come right home, and you need to go to bed early."

"But, can't I see Ken?"

"You'll see him tomorrow. He'll be here three days, so you will have plenty of time to see him."

"Oh, all right." Jeanie hung her head and headed into her parents' room.

At the dinner table, Maggie was excited and monopolized the conversation, telling the family about her plans to meet Ken. Her mother had offered to put Ken in Bill's room, so Maggie and he could spend more time together. That pleased Jeanie, because she could keep Ken busy playing games with her.

Maggie shivered in anticipation as she saw the bus roll into the station. It wasn't from being cold. After all, it was now June.

She waited, the door opened, the driver emerged, and then the passengers began to disembark. Finally, she saw Ken and ran right into his arms. Their kiss was long and hungry. She forgot about people being around. It had been too long since they had seen each other.

"Let's get your bag and be on our way," said Maggie.

He picked up a medium-sized duffle bag and said, "This is it. A soldier learns to travel light."

She took his arm and said, "Come on, we're wasting time."

"Did you find me a place to stay?"

"Yes, the best place in town."

"Where?"

"Mrs. McGee's boarding house."

Ken looked curiously at her.

"Yes, you're going to stay at the McGee house."

He smiled at her and gave her a quick kiss, "Well, let's go then."

The next three days were wonderful. Jeanie played with Ken whenever Maggie turned her back, and Ken didn't seem to mind.

The last night Ken was there, he took Maggie by the hand and said, "Come on, let's go into the den. I have something I need to tell you."

A chill was in the air, so her father had set a small fire in the fireplace. When they were nestled into her father's great big, red-leather chair, Ken said, "Maggie, when I get back to Fort Bragg, I'm being sent to Camp Crowder, Missouri. I'm being assigned to the Army Signal Corps. I don't know how long I will be there, but eventually I'll be going to Officer Candidate School."

Chapter 34

Maggie sat quietly for a while before it settled in that Ken was soon to be on the train, like all the other boys, to fight a war. She didn't know what to say.

Ken went on, "Please write me every day like you have been doing. Your letters light up my day."

"You know I will, and don't you forget to write to me."

"Maggie, there's something else I need."

"What's that?"

"I need a picture of my best girl to carry with me. Do you have one I can have?"

"I do. She rose and left the room. She told him she would only be a few minutes. Maggie went to her room and sat down at her desk. She opened the bottom drawer and took out the box that held the last picture — the one she had taken from the frame in her parent's room, when she exchanged it for the one that was returned to her, on which she had written "All my love, Maggie." She sat there and realized that she had known for sometime that Ken was different from any of her other boyfriends. When she looked into his eyes, she saw gentleness, a sense of humor, honesty, and yes, she saw that he loved her. Ken was not as handsome nor as tall as some of her other boyfriends, but he was just the kind of boy she had dreamed of to be her husband. Most of all, she loved to be with him, and she dreaded every time they parted. She realized he fit in with her family, and that all of her family seemed to feel comfortable with him, which made her feel that he was her prince. She started to write "All my love," but she didn't. After all, Ken had mentioned nothing about getting married. Maybe that would be a little premature. She closed the drawer, turned off the lights, went back downstairs, and gave Ken her picture.

"I hope you like it, and be sure to take care of it."

"Don't worry. It will go with me wherever I go," Ken said.

The rest of the evening they sat holding each other, dreading the close of the evening that approached with every tick of the clock. When they could no longer hold their eyes open, they decided to go to bed.

Sunday morning everyone woke up early, fought their way into the shared bathroom and got off to church on time. Maggie sang a solo part with the choir that morning, and it was the first time Ken had heard her sing. He thought, "She sings like an angel."

As they gathered around the McGee's dining room table for a delicious Sunday dinner, Maggie savored every moment, because they didn't have much time before Ken had to get to the bus station and back to Fort Bragg.

It was a sad parting, but Maggie managed not to cry, until after the bus had pulled away from the station. Maggie returned to the car, sat there a minute, and then asked her father to take her home. She went to her room and shed her tears in private.

Chapter 35

The summer of 1943 was one of routine and keeping a stiff upper lip. Maggie went to work every day with her father, and in the afternoons she and Lisa took turns taking Jeanie to the pool. Nancy was home from Peace College and they kept each other company going to the movies or meeting some of the other girls at one of the snack shops. She missed Ken terribly but looked forward to his daily letters. She tried to make her letters newsy, but it was hard to find things to write about, except how much she missed him. Jeanie, who was beginning to write, sent him something - a letter or a drawing - nearly every day inside Maggie's envelope.

Late July, she received a couple of V-Mail letters from James. His short letters sounded as if he liked what he was doing, but he indicated that it was a little boring when they were out too long. He reminisced as to how beautiful Winston was in the spring, and he also wrote about how much fun they had had together the past year. Of course there was nothing to indicate where he was. She only knew he was somewhere in the Pacific.

It was the first of August, and Maggie was late coming home from work, as was common the first few days of each month. When she came in the back door, her mother told her that James's sister, Susan Ferguson, had called her several times that day.

Maggie went upstairs and sat down in the upstairs hall to call Susan. The phone rang and rang until finally someone answered.

"This is Maggie McGee. May I speak to Susan?"

The line went silent, and after a few moments, "Maggie, this is Susan."

"Yes, what is it, Susan?"

There was a long silence, and Maggie began to fear the worst. She could hear Susan crying.

"Mother asked me to tell you that we have been notified that James and the entire crew of his submarine were lost in the Sea of Japan."

"Oh Susan! How awful," Maggie cried as she tried to hold back her tears. "I'll be over as soon as Daddy gets home."

"I'll tell mother you're coming. She'd like to see you."

Maggie went to her mother and told her why Susan had been calling.

Annie looked at Maggie and realized that the war was hitting her hard. She went over, dried Maggie's tears, and told her how sorry she was. "You and I need to go over to see the Fergusons as soon as your father gets home."

Ruben did not have time to get out of his car. Annie and Maggie were waiting to tell him the news and have him drive them over to the Ferguson's home. Maggie dreaded to enter, but her mother told her she must try to help the family with their sorrow.

Mrs. Ferguson greeted Maggie and Annie, and through her tears said, "I am so glad you've come. Maggie, you and James were such good friends. He wrote how you kept him in touch with the goings on in Winston. Thank you for being such a good friend to him."

"He was always so good to me," Maggie said, as she began to cry.

Susan came over to Maggie, put her arms around her, and they both cried. "He won't be coming back," Susan sobbed, "Nothing will be coming back." With that they began to cry uncontrollably.

Maggie could take it no longer and looked at her mother as if to say, "Please make this go away." Annie expressed her feelings to the family and excused herself. Maggie and Ruben followed her to the car.

Chapter 35

Maggie went inside the house, thanked her parents for going with her, and headed up to her room. As she had done one time before, she pulled out the bottom drawer, lifted out a set of letters, and she read them through her tear-stained eyes. James had been such a good friend all through high school and their first year of college, and now he was gone. She was having a difficult time grasping that he was actually dead. She gathered his letters together and tied them up with a royal-blue ribbon and placed them in the drawer beside Tim's letters. It seemed to her that the war had hardly begun, and she had already lost two of her very close friends.

Chapter 36

Maggie came home from work one afternoon late in August to find that her mother had received a V-mail from Jake. Annie called out to Maggie, "We have a letter from Jake. It's on the table in the front hall."

"What did he have to say?" Maggie asked.

"Not much. It was one of those V-Mail letters, and you know there's not much room to write. He did say he was happier now that he's flying."

"He says he hasn't heard from me lately. I'll go right up and write to him," she called to her mother.

Maggie made sure that she wrote to Ken every night, so she had let some of her other letter writing suffer.

The summer of 1943 was ending. Jeanie would start first grade in a few days. Maggie came home from work and as usual went to the hall table to see if she had a letter from Ken. There it was, and the news inside delighted her.

"I am being sent back to N.C. State to begin my junior year." Ken wrote, "I will still be in the Army, but I will be attending school like any other student. I don't know how long this will last, but at least we can see each other while I'm there."

She ran into the kitchen, kissed her mother, and swung her around.

"Maggie, for heaven's sake, what's the matter with you?"

"Ken's being sent back to State next week!"

"What will he be doing there?"

"I don't know. He said he's still in the Army, but he'll be going to school like any other student."

"That's wonderful, Maggie! I'm so happy for you. Now get busy and set the table for dinner."

"Yes, Momma!"

At the dinner table that evening, Ruben told them all that he had received a letter from Bill. "He has been sent to advanced gunnery school to become an instructor."

"Where will he be sent?" Annie asked.

"He will be staying in Charleston for now, but where he will be after that, he doesn't know. At least he won't be going overseas," Ruben answered.

"I'm sorry his ear was ruptured," Maggie added, "but if it keeps him in the states, I have to say I'm glad."

Annie closed her eyes as if she were saying, "Thank you, Lord."

"I wish Bill would come home," Jeanie said. "I miss him."

Everyone agreed with her.

Chapter 37

Bright and early on September 6th, the phone rang and Maggie intuitively knew it was Ken. She threw on her robe and ran down the stairs to pick up the phone first.

"Hello, beautiful."

"Ken! Where are you?" Maggie squealed.

"I'm at State College getting ready to start classes next Wednesday."

"Can you come to Winston this weekend?"

"I don't know yet what our rules will be, so I had better not plan to come this weekend."

"Then I'll come to Raleigh, if you want me to."

"You bet I do. I'll find you a place to stay tomorrow. I'll call you as soon as I find you a room. Will you be coming by bus?"

"Yes, I'll check the bus schedule in the morning so I can tell you when I'll be there."

"That sounds wonderful. I can't wait to see you, Maggie. I have to hang up now, because I have a curfew, and I don't want to be late. I love you!"

"I love you, too."

Maggie hung up, and went to her parents' room to ask them if she might go to Raleigh this weekend to see Ken.

"Where will you stay?" Annie asked.

"Ken will find me a room tomorrow."

"Ruben looked a little concerned, but he finally said, "If it's all right with your mother, it's all right with me. You're a young woman now, and this relationship seems to be serious."

"Thank you, thank you." Maggie swelled with excitement and ran out of their room, up the stairs, and into Lisa's room.

"Guess what, Lisa?"

"What?"

"Ken is back in Raleigh, and I'm going there this weekend to visit him!"

"That's great, Maggie, but get out of here now and let me study."

Maggie went to her room and started planning what to take. All the time she was smiling and dreaming, "I'm going to see Ken!"

Maggie took the bus to Raleigh that Friday morning. She was so excited at the thought of seeing Ken that she could barely stand to sit in her seat for three hours. She arrived at the bus station around noon, retrieved her luggage, and took a cab to the beautiful old Colonial Inn, where Ken had reserved her a room. She looked at the stately mansion and could not believe that she would be staying in there. It seemed to rise straight out of the pages of Gone with the Wind. She went inside, found a gentile older lady and said, "I'm Maggie McGee."

"We've been expecting you, Miss McGee." The lady smiled and said, "Come this way. I'll show you to your room. "She led Maggie up a long spiral staircase and opened the door at the top of the stairs. They entered a room filled with lovely antiques and a bed with a lace canopy. Maggie knew that she would feel like a princess when she lay her head down.

"I hope everything will be all right; that nice young man of yours wanted the nicest room we could offer," the kind lady said.

"Oh, it's so beautiful, and I'm sure it will be just fine," Maggie answered.

"Let us know if there is anything you need," The lady instructed Maggie as she left the room and closed the door.

Maggie stood in the middle of the room and smiled to herself, "I'm in Raleigh and I'll be seeing Ken soon!" She surveyed the inviting bed again and thought, "It's several hours before Ken picks me up, I think I'll take a nap." She slipped off her suit and blouse, turned back the covers, crawled into the bed and lay there looking through the lace canopy, dreaming of seeing Ken, until she finally slipped off to sleep. She had arisen very early that morning in order to catch an early bus, but she did not realize how tired she had become.

Right on the stroke of 4:00, she was awakened from a deep sleep by a knock on her door.

"Who is it?" A groggy Maggie asked.

"It's Ken! Who were you expecting? May I come in?"

Maggie hesitated, lying there in her undergarments. She could not wait any longer to see Ken, so she answered, "You may come in, but I'm not ready to go. I've been asleep."

Almost immediately Ken was kneeling by her bed, gathering her into his arm, and smothering her with kisses. She found herself wanting more. He began to caress her body and she lay there trembling with excitement. There he was so close to her, and she knew he wanted more, and for a little while, she considered giving in to their mutual desires.

Neither one said anything but they were just content to hold each other and taste those sweet kisses. There was nothing else to say, each kiss said it all. Their desires were growing more intense with each kiss. Maggie sat up in bed, careful to keep herself covered by the white damask bedspread.

"Ken, I think you better wait for me in the parlor downstairs. It won't take me but a few minutes to get dressed. We'll have all weekend together."

Ken kissed her one last time, agreeing it was best for him to wait downstairs; he went to the door, turned and said, "You know I love you, don't you?"

"Maggie answered, "Yes, and I love you. Now go."

Chapter 37

As he closed the door, Maggie's body ached in a strange, new sensual way. She closed her eyes and wished she had invited him to stay. She felt such a strong fight within herself. She loved him and wanted him, but she knew that would be wrong, and she did not want to spoil the day when she might marry him.

She dressed quickly, brushed her hair, and descended the beautiful stairs. She literally ran into his arms, and said, "Let's go! I'm hungry!"

"Sounds good to me!"

She and Ken made plans for the rest of the fall, and it turned out as planned - either Ken came to Winston or she went to Raleigh. They never missed an opportunity to be together. Despite the war all around them, it was a wonderful time for both of them.

Lisa was going to be 16 on a Friday late in September. Maggie had asked her father for the day off, so she could help her mother get ready for Lisa's party. She remembered how special her own 16th birthday party had been, and she wanted to be sure that Lisa's was just as wonderful. She rose early that morning to help clean out the garage and scrub the floor so the tables could be set up for the birthday dinner. The recreation room again became a festive flower garden with streamers and balloons hanging everywhere. She knew Lisa would be excited when she came home from school. The caterers arrived and began to unload delicious-looking trays of food. Maggie was so excited that she felt as if she were having her party all over again. "But," she thought to herself, "So much has happened since I turned sixteen."

Lisa and Jeanie came home from school and squealed with delight when they saw the preparations that had been made.

It was now 5:00, and Annie called out, "Girls, it's time to go get ready for the party!" They all scrambled up the stairs to get dressed.

"Jeanie, you come up with me, and I'll help you get dressed," Maggie said.

When they came downstairs, Maggie looked at Lisa and thought, "When did she become so beautiful?"

"Lisa, you look simply gorgeous!" Maggie exclaimed.

"Thanks, Sis. You don't look so bad yourself."

The guests began to arrive around 6:00, and the house was filled with the sounds of excited young people. Lisa was sitting on top of the world. She was sixteen now, and had a steady boyfriend.

After dinner they all went to the rec room and began to dance. She wished Ken's bus would hurry and come. It was due to arrive about 7:00, and there was just enough time for him to be able to participate.

As Maggie watched them dance, she thought how they all looked so young and untouched by the war, and she suddenly felt old. So much had changed for her since she was sixteen.

The doorbell rang and she dashed upstairs, knowing it was Ken. She opened it and fell into his arms. The rest of the evening was even more fun for Maggie now that Ken was there to dance with her. As they danced, she kept remembering that they also had all day Saturday together., and how grateful they were for any time together. How different it was for Lisa's friends who were still all in school and not scattered all over the world because of this war. In her heart she hoped that it would end before her sister's friends would have to face the same situation.

A few weeks later when she came home from work, Maggie found her usual daily letter from Ken, and a V-Mail from Jake.

Dear Maggie, *September 21, 1943*

Sitting here in England is pretty boring, the weather is always the same, wet, cold, and dreary. I can't tell you what I am doing, but to say the least, it isn't boring.

I had a letter from Bill saying he was being trained as a gunnery instructor. He sounds pretty happy, so I suppose he has gotten over his disappointment of not becoming a pilot. He might be the lucky one.

Maggie, I am sitting here looking at your picture. You sure look beautiful. I hope no one is cutting me out these days. When I come home, I'm going to rent an apartment, and maybe, we can begin a little serious dating. Don't get too serious with that guy Ken until I get home. Ha.

Give my love to all the McGee's *and tell them I think of them often.*

Maggie, I love your letters. They're always so newsy. Just keep them coming. Be Happy!

Love, Jake

Chapter 38

Maggie's favorite month was October, and this one was not disappointing her. The trees were lit up with shades of red, orange and gold. With the turning of the leaves, it was once again time to get out the rake and pile up the fallen leaves. Maggie was busy raking the leaves, but her thoughts were not on the task she was doing. She was thinking of Ken and how long it would be before he would be leaving for OCS. It must be coming soon, and she dreaded that day.

Jeanie popped out the front door and ran out into the yard squealing, "Maggie, will you play in the leaves with me?"

"Sure! Come on! Let's rake up a big pile, and then we can run and jump in them!"

They raked and played until they were exhausted.

Maggie finished the yard, and Jeanie went back into the house to get ready to go to town with their mother.

Jeanie and Annie arrived home around five, and, before she could get her coat hung up, the phone rang. Maggie heard her mother say in a gasp, "No! Mrs. Frazier, that can't be!"

Maggie ran to her mother's side, insisting that she tell her what Mrs. Frazier had said. Somehow she already knew that it was bad news, just by the tone of her mother's voice.

"Mrs. Frazier, is there anything we can do? Maggie and I will come over as soon as we can." She hung up the phone and began to cry.

Chapter 38

"Momma, what's the matter? Is it news about Jake?"

"Yes, honey. Jake's plane has been shot down over the English Channel. Jake saved his crew, but he did not survive." With that she broke down and sobbed.

"I can't believe that Jake is dead! It isn't fair, all these young men dying!" Maggie screamed out to her mother as she fled upstairs. She lay on her bed and cried until her eyes ached.

Finally her mother came to her room and sat beside her - both of them with blood-shot eyes. She stroked Maggie's beautiful auburn hair and consoled her, "We have to be brave. It's time to get ready and go over and see Jake's mother."

"Yes, Momma. I'll be ready in just a few minutes. Is Daddy home yet?"

"I called him, and he is on his way home to take us to see Mrs. Frazier right away."

Mrs. Frazier was sitting on the sofa, as they entered. She looked small and frightened. She rose as they entered, and she went straight to Mrs. McGee, flinging her arms around her.

"He's gone, Annie! I can't believe he's not coming back!"

At that, they both broke down and cried. Mr. Frazier came over, led them to the sofa, and sat them down. Mrs. Frazier reached out her hands to acknowledge Maggie and Ruben.

"Maggie, I am so glad you came. Jake was so fond of you. He wrote to me of how he could always depend on receiving a letter from you. Thank you for being a good friend."

Maggie thought, "This is so sad, and it's happening to so many families. We aren't the only ones going through this."

As they were leaving Mrs. Frazier's, Ruben told them that he was going to call Bill as soon as they got home. The rest of the way home everyone was silent.

Maggie opened the door to the car and slowly mounted the steps to the main floor of the house, and then on up the stairs to her room. She entered and closed the door. She went to her desk and opened the bottom drawer. As she had done twice before, she took out another set of letters, read them, stacked them, and tied them up with a red, white, and blue ribbon. As she laid them beside Tim's and James's, she thought, "That only leaves Bill's and Ken's letters. Please God, don't let anything happen to Ken or Bill," she silently prayed.

Maggie had not seen Ken since Lisa's party, and she was missing him more and more. She hoped that he could come the next weekend. Maggie was finishing two months of attending business school, and she was beginning to learn enough to assume more of Ruben's work. She enjoyed working in her father's office, for it gave her a chance to talk with him, especially when they went to lunch together.

When they left the office that Friday, November 7th, she was all excited because Ken was finally coming to spend the weekend. Maggie came home early that day, and found her mother busy in the kitchen. Maggie went in and pecked her on the cheek.

"Why are you so busy this afternoon, Momma? Can I help you?"

"I sure could use some help."

"Let me go hang up my coat, and I'll be right back."

Maggie left the kitchen, and in a few minutes she was back inquiring about what she could do.

"You can go over there and collect all the sugar that's left in each jar. Measure it and let me know how much we have left this week to fix a dessert for Sunday. I'm hoping I can bake a chocolate cake. We haven't had a cake in a long time."

Maggie went to the shelf, which was over the end of the breakfast-room table. On it were five mason jars, each with the name of a family member on it, Bill's and Jake's rations had been put away when they left for the service. Each week Annie put a week's ration of sugar in each jar. When you wanted sugar on your cereal, or in your coffee, or for any other reason, you took it out of your jar. At the end of each week Annie poured the remaining sugar out and made whatever dessert she could with whatever sugar remained. Sometimes it was bread pudding, sweet biscuits with blackberries, or if the family was frugal in their use of sugar, she baked a cake or pies.

Maggie finished emptying the five jars and refilling them for the next week. She took the sugar to her mother, and after measuring it, Annie joyfully announced, "I can bake a chocolate cake!"

"May I cut two pieces of the cake for our picnic?"

"I think that will be all right, if you don't cut them too big."

She met Ken at the bus station, and on the way home, she told him she was planning to pack a picnic basket for them for the next day.

"That sounds great, but where are we going on a picnic?"

"I thought we could drive up towards Pilot Mountain and view the autumn leaves in color. They are so beautiful right now."

"Whose car are we going to use?"

"With a little persuasion from me, Daddy said we could have his car for the day."

"Boy, that sounds great!"

Saturday morning was a warm fall day, and Maggie rose early to prepare their picnic basket. By the time Ken came downstairs, she had completed her preparations and was ready to get on the way. Her daddy came in the kitchen, handed Ken his keys, and said, "Drive carefully, and don't go too far, because I don't want you to be out past dark. Remember gas is in short supply, so don't drive around unnecessarily."

"Thank you, Mr. McGee. I promise we'll be back before dark."

Maggie ran over and hugged her father.

They loaded the car with the basket and an old patchwork quilt to spread on the ground. Maggie slipped over as close as she could to Ken, and they were off.

The drive toward the mountains was wonderful. The sun was shining brightly, illuminating the leaves, and all the world was aglow with autumn colors.

As they drove along, the highway began to curve and rise higher into the blue skies. At the top of the mountain they turned onto the Blue Ridge Parkway and began to look for a nice picnic spot. It didn't take them very long to pick a sunny spot on the Parkway, with an overlook that seemed to be the top of the world. Ken stopped the car, and they began unloading.

Maggie spread out the quilt and invited Ken to sit down. He pulled her over to him, kissed her long and hard, and said, "Do you know how wonderful you are to me?"

"No, but I hope you'll tell me."

With that he kissed her again. They rolled over on their backs and gazed up at the colorful fall leaves set against the crystal blue sky. Through the afternoon they enjoyed each other's company and talked about how grateful they were to still have time together when so many men were off fighting the war. Maggie sensed that Ken was holding something back.

Soon their hungry stomachs got their attention. Maggie spread out her picnic on a red-checkered tablecloth, opened the picnic basket and began uncovering fried chicken, deviled eggs, neatly trimmed triangle sandwiches, several kinds of pickles, and olives. Then she uncovered two slices of chocolate cake.

"Is this your handiwork?"

"Well, some of it. Momma fried the chicken, deviled the eggs, and made the cake. I made the sandwiches and fixed the rest."

"Gee, I can't wait to dive into it!"

"Maggie handed him a paper plate filled with food, a cup of tea and said, "Dive in!"

After they had finished, Ken stood up and took Maggie by the hand, "Let's put our things in the car and take a walk."

"I would love that. The mountain is so beautiful today," she said, as she packed the basket.

Ken folded the quilt and placed it in the car along with the basket, and then they were on their way. They entered the woods heading down a dark wooded path, covered with emerald-green moss.

Chapter 38

"Be careful, Maggie. This moss can be slippery," Ken said as he reached for her arm and pulled her close to him.

The farther they hiked, the darker it became. The trees were densely covered with red, yellow and orange leaves, making the walk incredibly beautiful.

"You're being mighty quiet today. Is something bothering you?" Maggie asked. Ken didn't reply. They strolled for a little while, when Ken stopped by a huge tree that had a low-hanging limb. He picked Maggie up, sat her on the limb, and said, "Maggie, rumors are that we will be leaving for OCS right after Christmas."

"Oh no, Ken! I was hoping you would be at State at least for the rest of this school year."

"Yeah, I know. I was too. Maggie, there's something else I want to tell you. When I finish OCS, you know I'll be going overseas, and I don't feel I have a right to ask you to marry me, but...."

Maggie jumped off the limb where Ken had placed her, flung her arms around him, and interrupted him saying, "Yes, yes, yes! Ken, I'll marry you!"

A bit shocked, he gathered Maggie into his arms and kissed her again, and again. They stayed there a long time talking about their plans.

Ken felt they should wait until he was out of the Army. Maggie wanted to marry as soon as possible. She knew so well that some young men don't come back, and she did not want to take a chance of not being Ken's wife. In the end, they decided to marry when he finished OCS. He would have a two-week leave, and that was enough time to get married and have a short honeymoon. As they drove down the mountain, they held hands and talked about their future plans together.

The world was so quiet and beautiful up there on the mountain, that it was hard to believe there was a war raging over most of the planet.

For now, this day belonged to Maggie and Ken.

Chapter 39

The next time she saw Ken was at Thanksgiving weekend. It seemed like an eternity since Ken had proposed. She wanted to tell her family, but they had decided to wait until he could buy a ring, and ask her father for permission. Maggie had caught him without a ring when she accepted his proposal before he finished it. Ken's idea was to "be engaged to be engaged" until after the war, but Maggie never let him get that far. He really didn't mind as he knew he really wanted it to be that way, but he didn't want to ask Maggie to possibly become a widow.

Everyone had gone to bed except Maggie when Ken arrived late Wednesday evening. Thanksgiving morning everyone awakened with aromas wafting out of the kitchen and up the stairs. Maggie jumped out of bed, dressed, and ran down to the kitchen to help her mother. As she reached the last step and turned to go to the kitchen, she saw Ken in the den talking to her father. She thought to herself, "He's asking Daddy for my hand in marriage. I wonder what Daddy will say?"

She was smiling as she entered the kitchen, and her mother asked, "You look mighty happy this morning."

"I am. Ken is in the den with Daddy, asking if he will give his permission for us to be married."

Her mother dropped her spoon and took Maggie in her arms and said, "I think that is wonderful! When do you want to get married?"

"When he finishes OCS."

"How long will that be?"

"OCS is a three-month course, and he thinks he will be leaving after Christmas."

"Oh, that gives us plenty of time to plan a nice wedding."

Maggie felt a little shiver go over her body as she listened to her mother talk of her wedding plans.

They all gathered at the table in the dining room for a delicious Thanksgiving Day dinner. When everyone was seated, Ruben asked for everyone's attention.

"I am sure you are all aware of how Maggie and Ken feel about each other. Well, this morning Ken has asked for your mother's and my permission to marry Maggie, and I have given them our blessings."

Lisa rose, went to her sister, and gave her a big hug and kiss. "I think this is wonderful!" She then went to Ken, hugged his neck, and said, "Welcome to the McGee family!"

Jeanie jumped up from her seat and ran to Maggie saying, "Can I live with you and Ken?"

"No, but you can visit us as often as you want to," Maggie answered.

"What would your Daddy and I do if you went to live with Maggie and Ken?" her mother asked.

"Maybe you could come and live with them too," Jeanie replied. With that everyone laughed.

"No, Jeanie," said Ruben. "I think we'd rather live in our own house with you. Now let's bow our heads and ask for God's blessings on this family, those absent from us, those brave men fighting for us, and this wonderful meal."

They all lingered over dinner, talking about the wedding and making plans for Christmas. Finally, Jeanie was tired of all the talk and wanted everyone to go out into the yard to play croquet. Maggie suggested that Ken and her father take Jeanie out to play while she and Lisa help their mother clear up the table and wash the dishes. Jeanie went running ahead to get out the balls and mallets. Ken came over, kissed Maggie, and said, "Thanks."

"Come on, Ken. It won't take them long in the kitchen, then you and Maggie can have some time alone," Ruben said.

Ken followed him out into the back yard, where Jeanie was waiting. After two hotly contested games, Maggie came out and rescued Ken.

"Come on Ken! Let's take a walk!"

"Can I go, Maggie?" cried Jeanie.

Their mother walked up and said, "No, Jeanie, you have to stay here and play with Daddy and me."

"Ok, what color ball do you want, Momma?"

"You know I love yellow. It's so sunny!"

Maggie and Ken walked away hand in hand.

When they returned, they went to the kitchen and fixed a coke, and then they staked out the den for the rest of the evening. Ruben had built a roaring fire after dinner, so the room was warm and cozy in the chill of the late afternoon, which felt good to them. They seated themselves in her father's big leather chair, big enough for the two of them. They sat there warming themselves and thinking of how much they loved the thought of the wedding they were planning.

"Maggie, did I really propose to you?"

"You surely did. Don't you even think of backing out!"

"Well, do you have any proof that I did?"

"No," she replied, and then she thought, "Where is this heading?"

With that Ken took a ring out of his pocket and placed it on her finger and said, "Now you have proof."

She extended her arm as far as she could and gazed at her hand with that dazzling ring on it. "Ken, this is the most beautiful diamond ring I've ever seen!" She turned and kissed him, and said, "I love you so much!"

Chapter 39

Ken held her for the longest time and whispered in her ear, "I love you, too."

Friday morning Maggie beat everyone to the kitchen. She was there to show her engagement ring to each one as they came to breakfast. When Ken came in the kitchen they all smiled at him and said, "Maggie's ring is beautiful."

Ken left Friday afternoon to spend the rest of the weekend with his mother. Maggie spent the weekend dreaming of the wedding she would like to have.

It was hard to go to work Monday morning, but she needed to, because she had taken over more and more of her father's office work, and he depended on her. She still loved working with her father, and she found that she was learning as much from him as she was learning at school.

On many days when she left work, Maggie would go through town, buying up every bride's magazine she could find, and shopping for silks and satins to start making her wedding trousseau. At night she was busy at her sewing machine making gowns and robes. She loved sewing with lace, silks and satins. Going to work, sewing, and Ken's daily letters filled her days and kept her from missing him too much.

Ken had not been able to come to Winston for several weeks, and she was anxiously awaiting his arrival one weekend in the middle of December. She kept dreading the time for Ken to leave for OCS, which would be real soon.

Ken arrived late Friday, and soon they settled down to talk. He told her it was now official and he would be leaving for Fort Monmouth, New Jersey, soon after the first of the year.

Maggie groaned, but she smiled and said, "Then we can be married in the spring. Maybe April?"

"I think that's about right, but we can't pick a date until I start OCS." Ken went on, "I can be here for Christmas, if that is all right with you and your family."

"Ken, that's wonderful! Bill is coming for Christmas. I know Momma will be happy to have the house full."

"Is Bill getting a leave?"

"Yes, he'll be home on December 22nd for ten days. He has been made a gunnery instructor and has been assigned to Charleston. We are ecstatic that he will not have to go overseas. At least not right now."

"That's great. I'd love to see him." Ken went on, "Maybe I had better get a room downtown for Christmas."

"You can share Bill's room," said Maggie. I'm sure he won't mind."

"You'd better check with your mother."

"I will." She kissed him, adding, "You're almost part of the family."

Ken smiled and kissed her. He was feeling very grateful and thought, "It's wonderful having a family. It hasn't been the same since my daddy died last year. Being an only child, I've felt mighty lonely."

Chapter 40

The first of December had been unusually mild. Maggie had spent most of her free time upstairs planning and sewing. She realized it was almost time to put up the Christmas tree and help her mother decorate the house. Jeanie had already started begging to put up the tree. Friday of that week when Maggie came home from work, Mrs. Frazier was in the living room talking with Annie.

"Maggie, come in and say hello to Jake's mother," Annie called out.

"Hello, Mrs. Frazier. It's so good to see you. I do hope you're feeling well these days."

"As well as can be expected, Maggie. Jake's personal belongings arrived yesterday, and I've gone through them and brought the letters from your family. It looks like he saved them all. I thought you might like to have them. I also brought Jake's wings for Annie to give to Bill. I know Jake would like for him to have them."

"Thank you for thinking of us, and yes, I would love to have those letters." Maggie extended her hand, and Mrs. Frazier gave them to her. She asked, "Did you find my picture among his things?"

"No, and I thought that odd since I know he spoke of having it with him."

Mrs. Frazier rose to leave.

"Bill will be coming home for Christmas, and I'm sure he will come to see you and your husband," Annie told Jake's mother.

"We would love to see Bill."

Maggie excused herself and went up to her room. She opened the bottom drawer, tied up her letters to Jake, and placed them beside Jake's to her. She took the box from the drawer, which had once held five pictures. She sat there quietly thinking about those five pictures and to whom she had given them. She had been so young and foolish when she first had the portrait made. She had hurt two young boys with her careless use of words. Pearl Harbor happened and we went to war. In a little over a year, one picture was lost in Africa, one lay on the ocean floor in the Sea of Japan, and now Jake's was who knows where. She closed the box and returned it to the drawer.

She prayed that Ken's picture would stay safe from harm.

Chapter 41

The morning of December 17th, Annie called Maggie to the telephone. Annie said she did not understand the young man's name, but he asked to speak to Maggie McGee.

She took the phone and answered, "This is Maggie McGee. How can I help you?"

"My name is Lt. Wade Jones. I'm sure you've never heard of me, but I have certainly heard of you. I was co-pilot with Jake Holden on thirteen missions."

"I'm so happy to hear from someone who knew Jake."

"I'd like to come by to see you. I'll be on my way home to Georgia for Christmas, but I can get off the train there to visit you and Jake's mother. I have not been able to get in touch with her, maybe you can."

"I'll be happy to, and I'll be anxious to talk to you. When will you arrive?"

"Tomorrow around noon, but I will have to catch the train on to Georgia at five."

"I'll expect you then."

When Maggie hung up, she went into the kitchen to tell her mother about the phone call.

"That is so nice of him, you better try and get in touch with Mrs. Frazier."

"I called, and her husband said she is out of town for a couple of weeks. He said she won't be home until next week."

"She will be very sorry to have missed him," said Annie.

The next day at 1:00 Lt. Wade Jones knocked on the door. When Maggie answered it, she saw a very handsome young flier, greeting her with a broad, friendly smile.

"Come in the house, I am so happy to have an opportunity to talk with you."

"Were you able to get in touch with Mrs. Frazier? I would like to see her, too."

"I spoke with her husband, and he said she is out of town and won't be back for another week." Maggie told him as she showed him into the house. "Would you like something to drink?"

"That would be very nice. The train didn't offer much in the way of refreshments."

"Let's go into the kitchen. I'll fix you something. Coffee, tea or a cold drink?"

"Coffee will do just fine, and maybe a glass of water."

Maggie, motioned to a chair and said. "Have a seat, and I will start a pot of coffee."

As Maggie sat down at the table, Wade pulled several items out of his pocket.

"Maggie, I have several things to give to you. I hope they will help you understand what a great guy Jake was, and please give this copy to his mother."

"Oh, I know what a great guy Jake was," said Maggie as she rose and poured a cup of coffee for each of them, sat back down, and asked Wade to proceed.

"First, this is a record of our fateful mission. The crew and I composed what happened and have submitted it to the proper persons, asking that

Jake's heroism be honored with a Silver Star citation. Please read it, so if you have any questions, I can answer them."

Maggie took the papers and began to read:

> This is an account of Mission 13, under the command of Lt. Jake Holden, written by Lt. Wade Jones with the help of the other crew members.
>
> Framingham, England, was shrouded in a heavy fog on the morning of October 9, 1943. It was like every other morning in England. The evening before it had been raining, but by 1:45 in the morning, the rain had stopped. It was as raw and cold as any morning we could ever remember. As we stumbled out of our warm beds, such as they were, we shivered. We thought of what this day was to bring, and realized our shivering might be from the cold, or it might be because this was to be our thirteenth mission. We kept reminding ourselves, this day in our life would be dedicated to doing our part in freeing the world from the tyrant that was turning our world into hell.
>
> Minutes before, we had been awakened by the "alert non-coms," and informed of the time of breakfast and the mornings briefing. As the ANC retreated out the door, he left the lights glaring in our eyes; there was no avoiding the inevitable, so we dressed and found ourselves heading out into the night groping and stumbling into the trucks which were waiting to carry us to the mess hall. The thoughts of a hot breakfast and those wonderful mugs full of hot coffee, made the cold bumpy ride to the mess hall almost seem pleasant. It seems that more and more, these little pleasures were what we lived for. We each seemed to be living for the present and the immediate future. Today, tomorrow, next week, even the events of the approaching day, which we tried to push out of our minds, were things that relieved the monotony that had begun to fill our lives.

We had been through this ritual a dozen times before, but this being the thirteenth mission, we felt a little more nervous. Sitting in the briefing room, waiting for the curtain to be pulled from the briefing map, we found out what our mission would be this day. It is then, and only then, that we knew the depth into which we would be flying into enemy territory. This morning the string that marked our route went deep into German territory where attacks were bitterly contested. Today's target was the synthetic oil plant in Marienburg, deep in central Germany. The second half of the briefing was the run down to the target and over the target itself. Next the intelligence officer gave us the name of the target, and its importance. He went over the bomb route, the number of probable AA guns to expect, the strength of anticipated fighter opposition, and what to do in emergencies. At the completion of this part of the briefings, the operations officer stepped forward and carefully went over altitudes, weather, the fighter escorts that were arranged, and where we were to expect to rendezvous with them. Questions were asked and answered, and finally the briefing was over. We were a somber group of men that filed out and loaded onto the trucks to be taken to the airfield.

The trucks rumbled along in the cold damp mist that we had become used to in these early morning exercises. The ground crew was busy at work checking the instruments and preflighting the engines. As we filed out of the trucks, the oxygen truck backed up to the ship to check the oxygen supply. The fuel trucks came next to top off their tanks with as much fuel as we could carry. The ordnance men showed up to check the ammunition. The gunners were first aboard, after armament had finished stripping, cleaning and oiling their guns. We climbed into position, ready to test fire our guns as soon as we were out over the channel, careful not to shoot towards the other airships in our formation. This was a busy time for each crew member, which left them little time to think about the coming mission.

Chapter 41

Finally the last truck lumbered away. The bombs were loaded and fused. They hung silently from the racks in the bomb bay area.

All was ready. The first hint of dawn brought an eerie glow to the predawn darkness. The huge B-17s stood silent, giving no hint of the mighty power of the six-thousand-pound bomb load they were carrying in their bellies. Now it was time for the crew to man our ship and get started on our day's mission.

Lt. Holden and his crew of nine climbed aboard. Jake and I, his co-pilot Lt.Wade Jones, began starting our engines one by one, while the crew donned their Mae Wests and parachutes, and each man checked the equipment that might save his life that day. Soon the roar of the mighty engines filled the early morning air. The big Flying Fortress lumbered out onto the runway, with the ground crew standing by to wave and give us a thumbs-up sendoff. We joined the other Forts in a procession to the take-off position. This was one of the scariest moments of our missions. With the Forts so heavily loaded with their fuel tanks topped off and loaded to their full capacity with bombs, it was always a concern if they would make it into the air. With only a five-thousand foot runway, it took a skilled pilot to get his Fort off successfully. On one of our missions, we saw one crash as it lifted off the runway, but went nose down just past the trees that lined the end of the runway. We had heard of Forts clipping trees as they took off. So there was always a sigh of relief that came when the wheels left the runway, and we were safely climbing. Once in the air, it was time to get into position with the other ships. Now it was hard to keep thoughts of the next eight to nine hours from creeping into our minds.

About two hours after taking off, the ships were in division formation and crossing the English Coast.

There was very little conversation; everyone was busy checking and rechecking his job. Occasionally someone attempted a little light conversation over the intercom to lessen the tensions that were mounting minute by minute, but it never seemed to help.

Before long someone said, "There's the Dutch Coast."

Lt. Holden cautioned, "Keep your eyes alert for fighters, any kind, and sing out as soon as our fighter escort shows up."

"We should pick up two groups of P-51s in sixteen minutes," the navigator reported.

From this altitude, perhaps 20,000 feet and climbing, the sun was well up, the air was clear and sharp, and cold, 30 to 40 degrees below zero F. We were grateful for our heated suits, even though it was tiring sitting in our cramped quarters for hours on end. Sometimes we had to chip huge chunks of ice off of our oxygen masks. Each crewman watched the skies until their eyes ached.

Someone up front called out, "Fighters at 2:00 high!"

The engineer in the top turret said, "They're P-51s."

We relaxed a little.

Another two hours of waiting, watching and thinking passed laboriously.

Someone said, "Those boys at 10:00 are catching hell."

We all looked and realized the formation to our left was flying over a flak area.

"We'll reach the IP in six minutes," the navigator announced over the intercom.

Chapter 41

The crew reached for flak suits, and checked their parachutes to see that the quick release cord was handy, just in case. The clouds below were patchy now, and great stretches of Germany were visible below.

"This is the turn at the IP," the navigator advised.

As the ships wheeled off gently to the right thirty degrees, we began to look for flak.

The navigator's voice came over the intercom again, "Fourteen minutes to target."

Lt. Holden called for an oxygen check to make sure their apparatus was working OK. The men sounded off in order from the tail forward. "Number one check." "Number two check." And so on.

"Flak at 12:00," came from the bombardier.

Lt. Holden stiffened and remained committed to flying his ship to the target point. Now the stuff was all around. A big black puff suddenly appeared and rushed back toward the tail. More and more came up, and closer and closer burst the flak.

Suddenly a ship in the formation to our right sustained a direct hit on one wing, and an engine was afire. Pieces of the wing flew off, and the plane quietly slipped out of line. We watched as it went down. As the plane started falling, the tail gunner's body fell out, but his chute opened. Then out came another, and one after another they jumped from the plane until the sky was full of chutes. Flames swept the full length of the fuselage, and then the bombs went off. Then burning debris filled the air as it plummeted earthward. We all wondered if we knew the crew.

"Bomb-bay doors on the lead bomber are opening!" I said.

Lt. Holden looked around at the other Forts and watched as their doors began to slowly open. He knew the doors on his ship were beginning to open to expose the load they were carrying. This was a time of mixed feelings, a deep feeling of regret, but a grim determination to get our job done. Lt. Holden turned over the controls of his ship to his bombardier. The bombardier flew right over the target.

Lt. Holden said. "Look out below! We're coming, in spite of all you can do!" If there is any comfort to be felt on a bomb run, this is it. Get there and deliver your bombs on the target and get out.

A voice called out, "A lot of bogies are dead ahead, and I think they're coming through." Five seconds later his voice rang out again, "Get ready, here they come!" And come they did. A dozen or more came barreling through the formation head on. Ominous white puffs appeared all around us. Cannon fire. The Jerries were throwing everything they had at us.

In another instant German FW-190s were all around us, but only for a split second as they passed through our formation and were gone to the rear. A couple of seconds later we heard, "Bombs away." Long strings of five-hundred-pounders headed for the German oil tanks below. The Germans put up a good fight, but they couldn't stop the formation. The flak began again as our bomb group turned their planes to head back to England. Another three or four minutes and we had run out of the flak area. We could still see the other Forts coming behind us.

As Lt. Holden took over the controls of his ship from our bombardier, he concentrated on his mission to bring his Fort back to England. The flak stopped as if it had received a signal. We were breathing a little easier, but no one really relaxed, because we knew the enemy fighters might still come after us. There came a string of idle chatter over the interphones. A little like letting off pent-up tension.

As our ship neared the French coast, the tail gunner shouted, "Fighters approaching at 1:00."

Suddenly the air was filled with exploding fire, ours and the Germans'. A voice rang out, "Bogies approaching, high at 12:00." No one had time to think; we just fired our guns and prayed.

Lt. Holden was intent on flying his Fort through this attack. Suddenly the ship was hit in the left wing, and the left engine caught fire. Lt. Holden was hit and sustained injuries to his face and chest, but he struggled to keep our ship in the air. He knew his ship could not stay in the air to reach England, but at least he would try to keep it in the air long enough to get over the channel, and save his crew. Lt. Holden announced over the intercom. "Our ship can't make it home. Prepare to jump immediately."

I turned to him, "Come on, let me fly this ship, so you can jump. I can exit the ship quicker than you can."

"No, I'm hit bad. I won't make it, but the rest of you can."

I started to argue, but he cut me short, "That's an order, Lt. Jones."

"Yes sir, Lt. Holden," I answered. As I moved to the center of the ship, I knew he was right. I didn't know if he could keep it flying long enough for all of us to get out. He called out, "Everyone get the lead out of your boots and jump. Damn you! Get the hell out of here!"

Lt. Holden was beginning to fade in and out of consciousness, but he willed himself to stay alert and keep his ship in the air.

I shouted to Lt. Holden, "I'm the last to jump. Good luck, buddy."

As I left the ship, Lt. Holden was peering out the window of his crippled ship at nine billowing parachutes.

As the crew floated down to the water, we watched our ship and its heroic Lt. Holden hit the surface and sink into the English Channel.

Lt. Holden's crew was picked up out of the channel and returned to our airbase by a British air rescue boat. The next morning we were summoned to headquarters for a debriefing.

After we gave our reports of our successful mission, each one of us had an opportunity to relate how our pilot, Lt. Jake Holden, had sacrificed any chance he might have had to survive. He had fought to keep the ship in the air, so that he could save his crew.

The debriefer asked us to write up our account of the mission and said that it would be duly recorded. He assured us that Lt. Jake Holden would likely be awarded the Silver Star for heroism.

A very solemn crew left the briefing room without exchanging many words. Each was reliving the events of our narrow escape, and thinking of the man who had made it possible, Lt. Jake Holden.

Signed, Wade Jones, 1st Lt. USAF

October 12, 1943

Maggie dabbed the tears from her eyes and let the papers fall from her hand onto the table before her.

Chapter 41

Wade rose, went to Maggie's side, and knelt by her chair. He continued telling her, "Three days later, I was given a Fort to pilot, and Jake's crew was assigned to me. We all met out on the airfield surveying the ship that had been assigned to us. I called for their attention and asked, "How would you like to name our Fort, The Flying Jake?"

The whole crew, including our newest crew member, our co-pilot, shouted, "The Flying Jake" it is!"

When he told her this she began to sob, "Jake would be so proud."

Wade reached into his pocket again and pulled out two other items. He held them for a long time as he said to Maggie, "When Jake ordered me to jump ship with the crew, he reached into his pocket with his bloody hand and gave me this unfinished V-Mail letter. Then he ripped your picture off the cockpit wall. He gave both to me, and asked me to deliver them to you whenever I could." As he handed them to her, he continued, "They're blood and water stained. He said he promised you that he would bring your picture back. I thought about not delivering them to you, but he did make me promise."

Maggie reached out with trembling hands and looked at her picture, stained with Jake's blood, then she turned to Wade and said through her sobbing, "He was like a brother to me. He was my rock. There's no one who can take his place. As devastating as it is to know this is his blood on the letter and picture, I am so grateful that you took the time to bring them to me. Wade, I need to know, will his body be recovered?"

"Sometimes the plane cracks under water and the body surfaces, but I have not heard that they have recovered Jake's body. It's not too late, maybe he'll still be found."

Wade rose and stood beside Maggie, "I must be going, it's time for the taxi to return to pick me up."

She took his hand and followed him to the front door, opened it, and as he walked down the front walkway, she waved farewell.

She slowly closed the door and climbed the stairs to her room. She sat down at her desk and opened the drawer, which now held so much sorrow.

Just a few years ago it held the letters of young and foolish boyfriends. She read Jake's letter.

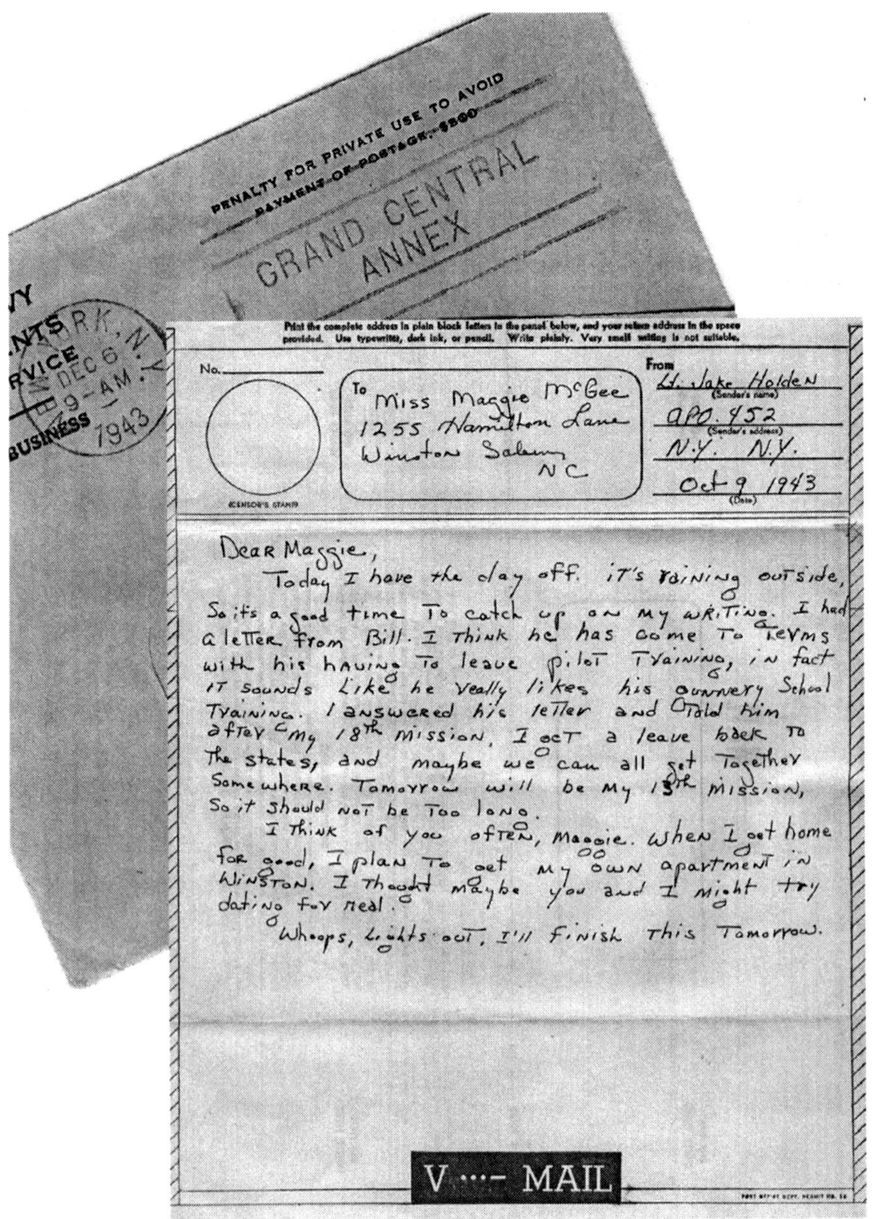

PENALTY FOR PRIVATE USE TO AVOID PAYMENT OF POSTAGE, $300

GRAND CENTRAL ANNEX

NEW YORK, N.Y. DEC 6 9-AM 1943

Print the complete address in plain block letters in the panel below, and your return address in the space provided. Use typewriter, dark ink, or pencil. Write plainly. Very small writing is not suitable.

No.

CENSOR'S STAMP

To Miss Maggie McGee
1255 Hamilton Lane
Winston Salem
NC

From Lt. Jake Holden
(Sender's name)
APO. 452
(Sender's address)
N.Y. N.Y.
Oct 9 1943
(Date)

Dear Maggie,

Today I have the day off. it's raining outside, So its a good time To catch up on my writing. I had a letter from Bill. I think he has come To terms with his having To leave pilot Training, in fact it sounds like he really likes his gunnery School Training. I answered his letter and told him after my 18th mission, I get a leave back to the states, and maybe we can all get Together somewhere. Tomorrow will be my 13th mission, So it should not be Too long.

I think of you often, Maggie. when I get home for good, I plan To get my own apartment in Winston. I thought maybe you and I might try dating for real.

Whoops, lights out, I'll finish this Tomorrow.

V ···– MAIL

Chapter 41

She folded Jake's unfinished letter, untied the packet of his letters, placed the unfinished V-Mail and the account of Mission 13 with the other letters, carefully retied them, and returned them to the drawer. She thought, "This war has certainly made me grow up in a hurry."

Maggie then took out the red-satin box, placed her blood-stained picture in it, and returned it to its resting place. She slowly closed the drawer, dried her tears, and thought. "I must go tell the family."

She took the account of Mission 13 that Wade had given her for Mrs. Frazier down to her parents, and shared it with them.

"It was very thoughtful of Wade to bring that to us. I knew Jake would always be a very brave man. Bill will be home on the 22nd. Be sure to show it to him," Annie said through her tears.

"I will. In fact, I'm hoping Mrs. Frazier will be home before Bill goes back, so he can go with me."

"That's a wonderful idea, you might call and find out exactly when she'll be back."

"I will. Thanks, Momma."

She went down to the rec room to play with Jeanie. She felt she needed to think about something besides war and death.

Chapter 42

Despite the grief they all felt over Jake, the family went all out for the holidays. The McGee house literally glowed with Christmas decorations. Jeanie was running from one to another, chattering. It was hard to tell which visitor she was more excited about - Bill, Ken or Santa Claus. The whole household was nearly as excited. Everything was ready - the house was decorated, gifts were wrapped and under the tree, and the china cabinet was full of Annie's baking.

The door popped open on the lower level, and Bill came in, saying, "Is anyone home to greet me?"

In seconds all the girls were hanging on him. Ruben followed Bill, carrying his duffel bag. The girls let go of Bill when their mother arrived. She took him in her arms saying, "Welcome home, son."

Maggie waited patiently, and when all the greetings were completed, she stuck her left hand out right in front of Bill's face.

"See?"

"Wait! Let me get my glasses so I can see."

"Oh, Bill, don't make fun of the most important thing in my life."

He took her hand, kissed it, and said, "Sorry, Sis, I was just teasing. It's a beautiful ring, and it comes from a great guy. Congratulations! When's the wedding?"

"This spring after Ken finishes OCS."

Chapter 42

Maggie followed Bill to his room, "Bill, would you mind if Ken uses the spare bed in your room? Momma has been letting him stay in here the last few times he has visited. I asked her, and she said for me to ask you."

"Sure, that will be fine. When is he coming?"

"Saturday afternoon. His mother is letting him borrow her car, and he'll drive here Christmas Day afternoon. He'll be here until Tuesday."

"I think I can handle a roommate that long. It's not like I haven't been sharing a room with fifty other guys. This will give me a chance to get to know my new brother."

Maggie gave Bill a great big hug and fled down the steps to tell her mother that the room arrangement was all right with Bill.

Maggie began setting the table for dinner. It seemed wonderful to be setting the table for the entire family, as she had done so many times before.

After dinner, they all gathered in the den by the big roaring fire, listening to Bill tell of his Army experiences. Jeanie sat on Bill's lap all evening. Finally, she couldn't keep her eyes open any longer, and she fell asleep in his arms. Bill said he would take Jeanie to her room and tuck her in to her bed for the night. Annie went with him to help. As he laid Jeanie down, an eye popped open, and she reached up and kissed Bill on the cheek. Then she fell fast asleep. Bill and Annie slipped out of the room and went back to join the rest of the family in the den.

"Let's play Monopoly!" Lisa suggested.

"Not tonight," Bill replied. "I've been on a bus all day, and I'm bushed. I'll take you up on that challenge tomorrow night."

They all decided it was time for bed. Maggie followed Bill up the stairs. He stopped at the head of the stairs and asked, "Maggie, will you go with me to visit Jake's mother?"

"I'd love to go with you. I have a copy of an account of Jake's last mission that his co-pilot brought to Mrs. Frazier and me. She was out of town, so he asked me to take a copy to her. I'll check to see if she is home now."

She went to her desk, took out the copy, and gave it to Bill. "You will want to read this," Maggie said.

Bill took the papers and headed for his room.

"We can go as soon as I get home from work," she called after him.

"When's that?"

"I get home around four."

"I'll be here. Thanks for saying you'll go with me. You know it's going to be tough for me and for Mrs. Frazier, too," Bill said.

"I know," said Maggie. "I've been through this before." Maggie kissed Bill goodnight, and they went to their rooms.

She lay in her bed and thought, "It feels so good to have everyone in the house. Oh, how I wish Jake could be here." She could only try to imagine how her parents were feeling.

A soft knock came on Maggie's door.

"Yes."

"It's me, Bill."

"Come in."

Bill handed the papers to Maggie and said, "It must have been a tough day for those guys. I'm not surprised at what Jake did: he was that kind of fellow." He turned and left her room. There was nothing else he could say.

The next few days were busy and happy ones for the McGee family. Christmas morning Maggie was awakened by Jeanie, "Come on, Maggie. Get up! Santa Claus came last night!"

"OK, OK, I'll be down shortly. Are Bill and Lisa up?"

"Bill is downstairs having a cup of coffee with Momma and Daddy. Lisa said she would be down in a few minutes."

When Maggie came down, everyone else was in the kitchen already.

"It's unusual to find you up so early, Bill," Maggie chided.

"You forget. I'm in the Army now, and they don't let us lie around in bed."

"Let's go out by the Christmas tree," Mother said. "Jeanie wants everyone to see what Santa brought her."

They all began opening their presents, like so many other Christmas mornings they had shared, strewing boxes, papers, and ribbons everywhere.

After breakfast, they all scattered around in the house. Jeanie dragged all her presents to her room. Lisa was getting ready for her boyfriend to come. Ken was due around 4:00, so Maggie went to her room to get dressed. Annie was planning their Christmas dinner at five. Maggie wanted to get ready early so she could help her. The house was full of excitement.

Ken arrived right on time. Maggie ran out the door to greet him and wished him a Merry Christmas. They came into the front hall hand in hand. Bill was there and stuck out his hand to Ken, and said, "Welcome, buddy. I hear you're going to be part of our family."

"That's my intention."

"You can put your gear up in my room. I think you know where it is."

"Yeah, I do, and thanks."

Ken came back downstairs and took Maggie by the hand. "Come with me to the recreation room."

"Why? It's too cold down there."

"Don't ask questions, just follow me."

When they were in the rec room, Ken pulled a cover off the most beautiful cedar chest Maggie had ever seen. Ken said, "Merry Christmas. I hear every young girl needs a hope chest when she's planning to get married, and this one is yours."

Maggie knelt in front of the chest and opened it. It smelled like her grandmother's chest, where she kept her fine linens. She stood, and threw her arms around Ken, and said, "I love it, Ken! I already have some dishcloths and doilies that my grandmother crocheted for me. Now I have my very own hope chest, and they will go in there first."

She ran upstairs to tell her mother about her cedar chest. Ken followed her close behind. "Momma! Guess what Ken gave me?"

"A lovely cedar chest."

"How did you know?"

"Your mother shopped for me," Ken said with a laugh. "Boys don't know how to pick out a hope chest."

"Momma! It's beautiful! You both did a great job of surprising me!"

Later in the day the family enjoyed the turkey and ham and all of Annie's special dishes. The dining room resounded with incessant conversation.

"Lisa, you sure have grown up to give Maggie some competition." Bill chided

"How many pictures do you need for your boyfriends?"

"Oh, Bill you know me, I am much too serious to compete with my older sister."

Maggie jumped in and said, "Watch out how you use that older sister stuff."

"Now, now, girls, I was just kidding. I must say though, Lisa, you sure have grown up pretty."

"Thanks, Bill."

Maggie's wedding plans were discussed at length, and Jeanie twisted Bill's ear about all of her new friends at school, what she was playing on the piano, and showed him the ballet dance she was learning. It was hard for Bill to take it all in.

Sunday everyone went to church together, and shared Sunday dinner. Tuesday came all too soon, and Ken had to leave. After saying goodbye, Maggie returned to the house, wiping tears from her eyes. When she was inside, Bill put his arms around her and just let her cry.

"Sis, it's not going to last too long. Before you know it, you'll be married to the guy. And besides, you'll see him in a week for New Year's Eve."

Maggie brightened as she realized it was only a week before she would see Ken again.

"I had almost forgotten," she laughed.

"I guess minutes seem like hours to those in love," Bill teased.

"Hey, someday you'll understand." She smiled at Bill and went upstairs.

Chapter 43

On New Year's Eve, 1943, Ruben was a taxi service to the bus station. First, he took Bill who was returning to his new assignment as a gunnery instructor in Charleston, and then later he had to go back to the station for Maggie's bus to Raleigh for her to celebrate the arrival of 1944 with Ken. He wondered why they couldn't have coordinated these bus times!

When Maggie arrived in Raleigh, Ken was waiting at the bus station with open arms. He dropped her off at the hotel where he had reserved a room. After resting for a little while, she excitedly got dressed for their first New Year's Eve together as an engaged couple. Ken came back around 6:00 and they went off to a glitzy restaurant to celebrate New Year's Eve with a few friends. Maggie was so happy to be dancing in her future husband's arms. It hardly seemed possible that she was going to be married soon. She looked up and smiled at Ken, and she knew they were both thinking that this could be their last special time together for quite awhile.

New Year's Day Ken picked Maggie up around noon, and took her to lunch at the Canton restaurant. Then they were on their way to Kinston, so Maggie could meet his mother and relatives.

"I don't have an immediate family as big as you do, Maggie, but my extended family is big with my mother, grandparents, aunts, uncles, and cousins. I hope this doesn't overwhelm you."

"Don't worry. You've only met my immediate family. I have lots of aunts, uncles, and cousins too."

Chapter 43

Ken pulled up in front of his house, went around, and took Maggie by the hand. He looked up as his mother was emerging from the front door smiling. She descended the step to greet them.

"Mother, this is Maggie. Maggie, this is my mother, Nora"

Nora took Maggie by the hand and led her into their home. As she opened the door, she said, "Please come in, and make yourself at home."

Ken followed them into the house, carrying their luggage.

The next few days Maggie met all of Ken's relatives, who made her feel very much at home among them.

Wednesday morning Ken and Maggie packed the car and headed for Winston- Salem. Maggie sat as close to Ken as she could manage. She knew that this was to be their last night together for the next few months. They rode along immersed in their own thoughts, until Maggie interrupted the silence.

"Ken, I really did like your mother. She was so nice to me, and she told me she welcomed having me as her daughter, which she had always wanted, but never had."

"Yeah, Maggie, I think you made a good impression on her."

The car pulled into the driveway at the McGee's, and that night Ken and Maggie took over the den. They sat in Ruben's big leather chair and hoped the night would never end.

The next morning arrived too quickly and it was time for Ken to go back to school. They went for a long walk, and when they returned it was time to say good-bye. Ken went inside and gave each family member a personal good-bye. Maggie stayed outside, and when he came out of the house she walked him to the car. He took her into his arms and kissed her good-bye. A tear fell down her cheek. Ken kissed it and said, "Maggie, it won't be too long before we'll be together all the time."

Maggie smiled up at him and said, "I love you, and I'll miss you terribly."

Ken kissed her one last time, jumped in the car, and drove away, back to do his duty.

January 7th, Ken called to tell Maggie that he was being shipped out the next morning to Fort Monmouth, NJ. He would start OCS the following Monday morning. Maggie began counting the weeks on the calendar and said to Ken, "That means we can be married around the middle of April, doesn't it?"

"I think you can count on that. I gotta go, honey. It's time for me to be checked in. I love you. Bye, Maggie."

"Good-bye, Ken. I love you, too."

Maggie went to tell her parents Ken's news. "Momma, that means our wedding will be around the middle of April."

"Did you set the date?"

"No, we have to wait until they give him a graduation date before we can set our date."

"Maggie, I think we should announce your engagement soon. Three months isn't long to get a wedding planned."

"When should it be announced?"

"Soon."

"Well, let's announce it on my twentieth birthday - January16th."

"I think that's a great idea."

"You will need to go to Carroll's studio and get a glossy print made to give to the newspaper," Annie told Maggie. "Why don't you go Monday morning before you go to work?

"I'll get Daddy to drop me off on our way to work." Maggie went straight upstairs to her room, sat down at her desk, and began writing out her announcement.

She took it downstairs for her parents' approval.

The next morning, when Maggie entered Carroll's Studio, Mr. Carroll said, "Come in, Miss McGee. Do you need another picture made?"

"Yes, I need a glossy print made of that picture you took of me several years ago. My parents are announcing my engagement."

"Well, the picture must have worked. Did you use them all?"

"Yes, but you wouldn't believe what happened to them," Maggie said somewhat embarrassed.

"When do you need this one?" Mr. Carroll teased.

"As soon as possible, I want my engagement announced January 16th, on my twentieth birthday.

"That's no problem, I can have it for you tomorrow around noon."

Maggie descended the steps thinking about the pictures, which she had made to give to any young man whose eye she could catch. She felt very foolish as she admitted this to herself. Now her mind went over each young man who had received one. "Two she had misled and got back — one torn to bits and the other with a reprimand for her to grow up. Then came Pearl Harbor and grow up she did. James lay with all his crew in a submarine half way around the world lost in the Sea of Japan. Tim, who was so sure he would never return, didn't. He was in the desert of Africa somewhere near Tunisia where my picture blew away into the hands of another young fighting man. Then there was Jake. Sweet and gentle Jake who gave his life to save his crew - his coffin a B19 bomber lying on the bottom of the English Channel. Now I have two pictures left — Bill's and Ken's. Luckily Bill has been spared by the loss of his hearing, but is still training young men to go kill the enemy. And Ken. Oh, I can't even think that he will go to fight, but it may be something I'll have to face."

By now Maggie was walking along the street with the crowd of people, probably going to work. Each of them may have a love — one or two in the service, or maybe lost. She managed a smile for each one she met, hoping to let them know that we're all in this horrible war together.

Maggie sighed and boarded her bus for another day at work. She acknowledged to herself that she was definitely a woman now — one who could face whatever she needed to face.

Chapter 44

Sunday morning, January 16, 1944 was Maggie's twentieth birthday. She couldn't wait until the daily paper arrived because the following announcement appeared on the front page of the society section in the Winston-Salem Journal and Sentinel.

Mr. and Mrs. Ruben Edwin McGee
announce the engagement of their daughter Miss
Maggie Eileen McGee to Cpl. Kenneth William
Winters. A spring wedding is planned.

Epilogue

On May 20, 2004, Katie Winters awoke and realized this was her grandparents' sixtieth wedding anniversary. She leaped out of bed to get ready for the day she had been working long and hard for. She was going to present her manuscript to the family in honor of her grandparents.

She had worked tirelessly, day and night, pouring over her grandmother's letters and documents. There was much more to do before she could publish her book, but it was ready enough to let the family read it.

As she drove up in front of her grandparents' home, she felt goose bumps all over. She was proud of what she had accomplished with her grandmother's help. She knew that her grandmother would be surprised to see a finished copy.

As she neared the front door, she thought, "My grandparents are remarkable people. They were married May 20, 1944, during the height of World War II. They lived in New Jersey for one year while Grandpa trained in the Army Signal Corps. Then after he returned from a year in the Pacific, they bought a small home in Kinston and began their family of four. Through the ups and downs of raising a family, running a business, and the loss of their first child, they remained committed to each other and very much in love. The last 20 of their 60 years together, they were blessed with four grandchildren - three boys and myself. They've had a good life."

She was deep in thought when her grandfather opened the door.

"Come in Katie, everyone is here anxiously awaiting your arrival."

"Hi, Grandpa." Katie said as she gave her grandfather a hug.

Katie went straight to her grandmother, and after kissing her, she whispered, "Here is our manuscript."

Maggie looked up at Katie, with tears in her eyes and said, "It's actually finished! Thank you, my darling granddaughter."

Everyone gathered around Maggie, anxious to have a copy of the manuscript.

"They're in my car, and there's one for each of you."

The boys flew out the door and returned with the extra copies.

Ken was pouring champagne for everyone, and, when the boys came back, he turned to Maggie with that beautiful picture sitting beside her, raised his glass and gave a toast. "Here's to the hard work of Katie and Maggie. Their book tells of a time of sadness for our family and our country, and a romance that has lasted for 60-some years. How time flies when you're having fun!"

They all laughed and raised their glasses.

Biography

Peggy Taylor Winstead, was born in Winston-Salem, North Carolina. She was the second child in a family of five, and this is the background for *The Picture*, a fictional novel, and her third book.

Peggy began writing in 1999 at the age of seventy-five. Writing was about the only artistic endeavor she had not tried; even though it was one she secretly wished she could accomplish. She and her husband took a writing class at the Polk County Community College, and this opened the door to her writing.

Peggy's first effort was her memoirs, *Peggy's Story*. Soon after came a book called *In Passing*, which was a combination of favorite family recipes, old family stories and the history behind the family heirlooms - a legacy much appreciated by her family.

Still not satisfied, she kept remembering a story she longed to write about a young girl, whose life was forever changed by that fateful day, December 7, 1941.

It seemed an impossible task for an eighty-year-old, but determined not to give up, she began to write, and thus she finished, *The Picture*, and completed her dream.

Made in the USA